Please feel free to send n
filters these emails. Good

Rua Hasan – rua_hasan@awesomeauthors.org

Sign up for my blog for updates and freebies!
rua-hasan.awesomeauthors.org/

About the Publisher

BLVNP Incorporated, A Nevada Corporation, 340 S. Lemon #6200, Walnut CA 91789, info@blvnp.com / legal@blvnp.com

DISCLAIMER

Fangs vs Claws

By: Rua Hasan

ISBN: 978-1-68030-880-8

Table of Contents

I would like to dedicate this book to my wonderful twin sister, Raneem Hasan who helped me start writing and inspired me in publishing this book from the very beginning. I would never have been here if she never encouraged me to write.

FREE DOWNLOAD

Get these freebies and MORE when you sign up for the author's mailing list!

Chapter 1

Stella

"Alice!" I yelled.

"I swear to God, if you don't come out from where you're hiding, I'm leaving!" I threatened.

Again, I was met with silence.

I swear this girl is crazy; she does this all the time — tells me to go grab something, and when I'm back, she's gone. Yes, she's my best friend and is like a sister to me. But come on, let's face it, she can get distracted pretty easily.

A couple weeks ago, I gave her one thing to do. One thing! And that was to watch over Billy, a six-year-old human that can get a little too excited at times. His parents were out celebrating their seventh year anniversary, and they left him in my care.

I was so busy that day; I had a dance rehearsal at two, and then had a choir concert at three. Living for so long gives you the advantage to try out new things. Anyway, I had to watch over Billy at to two thirty. I was so stressed out to the point where I called Alice to watch over him for one hour. One freakin' hour!

And you know what I found when I came back? A pile of Billy's dad's collection of shoe laces put together to make a piece of art by my not so smart best friend.

And you want to know where Billy was at the time when Alice decided to become an artist and touch things that don't belong to her? At his grandmother's house which was five blocks away. That little troublemaker walked all the way there, and when I came back, Alice didn't know where he was and started to panic.

We looked for him everywhere while I was giving Alice a useless lecture that I wish actually helped. Half an hour passed, and his pissed off parents came home with an annoyed grandmother holding a sleeping Billy.

I swear that day I heard so many "You should know better than this," and "How can you leave a child alone out on the street?" and also some complaints from Billy's dad on who touched his collection.

A sound behind a couple of bushes broke me out of my thoughts. I stopped and started to tiptoe to where the sound was coming from. Once I was near it, I bent down, getting ready to attack. I counted to three in my mind then I jerked up and jumped over the bush.

I landed heavily over Alice eating a bag of chips.

"Oh my gosh. Stella, get off me. You're too heavy. What did you eat for breakfast? A horse?"

I got off her, ignored her comment, and gave her a pointed look.

"Really, Alice? What on earth are you doing?" I yelled. "You know I'm supposed to be home by four. My parents think I'm at school studying with a couple of vampire friends."

She gave me a lazy smile while she continued to stuff some potato chips into her mouth.

"Oh, relax. It's only three thirty. See!" She pointed at her watch.

"And besides, I was hungry. I just went to grab a snack," she said, pointing at the large supermarket a few blocks away.

I raised one of my eyebrows at her.

"You do realize that I went to grab some sandwiches from the car, and it would have taken only a minute. How on earth did you get there and come back that fast?" I asked.

"There's something called werewolf speed, my vampire friend. It helps to use it," she said with a full mouth.

I just slapped my forehead and gave her an annoyed look. "Well, my werewolf friend,"—I threw my hands up, making air quotes—"your stupid watch is broken. It's four already, and I'm going to get into so much trouble."

Her eyes widened then she got up from the ground, grabbed, and shook my shoulders.

I gave her a questioning look and tried to stop her from shaking me, but it was no use. She just kept on shaking me.

"What are you doing?" I yelled at her.

"Get up," she said. "You've been sleeping for hours."

* * *

What?

Slowly Alice's voice started to fade and grew more like my mom's. I opened my eyes to find my mom shaking me from the front seat while holding a sandwich and a blood bag.

"Hey, sweetie. You've been sleeping for hours. Have a bite," she said while handing me over the sandwich and the blood bag.

I was lying down in the back seat of our car. It's probably been days since we first landed in America. We were in London before and now traveling to California by car. It was a usual thing for us.

My mother, my father, and I have been traveling ever since I was born. It was normal for us vampires because we stopped aging at the age of twenty and wanted to avoid any unnecessary questions from humans. I'd been everywhere. Just name it. Living for two hundred years became quite boring at times, so traveling helped.

I smiled at my mom while taking a bite from my sandwich, and I crunched my nose when I realized that my dad was singing some Backstreet Boys song while driving. I wasn't such a big fan of his singing.

My parents were around six hundred years old but looked like they were in their twenties, while I was born in 1816, which made me two hundred years old. I stopped aging one hundred and eighty years ago when I turned twenty.

Usually, when humans asked how we were related, we would say we were siblings because of how we looked. Yeah, I know. Weird.

I took a sip from the blood bag, enjoying the wonderful taste. We didn't drink blood from humans. We believed they deserve to live as much as we do, so we learned to control ourselves around them. It was not a problem for us. We learned to hide our cravings around them throughout the years.

Besides, we usually drank from rabbits and blood bags. One of my mom's human friends was a doctor who lived in the Philippines, and she sent us our blood supplies.

"Where are we?" I asked my parents.

My dad looked at the GPS and said, "We're somewhere in Los Angeles."

He paused.

"Or is it Orange County?" he said more to himself than to us.

My mom looked at him with an annoyed expression and started to rub her eyes with the palm of her hands.

"Lucas, please don't tell me we're lost again."

He glanced at my mom then looked back at the road and said, "Bella, sweetie, relax. I know what I'm doing."

Sure.

He said that all the time, and the next thing we knew, we were in China. Don't ask.

I lay my head on the back of the seat and got comfortable.

This is going to take a while. We're definitely lost.

My mom always tried to convince my dad to ask for directions, but he always refused, saying that he knew what he was doing.

I couldn't help but notice that something in the air smelled funny.

It smells like wet dog. Or maybe I'm just imagining things.

I shrugged off the thought when the memory of the dream I just had came into mind. Sadness crept into my heart. I tried not to let it get to me, but the memories overtook my mind.

I held back the tears threatening to come out. Thinking of Alice always did this to me.

I took another sip from the blood bag when the car came to a sudden stop. My head was about to hit the front seat, but I was held back by the seat belt.

I heard my dad cursing some colorful words which increased my confusion.

Suddenly that strange smell I noticed earlier hit me like a brick in the face. It smelled so familiar, but I couldn't seem to figure it out. I heard my mom gasp. But that was not what caught my attention. It was what she said next.

"Werewolves."

My eyes widened when I realized what was going on.

Oh shit. No, this can't be happening.

I looked at my dad who had a worried expression on.

"Dad, please don't tell me you led us into a pack."

He looked at me but said nothing.

So that was why the strange scent smelled so familiar. It was the smell of werewolves. It was similar to Alice's smell.

My mom was lecturing my dad, saying how reckless he was to lead us into a suicide mission.

Let me tell you that werewolves and vampires didn't get along. They hated each other. Which was the reason why every time Alice and I met, it had to be done in secret. My parents didn't like the fact that I was hanging out with a werewolf. But that didn't stop me. I didn't exactly hate werewolves; it was just I respected anyone who respected me.

The smell got stronger, and my parents got out of the car when a strong voice boomed through the forest.

"You bloodsuckers are trespassing."

When I got out of the car, I was met with about ten werewolves standing side by side. The guy standing in the middle of the group had power radiating from him; but thankfully, I could guess that he was not the Alpha. I guessed he was the one who was just talking.

Wait. Did he just call us bloodsuckers? That mutt!

Chapter 2

My dad stepped forward, and my mom grabbed his wrist.

"What did you call us, dog?" my dad asked.

The veins on his forehead looked like they were going to pop out.

My mom hit his stomach with her elbow so he would keep his insults to himself. Otherwise, he would get us all killed.

Well, at least, painfully. We're all going to die anyway since we trespassed.

Us as vampires didn't really help the situation. It just gave them another reason to kill us. I gulped in fear as I realized that this might be my last day.

I didn't get to live. I'm only two hundred years old.

Okay, that might seem a lot. But it's not!

The guy in the middle growled at my dad's insult. He took one step forward, glaring at my dad threateningly. I stood there watching the scene, hoping that my mother won't pass out due to my father's carelessness.

"This dog right here"—the guy pointed to himself—"is the Beta of this pack, and you are trespassing."

He looked at the men around him and said, "To the dungeons until the Alpha gets back."

My dad hissed at him, and my mom pleaded to let us go.

One of the guys grabbed my arm, but I jerked it from him and punched his face. As I said before, you respect me, and I shall respect you. But it looked like Mr. Wolf here was getting a little too close to my comfort zone.

"You shall not touch me, you ugly mutt," I hissed at him.

He slapped my face.

I held back the hiss of pain threatening to come out. My cheeks were throbbing, and I was pretty sure that would leave a bruise. Not long, though, my dad's fangs came out as his eyes turned red. He started to shake with anger and hiss threateningly.

"You bastard," he yelled.

He was just about to lunge at the guy who hit me when the Beta growled at him, daring him to fight on his land.

One guy dragged my mom away, and five guys held my dad down. The guy who hit me grabbed me by my hair and dragged me into a car. I tried to fight back, not wanting them to underestimate me, but it was useless. Yes, I was strong, but my vampire's strength wasn't anything compared to a male werewolf with a higher ranking. That was just how it worked.

If I were fighting against a pup or a normal wolf, then I would have been able to get them on the ground in an instant. But a warrior wolf was a challenge.

"We've got a feisty one," said one of the guys. The way he was looking at me disgusted me.

"Too bad she has to go. She would have been useful."

Oh no he didn't!

As they were snickering, I swung my leg backward and hit the guy holding me where the sun doesn't shine.

He yelled in pain as I grabbed the heads of the two guys with him and hit against each other with all my force. They both fell to the ground as two others came my way.

If I am going down, I certainly won't go down without a fight.

My fangs came out as my eyes reddened. I punched one of the guys in the stomach, but that seemed not to do anything. He lunged at me, but I quickly dodged it. I was about to make a run for it and help my parents when something hard hit my head. I yelled in pain as I fell to the ground. My vision started to blur, and I felt the darkness creep closer. The last thing I heard before being engulfed by it was, "Take her to the torture chamber."

* * *

My head throbbed in pain. The light in my room was too bright.

I thought I closed the curtains last night.

I opened my eyes but ended up regretting immediately. I closed them again and tried to rub the sleep out of me. But somehow my hands wouldn't move.

I opened my eyes again, widening them.

I wasn't in my room.

Shit.

Memories of what happened started to flow into my mind—memories of my parents and me trespassing and of me getting hit on the head.

I looked around to see that I was chained to a wall in a dungeon. There was a small window with bars through which light shined into my face, and it was really starting to annoy me. There were weird looking tools hanging on the walls. I started to panic when I saw several stakes lying on a metal tray.

Where are my parents? Are they okay? What's going to happen to us? Should I be worried about the tools on the wall?

I yanked on the chains binding my wrists, trying to break free, but it was no use. I took a moment to look at my surroundings, seeing if there was any way of escaping. The only way out was through a big metal door that had a lock.

The place smelled horrible like dead mice and something I know too well—blood.

Footsteps outside the dungeon door broke me from my thoughts. I stood still—well, not like I had much of a choice when I was chained to a wall. I held my breath, getting ready for what's coming.

The footsteps became louder every second it grew closer.

I heard a clicking sound as the steps stopped right outside the dungeon. The big metal door creaked open and more light shined into the dark room, blinding me. I turned my head to the side and squeezed my eyes shut. I heard someone walk into the room and close the door.

Once I opened my eyes, I was met with the Beta. He was standing a couple feet away from me, swinging keys in his hand. I lifted my head up high, showing no fear as he walked closer.

"You know for a little one like you, you sure know how to get into trouble," he said with a hint of amusement. "I don't think James will be able to walk for a few days."

I could see the corner of his mouth twitch upward as he said that. I gave him my best obvious fake smile and said, "I try."

He raised one eyebrow at me then walked over to the metal tray while swinging one stake around.

"What are you doing here?" he asked

His voice was now serious, not a trace of amusement left.

I pretend like I was thinking and said, "Well, I would not know. I think the hit on the head affected my memory. Maybe if you unlock me from these chains, I will remember."

There were a couple seconds of silence before his laughter boomed through the room. He wiped an imaginary tear from his cheek and walked closer to me.

"Yeah, sure. When the tooth fairy pays me a visit."

I huffed and rolled my eyes at him and said, "Listen, we weren't plotting some kind of evil attack if that's what you persist on thinking. My parents and I were only passing by."

The mention of my parents made me tense. I didn't really care what they would do with me as long as my parents were fine. They were always there for me; I was and still am their number one priority. The same thing goes for them. I was about to ask him where my parents were when he beat me to it.

"Your parents are fine—well, for now. Once the Alpha gets back, he will decide your fate."

I raised my eyebrows at him but let out a sigh of relief knowing my parents were okay for now.

"Well, when is that?" I asked, trying to keep my voice strong and hide my anxiousness.

He put the stake back on the metal tray and stepped back looking at his watch. "In about an hour," he answered looking up.

I gulped in fear.

An hour is a very short time—well, not that short when you're sitting in class wanting to go home. But that isn't the point. The point is that I might die in a few hours without saying goodbye to my parents. I'm too young to die.

I know what you're thinking, and yes, two hundred years is a very short time.

I just hope they don't cut my limbs out and use my head as an ornament to hang on the wall. That won't be pretty.

I looked at the Beta and asked, "Which pack is this?"

The Beta lifted his head up high and proud and said, "Black Blood pack."

The way he said it was expecting me to shudder in fear. Black Blood was one of the dangerous packs in America. I know, cliché, but they had the strongest men and more than one thousand pack members. They were known for their cruelty and harsh punishments.

I gulped in fear and looked at the tools hanging on the wall.

Yeah, I am going to go through hell.

The Beta gave me one last look then turned around so his back was facing me. He began to make his way to the door, and he stopped. He looked at me hesitantly before asking, "What's your name?"

A couple of seconds had passed before I realized what he asked.

"Stella," I said. Well, more like whispered.

He gave me a small smile while nodding his head. My mouth fell open at the slight gesture. I did not expect that this man in front of me had a single nice bone in him.

"The name's Liam. I'll try to convince the Alpha not to make your death painful."

With that, he exited the door.

Excuse me?

Wow, how sweet of him. Note the sarcasm.

* * *

It had been over an hour, but it seemed like only a minute. Time was passing by too fast for my liking.

Come on, why can't this ever happen when I'm in a meeting or attending a class?

I remembered the days when Alice and I would attend high school and sometimes skip class, spending our time in the bathroom making stupid jokes. I could still remember those days as if they were yesterday and not like they were a hundred years ago.

The thought of Alice made me smile sadly.

Maybe I can see her again. I guess now it won't be that bad.

Wait. What's that smell?

It smells like cinnamon and vanilla, which is strange. How can I smell something like that in a place like this? The walls are filled with mold as there's blood scattered everywhere. There's something in the corner of the room that seems to be puke. Ew.

Suddenly the smell got ten times stronger. Man, it smelled like heaven. I think I was drooling a bit.

The metal door opening caught my attention as more light once again shined into the room. The male standing in front of the door made my jaw drop.

There stood a muscular man all tall and proud. He had so much power radiating from him. It wanted me to submit. I didn't get a better look at him until he walked into the room. He was breathtaking; he had beautiful dark black hair that made me want to run my hands through them. And wow, don't get me started on that jawline.

Wait, what's wrong with me? Stella, snap out of it! This might be the dude who will kill you!

My eyes made their way to his, and that's when time stopped. His beautiful blue eyes glowed in the dark as he looked into mine. For a second I saw them darken as he let out a growl. My eyes widened in realization as I stood still, feeling like a deer caught in a lion's den.

No. No, this can't be happening. How can this be? It's impossible!

The guy stalked his way to me, and he wrapped his arms possessively around my waist and said one thing. One thing that could probably change my life for the better or worst.

"Mine."

Chapter 3

I was completely speechless. I tried to bring the words out of my mouth but failed.

This stranger right here in front of me is not just the Alpha of the most dangerous pack. But he is also my mate!

It had been years since the last time I heard about vampires and werewolves being mates. It's quite rare. And the hatred going on between them doesn't help at all. I've heard that the minute they lay eyes on each other, they will reject one another.

I don't see how that can work. I mean, your soul mate is supposed to love you and spend eternity with you.

How can I be with someone if they're going to die sooner or later and leave me all alone? How can I have a mate if I'm immortal and will never age?

My mate snuggled his head into the crook of my neck, and he inhaled my scent. I heard him whisper something that sounded something like, "Strawberry and chocolate."

I would have pushed him away, but I was still chained to the wall. I squirmed in his arms, trying to break free from his grasp, but that only caused him to tighten his hold. He rubbed his hand on my back, moving them up and down, while the other hand played with my hair. I felt his teeth graze my neck, and I panicked.

"Stop. What are you doing?" I yelled.

He ignored my question, and he lifted his head to look at my face. His eyes darkened when he saw my bruised cheek. He growled, and I could feel his chest vibrating.

"Who did that?" he asked huskily.

Damn, his voice is beautiful. I think I just heard bells jingling.

If he wasn't holding me, I think I would have fallen to the ground because my knees became weak.

Dammit! Stella, snap out of it. You can't fall for him. He's a mortal!

I shrugged my shoulders, not giving him an answer. I think I heard someone say his name was James.

I didn't really want anyone to die because of me, and the way my mate was looking at me, it looked like he was ready to kill.

He caressed my bruised cheek with his thumb as if that would make it feel better.

I gasped at the tingling I felt every time his thumb made contact with my skin. I pulled away, not wanting to give in. I put my best bored face on and started to move my chained hands.

"Do you mind unchaining me?"

He looked at the chains then growled again.

"Liam's in so much trouble," he grumbled more to himself. He grabbed some keys from his pocket and unlocked the chains. My wrists were red and bruised. I rubbed them, trying to make them feel better, then my mate grabbed and inspected them.

I pulled away, not wanting him to touch me or else I would give in. I took a couple steps back, creating a large distance between us. There were a couple moments of silence until I broke it.

"You know I'm a vampire, right?"

He nodded his head but said nothing. It's like he was looking into my soul. His eyes were roaming all over my body which made me insecure. I shifted my feet a little before continuing.

"Well, aren't you going to reject me?" I asked.

Probably not the best idea.

His head jerked, and he looked into my eyes as his got darker again. He walked over to me with inhuman speed and was towering me in just a second. He wrapped his arms possessively around me, bringing me to his chest as he growled.

"Mine! You're mine, and you're not going to leave me. I'm not going to reject you because you belong to me," he yelled.

Excuse me? Who does he think he is? Talking about me as if I were one of his possessions.

I used as much strength to push him away, only leaving inches of space between us. I furrowed my eyebrows.

"Since when did I belong to you? In case you haven't noticed, my kind hates you as much as you hate us. I don't belong to anyone and certainly not to you! Now, tell me where my parents are so we can get going."

I think I saw a vein pop. He was shaking with so much anger, I could see the tip of his claws come out. His wolf was probably surfacing. He pushed me to the nearest wall, resting each arm on the wall to my side, caging me. His scent was so strong which made it harder for me to resist.

"Listen here and listen closely."

His voice came out as a whisper, but I heard so much power in it.

"You aren't leaving. You and your parents will live here. You will become the Luna of this pack, and I don't care if you're a vampire. You belong to me and only me, the same way I belong to you. If you think about escaping, try all you want, love, but I will find you and drag you back here."

I was speechless... again.

How can I become the Luna of this pack when every single werewolf who lays eyes on me wants to rip me to shreds? How can my parents and I live in peace in a pack?

I was about to mention this to him when he beat me to it.

"If anyone disrespects you or so gives you a wrong impression, you tell me, and they will be punished."

Before I could say anything, he leaned in and rested his head on my neck, and he inhaled my scent to calm him down. I put my hands on his chest and pushed him away. I decided to drop the subject for later because he already seemed angry, and who knew what he could do when his wolf was in control.

"I want to see my parents."

He took a moment before nodding his head and grabbing my hand. I felt sparks at his touch. He pulled me to the metal door and said, "Go clean up first. I'll have someone grab you some clothes, and then we can meet up with your parents."

I nodded my head, and we walked for a minute in silence until he pushed me into a room that was filled with is scent— cinnamon and vanilla.

He exited the room after showing me the bathroom. I took a look around his room. The walls were white, and there was a king-sized bed in the center. The room was huge and had a door lead to a balcony.

I walked into the bathroom and made sure to lock the door. I did not want anyone to see me butt-naked, especially if he had so little control over himself. I turned on the water and adjusted its temperature. It took forever to warm up, but I finally got it right. I stripped off my clothes and got into the shower. There was no shampoo for women, so I used my mate's.

I don't even know his name. Geez, what a sweetheart, telling me that I will spend all my days here when I don't even know what to call him. It seems as if we skipped first base. There is no way I will give in, I mustn't

I'm a vampire for Pete's sake, which means that he will grow old and die and I will still look like my sexy self.

I started to scrub my body and wash my hair.

I'm pretty sure once I come out I'll reek of him.

Once I was done, I got out and covered myself with a towel then brushed my hair and left it down.

I slowly opened the door and peeked into the room, not wanting to bump into him while I was in only a towel. Thankfully, there was no one in the room, and at the center of the bed, I spotted a pile of new clothes and my suitcase.

I ignored the new pile of clothes, and I opened my suitcase and took out a pair of black underwear, a pair of tight jeans, and a t-shirt. I quickly put them on then walked over to the door. I opened it, and there seemed to be no one in the hallway.

Oh great. Now, where do I go?

I made my way out of the room and into the empty hall. I didn't leave my guard down, not wanting to bump into the wrong person. I was in a place that despises vampires; if I ran into the wrong person, then that would have surely caused some trouble.

I was lost in my thoughts when I bumped into a girl—well, she bumped into me.

She was carrying a huge stack of books covering her face. She must not have seen where she was going because she came crashing into me and we both fell as each book scattered onto the ground. I lay on the ground groaning as a book hit my already bruised head.

"Oh my gosh, I'm so sorry," she said as she got off the ground and helped me up.

What really surprised me was she gave me a small smile as if I was completely not a threat to her. She then got on the ground again, picking up her books. I kneeled down to help her.

Wow, there are so many books. Well, it looks like we've got a bookworm over here.

Wait a minute!

"Is that *The Giver*?" I asked excitedly while pointing at a book she just grabbed. She looked at me smiling then nodded her head.

"Yeah, it's one of my favorites. Read it three times," she said and chuckled.

I raised one eyebrow at her and said, "Three times? I read it about fifteen."

I had a grin on my face when her eyes widened. "Living for two hundred years tends to get boring sometimes," I continued and shrugged my shoulders.

"Woah, two hundred years is a long time," she said as she collected her books from me. I smiled at her comment and nodded my head.

"My name is Marie Lundgren. What's yours, immo?"

"Immo?" I asked as I raised one eyebrow at her.

She laughed at my expression and continued, "Yeah, immo, as in short for immortal."

I laughed at her nickname for me.

I love this girl already.

I reached my right hand out for her to shake.

"The name's Stella."

She ignored my hand and gave me a bone-crushing hug. I smiled at her friendly gesture. Something about her reminded me of Alice. I don't know what it was, but it's probably the way she was so outgoing. I hugged her back then pulled away.

"Nice to meet you, immo," she said, completely ignoring my name. "What's a vampire like you doing here in a pack?"

I sighed at her questions.

Well, at least, she doesn't hate on me. It's really rare to find werewolves who don't hate on vampires. In the two hundred years I've lived, I've only met a couple of wolves who don't hate us. Alice was one of them.

"My parents and I accidentally trespassed into this pack," I answered, leaving out that her Alpha was my mate.

She nodded her head but then asked, "Not to sound rude, but how are you not dead?"

I shrugged at her question, not really having an answer for that.

Our conversation was interrupted when Liam walked toward us. He smiled when he saw me stand next to Marie. I still couldn't believe this was the dominant guy that stopped us in our tracks yesterday. Well, at least, that's what I thought. I turned to Marie and asked her, "What's today's date?"

By the time I asked, Liam was standing right next to me and answered for Marie, "April third."

His answer caused my jaw to drop and my eyes to widen. "Three days? I've been out for three days!" I yelled.

What about my parents? How were they treated in these past few days?

My anxiousness increased by the second but disappeared when Liam spoke.

"Your parents are fine. They weren't hurt. They're just worried about you. Of course, it did take a while for your father to calm down, but in the end, all is good," he assured me.

I sighed in relief. I swear this guy could read minds! I was about to ask Liam what he was doing here when he beat me to it, again.

"Aiden sent me here to grab you and take you to your parents," he explained.

My eyebrows furrowed in confusion.

"Who?" I asked.

Liam smirked at me and gave me a teasing look.

"Oh come on, don't tell me you don't know your own mate's name?" he said with a hint of amusement.

Dammit! So that was his name—Aiden.

Before I could throw some kind of comeback at him, Marie's voice boomed through the hallway.

"What! Your Aiden's mate! Oh my god, oh my god. That's wonderful. So that explains it. You're going to become our Luna," Marie shouted as she jumped up and down.

The mention of me becoming Luna of this pack worried me.

What will my parents say? Will they be disappointed that their only daughter is mated with an Alpha, let alone the Alpha of the most dangerous pack in America?

I felt a lump in my throat as I realized that I might lose my parents because of my fate.

Well, not if I can help it. There's only one thing to do.

And that's to reject Aiden!

Chapter 4

I could tell right away that Liam, Marie, and I were going to become good friends.

Too bad I can't stay here much longer. I don't belong here, especially if I'm going to become the Luna. Never in my life have I heard of a vampire being the Luna. Besides, how can the pack respect her if they hate her kind? It just doesn't make sense. Anyway, I have the plan all sorted in my head. Well, kinda.

Reject Aiden.

Grab my parents.

Then get out of here.

I hope it will be easy as much as it sounds. Yes, I know I said that rejecting your mate is something horrible to do, but it's not like I have much of a choice. Aiden really expects me to stay by his side while I watch him grow old then die?

Not going to happen!

Marie left to go put her books away while Liam took me to see my parents. While we were walking, I could tell that my first impression about Liam was wrong. He wasn't the serious type; he's outgoing just like Marie and could be really funny. He had so many jokes up his sleeve; I don't think I ever laughed this much in just two minutes. He seemed to be a little cocky since he's the Beta of this pack. This I knew at first glance.

We finally made it in front of a big door. While we were walking, I noticed that this was a pack house—which is really huge, by the way. Every time I would pass by someone, I would get anxious. Some would glare at me, while others gave me questioning looks, wondering what a vampire was doing walking with the Beta. But no one said anything. Would they dare when I was standing next to their Beta?

Liam opened the door, and the fresh smell of cinnamon and vanilla hit me. I walked into the room to see my parents standing with Aiden. This got my guard up. Aiden being in the same room with my father was probably not the best idea, especially because he was a werewolf.

My mom was more like me. She always saw the glass half full. She was more of a peaceful person, and she hated the hate going on between two sides. But if someone gave her something to hate on, then that's when shit broke loose. You don't want to see my mom's bad side.

My dad. Well, that's another story. I can say he's the total opposite. You gave him lemons, he wouldn't make lemonade. You know what he would do? He would squeeze it and pour it all over your new cuts that he made and watch you suffer as it burns you.

Yes, harsh, but he had a soft spot for my mom and me.

My parents met somewhere in the sixteen hundreds. They were both turned into vampires sometime before and were very lonely. To watch all your relatives and loved ones die while you never age can lead to depression. But my dad was there for my mom, and my mom was there for him.

You can either be born as a vampire and stop aging at twenty or get turned into one like my parents. My mom and dad were both turned into vampires sometime in their twenties. My mom was about to die from the plague when her vampire uncle saved her life by turning her into a vampire. To this day, she and Uncle Robert are very close.

My dad's tragic story is probably why he is himself these days. My dad used to date someone in the fifteen hundreds. Her name was Alexandra. She and my father were very close. One day, they were out on the streets going home when a gang attacked them. One member was a vampire. As the other guys had their way with Alexandra, my dad was held to the ground watching. The vampire decided to turn him into his kind just for fun. That night was probably the worst night of dad's life, watching as the life drained out of Alexandra and into his.

As I got closer into the room, I could tell that my mom had a worried expression on and my dad seemed to be raging. My mom was standing next to him, rubbing her hands on his arm up and down, trying to calm him down. Once they both noticed me, my mom rushed to my side, giving me a crushing hug.

"Oh, sweetie, are you okay? We were so worried about you."

My mom inspected me for any harm done. The bruise on my cheek and head were already healing thanks to my vampire healing. I smiled at my mom hugged her back.

I looked at my father and saw his eyes soften. He came my way and pulled me to his chest. There were a couple moments of silence.

Why is my dad raging? Is it possible that Aiden told him I was his mate and that I have to become the Luna?

Once my dad pulled away, I looked at Aiden to see him looking at me with cold eyes. For a moment, I saw them soften. Something inside me broke when I remembered my plan. Something told me not to do it. It was probably the mate bond, but I just ignored it. I looked at my parents. They were my number one priority. I had to focus on them and no one else.

"Mom, Dad, can you leave us alone for a bit?" I pointed to Aiden and myself.

My dad raised one eyebrow at me while my mom gave me a confused look. It looked like my dad was about to refuse, but my mom intervened.

"Of course, sweetie. Take your time. We'll be outside waiting."

She pulled my father by the arm and dragged him outside of the room with Liam.

Once the door closed, I looked at Aiden and prepared myself for what's coming. I took a deep breath and saw that he was looking at me with questioning eyes. I walked closer to him so that I could tell him what I wanted to say. But he wrapped his arm around my waist and rested his head in the crook of my neck.

I sighed out of annoyance. *Wow, does this guy like to cuddle.* I didn't want to admit it, but it actually felt good to be in his arms. *Too bad it can't last.*

I put my hand on his chest and pushed him away with all my force and stepped back.

He growled disapprovingly and filled in the space between us.

"Stop. We can't do this. I can't be with you! Just let my parents, and I return to where we came from," I yelled.

His hands dug into the skin of my back. His claws were now coming out. This meant only one thing, and that was his wolf was surfacing. *Yup, he must be furious.*

I could feel the blood dripping from my back as he started to shake.

This guy is unbelievably moody

He pushed me to the nearest wall with all his force. I yelped in surprise when my back hit the wall. He pushed me up against the wall to the point that I felt like a sandwich.

I was about to complain when he did something that I wish he didn't.

He kissed me.

Yup, I knew this was going to be hard to resist. His lips were a perfect fit against mine. They tasted so good; I've never tasted anything like them. They tasted like cinnamon and vanilla, which had me wanting for more. As cliché as it sounds, I saw fireworks behind my eyes as he started to move his lips against mine. It took me a moment to realize what was going on, then I started to move my lips with his.

Shit. Bad, bad move. Little did I know that this seemingly innocuous action was me opening my arms wide to fate.

This kiss was no sweet and gentle one. No, it was rough and aggressive. I knew his purpose; it was to show me that I belong to him, and only him.

In all my two hundred years, I've never met a better kisser than Aiden. Yes, I had my fair share with the guys I've dated, but not one had this much effect on me. I was no virgin.

You really can't expect a vampire who's lived for more than a hundred years to be one.

If one kiss is doing this to me, then how will it be like when we move to the mating process?

Ugh, I did it again!

No, Stella! That can't happen! I mustn't lose control. I can't lose another important person once again.

I was about to stop him, but his hold on me was so tight. His teeth were biting the bottom of my lips, asking for access. I, of course, refused. I shut my lips together so tight not giving him the satisfaction.

But I should have known he wouldn't give up until he got what he wanted. All Alphas are like that.

One of his hands slid down my back going lower and lower. His hand stopped at the hem of my shirt. It slid right under my shirt, and I gasped every time it made contact with my skin. Aiden then took the opportunity to slide his tongue into my mouth. At first, I tried to resist, not kissing him back. He started to growl, not liking my behavior, but after a while, I finally gave in. I could feel him smile against my lips in approval.

We were fighting for dominance—well, I was trying to show him who he was messing with. Kissing him was such a bad idea. *Now the bond is going to get stronger, and it will be harder to leave him.*

In the end, he won. He was too strong compared to me. His giant frame was towering my little one as the hand under my shirt was teasing my skin.

It was such an amazing feeling. I remembered the first time I lost my V-card. It was before I turned twenty. I was in high school—I think I was seventeen. I remember dating this guy for months, and one night, he invited me over, and it just happened.

I can never forget the look on Alice's face when I told her. She was so happy for me but shocked at the same time. She told me that she didn't want to become an aunt yet, and that I was still too young to get pregnant. Those were the days.

My thoughts were cut off when Aiden pulled away for air. He and I were panting heavily, and only our breathing was heard in the silent room. He laid his forehead on mine as he stared into my eye. My lips were red and swollen. I think there was a cut from where he bit. I was speechless.

"How many times do I have to tell you until it gets through your thick skull? You aren't leaving, and that's final. This is your home now, and I already informed your parents. They know that you're the Luna of this pack and my mate."

Dammit! I knew it. That's why dad was raging. God, I hope he doesn't hate me. What will I do? I can't stay here and repeat history all over again.

"You do not understand, do you? I am immortal. I shall never age! You expect me to stay by your side as I watch you grow old and die? Well, I shall not let that happen. I'm not going to let history repeat itself," I yelled in his face.

I was about to run out the door when he grabbed my wrist and turning me around. My body hit his chest. I could feel the abs under his shirt.

I think I'm drooling. Oh God, what he does to me!

He leaned over so he could reach my eye level. His eyes were dark blue. He was breathing heavily as his eyes looked into my soul, sending shivers all over my body.

"What did you say?" he asked. His voice was husky; his wolf was taking over.

"What?" I asked, not understanding what he was asking.

"What did you mean by history repeating itself, huh? There's someone else, isn't there? Is that why you keep resisting me? Well, let me tell you this—you should get over him. He's gone, and you're mine," he yelled.

I mentally slapped myself. His possessiveness was overwhelming. I've heard of possessive Alphas before, but I never thought that they would step up to this level. While I was talking about Alice, Mr. Smartypants right here thought I was talking about another guy. Ridiculous!

I rubbed my eyes with the palm of my hands. It was getting dark outside, and that day had been a very long. I ran my hands through my now dried hair and said, "Oh my God, you've completely misunderstood."

By this time, all I wanted to do was sleep and forget all about my problems.

He looked at me like he didn't believe me.

"Really? Then care to explain what you meant by that? Who did you lose, and why are they so important to you that you want to reject me?"

His voice was calm, but I could hear the anger and confusion in them.

"Can we talk about this later? I'm tired. I've been locked up in a dungeon chained to a wall for days. All I want to do is sleep," I said more to myself than to him.

He looked at me with worried eyes. He nodded his head and said, "Fine. But this isn't over. Let's go to bed. Our room isn't too far away from here."

Yes, finally.

Wait.

Did he just say our *room?*

Chapter 5

"I find it very funny how you think that I'm actually going to sleep in the same bed as you," I said and chuckled.

This guy is hilarious!

I put my hands on my hip and started to look around the pack house.

"This place is huge. I'm pretty sure there are other rooms available."

He shook his head while frowning. "Why do you have to be so stubborn? I swear I've never met anyone like you," he grumbled while running his hands over his face and through his hair.

"You're not sleeping in another room. Everything that belongs to me belongs to you. Got it?" he said.

I shook my head at him, not wanting to be defeated.

"Either it's that, or I sleep on the floor," I exclaimed.

He sighed in annoyance then grabbed my hand and started to walk us to our room.

Once we made it, he grabbed a pillow and a blanket then threw them on a couch right across from the bed.

"I'll sleep here. Happy?"

I smiled in satisfaction. Then the thought of my parents came to mind.

"What about my parents?" I asked.

I got some clothes out of the suitcase to sleep in.

Aiden looked at me then answered as he walked into his closet, "I already had Liam show them to their room."

I followed him into the closet and gasped in surprise. Not because it was huge, but because half of it was filled with new female clothes that looked like my size. I looked at Aiden for an explanation, but he only shrugged his shoulders.

"Had someone bring them over a couple hours ago."

I gave him my best are-you-crazy look while shaking my head.

"You know this wasn't necessary, right? I mean, I already have clothes in my suitcase," I told him.

He only stuffed one of his hand in his pocket, grabbed boxers from a counter, and walked out leaving me behind.

I walked into the bathroom and locked it. I stripped out of my clothes and got into my sleeping ones. Once I was done, I brushed my hair, tied it up into a ponytail, and then brushed my teeth. Once I got out, I was met with a half-naked Aiden.

I couldn't believe what I was seeing. He stood right in front of me with all his glory, looking like a sexy god. *Damn, those abs. He has a six-pack that had me begging to lick. And that V-line. Don't get me started.*

Dammit, I did it again! I really need to shower myself with some holy water.

I think he noticed me ogling him because he had a wide grin that showed his beautiful straight white teeth.

"Like what you see, babe?"

I hide my blush then put my best bored face on and rolled my eyes.

"I've seen better," I told him.

I know I was lying to myself. No other guy I've seen before was this sexy—with those muscular arms and lickable chest. I think I was drooling.

In a flash, Aiden was towering over me with his huge frame. I had to tilt my head upward to look at him or else I would have been staring at his abs. One of his arms wrapped itself around my waist while the other one caressed the spot where my neck and shoulder met.

"I wonder how my claim would look on you," he whispered.

I held my breath.

That brought shivers down my spine.

I hate to say this, but I love his touch. How can I not? I am his mate. It's just things can never work out between us.

I remembered all those years watching Alice grow old. Humans would always ask me why I'm best friends with a grandma. I was there for her every step of the way. I wouldn't expect the humans to understand. How could I tell them that I've known her ever since high school and I'm just not aging?

I tucked the memories deep back into my mind, not wanting to think about it at the moment.

I took a step back from Aiden and walked over to the bed. You're probably thinking this is going to be one of those cliché moments where the girl gets to sleep in the guy's bed while he sleeps on the couch, and then she feels guilty, so she invites him over to sleep next to her.

Yeah, not going to happen.

It's not that I was cold-hearted or something. It's just that I didn't think I could hold back if we shared the same bed.

I got under the sheets as Aiden walked over to the couch. He turned off the light and lay down on the couch which was a bit small for his tall frame. I lay my head on the soft pillow as I get ready for sleep to consume me. But before I dozed off, I heard Aiden's voice.

"Good night, baby."

* * *

I walked pass the forest, wiping the blood off my face with a napkin I had in my pocket. I didn't want to run into a human with rabbit blood all over my mouth. They would certainly freak out.

I made my way toward Alice's house. The sun was bright that day, and the birds were singing. Once I knocked on the door, Jimmy opened it while holding a lollipop. He smiled at me, grinning with missing front teeth. I walked into the house to see Alice reading a book to her other two grandchildren. Once she saw me, she tried to get up from her rocking chair, but I rushed over to stop her.

"No, Alice. Don't get up. You know what the doctor said."

She nodded her head then closed the book she was reading to the kids. She gave it to Jamie, her daughter.

I sat down next to Alice.

I don't have to meet her in secret anymore, not like when we were in high school. My parents accepted the fact that I was best friends with a werewolf a long time ago. It's been about fifty years since we met in high school in 1831.

Alice was getting weaker and weaker by the day. She got sick very often and showed signs of dementia. Her state was worrying the hell out of me. It hurt so much to watch and not being able to do anything.

"How was your day?" Alice's voice came out as a whisper.

I smiled at her and started telling her how my day went by.

Seeing Alice smile as I told her funny stories about me bumping into werewolves and getting into fights with them always made my day. She would always tell me that I was a feisty one, never to lose a fight.

There was once in senior year, Alice's boyfriend cheated on her. He was one of those jerks—what do you call them? Oh yeah, manwhores. I warned Alice several times, not wanting to get her heart broken, but she didn't listen.

I mean, come on, when did she ever listen?

And can you guess what I did once I found out that bastard was sleeping around with other women? I got one of those big hairy spiders I found in the forest and made sure to put it in his lunch while he was around everyone in the cafeteria.

That day was probably the worst day of his life. He was so humiliated! Of course, he blamed it on me, but he had no proof. Alice and I went home cracking up. Seeing her smile was one of my goals in life. She was and forever will be my sister.

Jimmy came over to us while holding a book in his hand. He was always Alice's favorite grandchild. I think it was the way they thought alike.

He gave the book to Alice so she could read it for him. Alice was just finishing up the first page when she dropped the book and fell to the ground.

I got up immediately trying to stop what I knew was going to happen. But deep down inside, I knew it was too late.

That was when my world stopped.

* * *

My eyes snapped open. The sun was shining into the room, making it perfectly clear that there was no more room for sleep.

That's when I remembered the dream I just had last night. It was enough to keep me wide awake.

Well, it was more like a memory.

My heart was still racing, and I was sweating a lot for some reason. Yes, it was spring, but it wasn't hot that I would sweat in bed. I decided to get up and have a nice long shower before seeing my parents, but when I tried to get up, I was held back down.

What?

Oh please don't tell me I'm chained to the wall again.

I looked around to see that I was in the same place I slept in last night.

But why can't I move?

Suddenly someone mumbling in their sleep made me realize what was going on.

Oh no he didn't! He is so dead.

I turned my head to the side to see Aiden's sleeping face. His arms were securely wrapped around my waist as his bare chest was pressed up against my back. Aiden was practically a second blanket.

For a moment, I stared at his sleeping expression. He looked so peaceful, not the serious Alpha I met yesterday.

I stopped my thoughts from wandering off, grabbed a glass of water that was resting on the counter next to me, and poured it all over his face.

That will show him!

He got up as soon as the water touches his face. He looked around. I could hear his heart beating so fast. I bet I scared the crap out of him. Once he saw me, he relaxed a bit but seemed pissed. He ran his hand through his wet hair while groaning.

I was trying so hard not to laugh.

"What was that for?" he asked.

I ignored his question.

"What on earth were you doing sleeping next to me?" I asked, hiding my amusement.

He got up, displaying his gorgeous body.

"Geez, you're such a pain to deal with. I couldn't sleep last night, so I came here. Besides, that's my bed," he grumbled.

I lifted one of my eyebrows at him and crossed my arms over my chest.

"I gave you a choice yesterday, and that was to give me a separate room," I said.

He looked at me then shook his head.

"Not happening."

God, he is so stubborn! Looks like he wants to wake up like this every morning.

I got off of the bed and made my way to the bathroom. I did my daily morning routine: took a shower, braided my hair, and brushed my teeth. Today, I chose to wear a floral dress, which was one of my favorite.

I walked out of the room to see Aiden gone and Marie sitting on the bed eating a granola bar.

Once she saw me, she got up and gave me a hug.

"Hey, immo. How was your first night here? Well, I mean first night here not chained up," she hesitantly said the last part which made me laugh.

I nodded my head at her and spoke, "It was delightful."

She smiled at me and handed me a granola bar.

I took it thankfully because I wasn't planning on eating breakfast with Aiden. All I wanted to do was see my parents and clear up what happened yesterday.

"Do you know where my parents are?" I asked Marie.

She shook her head while stuffing the last piece of granola in her mouth.

"Let's go look for them."

She grabbed my arm and dragged me out of the room.

Marie kept on telling me about the pack while she gave me a tour of the pack house. I found out that she, Liam, and Aiden were actually childhood friends, which surprised me. Yet that was not the only thing which surprised me. It was the vision everybody outside of this pack had of Aiden.

The cruel and serious alpha turned out to be only rumors. Aiden was nothing like that at all.

We were walking through an empty hall when I bumped into some guy. I looked up to apologize, but when I saw who it was, I immediately changed my mind.

Great, I just had to bump into him!

James, the guy who slapped me, and I kicked his balls.

He growled when he noticed it was me then gave me a threatening look.

"What are you doing out of the dungeon, you bloodsucker?"

Looks like Aiden hasn't spread word that I'm his mate.

That's supposed to be a good thing right?

I was surprised when James came my way and pushed me against the wall. He held my neck in his hands, and I rose a little from the ground. My body pleaded for oxygen. I was paralyzed in shock, but once I recovered from it, I tried to break free.

Yeah, but here's the thing. James was a warrior, a wolf with a higher ranking than mine, so my strength wasn't completely near his.

Marie was begging him to let me go, but he wouldn't budge. I saw Marie's eyes roll up, looking toward the ceiling, as she stood still. I bet she was mind-linking someone.

I started to squirm in his hold, getting a little dizzy. Black spots blurred my vision. I wasn't going to die from this, but I was surely going to pass out.

I heard James's voice whisper in my ear, "You think you can trespass then hit me and get away with it? You are going to pay, and I'm going to make sure your death is painful."

Okay, this dude has some issues. I don't know if it's because I'm a vampire or because I hit him, but he definitely hates my guts.

I felt like my lungs were about to explode, and Marie's screaming started to fade as darkness took over my vision. But before I could completely pass out, a vicious growl was heard throughout the hall.

James released me, and I fell to the ground coughing and sucking in as much air as I could get. I looked up to see a furious Aiden.

And he looked ready to kill.

Chapter 6

Aiden was shaking with rage, and it meant only one thing.

His wolf.

Before I could blink, he was already shifted.

And wow, was he gorgeous.

His wolf was huge. I don't think I've ever seen anything like it. He had so much power radiating from him; it made me want to submit. But my stubbornly side never wanted to give in. His amazingly gray fur stood out so much. I've never heard of an Alpha with gray fur; they're usually black, which is why Aiden was so special in a way. All I could think of was running my hand through it.

While I was lost in my thoughts, I didn't notice that Aiden ran toward James and attacked. I was surprised when James shifted just before Aiden could touch him.

Will he dare fight back against his Alpha? I don't really blame him. I mean, he is fighting for his life after all. I wouldn't want to go down without a fight either.

James's wolf was dark brown and bigger than an average male wolf but not larger than Aiden. When James bit on Aiden's leg, I started to panic.

Oh, I hope Aiden doesn't get hurt.

Wait, since when did I start to care about him? I mean, I only met him yesterday. Curse you, stupid mate bond!

It was like I kept going in a circle. My mind and heart were racing, and I couldn't control them. One minute I was listening to my mind, then the other I was being controlled by my heart.

Aiden was growling at James viciously. His eyes turned black, which meant he was furious. I would hate to be James. Aiden was sure going to kill him.

Aiden's wolf was on top of James. As he bit into his chest, you could hear James's wolf barking in pain. He didn't stand a chance against Aiden.

What surprised me was that Aiden didn't go for the neck. No, he went for the legs, then the arms, then his stomach. I knew why. He was making his death painful.

I remembered Alice once telling me that the neck was the wolf's Achilles heel. A direct kill.

But Aiden wasn't looking for one. He wanted him to suffer.

There was blood scattered all over the ground, which made me hungry. I always had a weakness when it came to blood. It's just so good. I mean, you can't really blame me. What do you expect from a vampire?

Marie wrapped her arms around me, comforting me. But it's not like I needed the comfort. I thought the brown wolf under Aiden who's losing a lot of blood needed it more than I did. She was whispering words that I could not make out. All my concentration was on James's lifeless body lying on the floor as Aiden continued to rip his body to shreds.

You might be thinking that this will traumatize me, but no. I've seen worse. Like maybe the day Alice died right in front of my eyes. That, my friend, was traumatizing.

Once Aiden calmed down, he came over to me and licked my bruised neck. I bet by tomorrow it would be healed. He nuzzled his nose in the crook of my neck, and he inhaled my scent. It was very hard for me to resist. I couldn't hold back, so I did the thing that my mind was begging me to do. I ran my hands through his soft gray fur.

I think I just heard him purr. Wolves don't purr, right?

His wolf licked my cheek in approval.

How can this be the same wolf who just killed someone?

Marie went to grab some clothes for Aiden to wear because when he shifted, they were ripped to shreds. Once she was back, Aiden shifted to his human form and, oh my gosh, I think my face was red as a tomato. I looked at the ground as I turned around, leaving my back facing him as he changed. I heard him chuckle at my reaction. Once I was sure that he was done, I turned around and was pulled to his chest.

He smelled like blood, and if I weren't a vampire, I would have found this disturbing. Something deep down inside me was relieved to see him okay and not hurt. His leg was healing really fast since he was an Alpha.

His thumb stroked my neck as he inspected me for any other injuries. I pulled away and spoke, "You did not have to kill him."

He shook his head at me as his eyes darkened.

"You're defending him when he was about to kill you? He deserved it. No one should lay their hands on you. No one!" he growled.

I decided to drop the subject. Even though I didn't like James, I don't think anyone deserves death. Everyone should be given a second chance.

I pulled away from Aiden, and he growled. But I just rolled my eyes.

"I want to go see my parents. Do you know where they are? Oh, and you should probably go take a shower. You smell like blood," I mumbled the last part.

He grinned widely.

"Oh, but you know you like it. Don't you just want to eat me up?" he asked.

Wow, someone's a little too cocky.

I rolled my eyes at him and shook my head.

"Please, I'd rather eat garlic."

He laughed really hard. His laugh was music to my ears. Beautiful.

* * *

Half an hour later, I was sitting with my parents in the same room they slept in last night. Aiden had some pack work, so he showed me to their room and left. I was so nervous.

What will my parents say? Will they hate me, or will they accept the fact I am mated to a werewolf?

My mom seemed completely fine when she saw me, but I could tell that she was worried. While my dad wasn't raging, I could tell he was pissed. My parents meant so much to me since they were the only ones left around, so I needed their approval.

Their thoughts mean the world to me and knowing that something could get in the way scares me.

Being a vampire means one thing—immortality. Which means that everyone around you will die. You will have to grow up and live with the fact that sooner or later you will be alone.

Swallowing the lump in my throat, I tried not to think about Alice. But I knew deep down inside that my experience with her was the greatest example of how being a vampire is like. Which was why I was so attached to my parents.

We weren't like humans who separate after a certain age. We stuck together just like any other vampire family.

"Mom, Dad, I really don't know what to tell you. I really don't know what to do about this situation. I just hope you guys aren't disappointed in me," I whispered the last part.

My parents got up from where they were sitting and gave me a warm, loving hug.

"Oh, sweetie, why would we be disappointed in you?" my mom began. "It's just when we heard the news we were both shocked and worried. We just want you to be safe and happy."

I looked at my dad then asked, "But why were you so mad yesterday when Aiden told you I was his mate? It's because he's a werewolf isn't it?"

My dad shook his head while chuckling.

"Oh, sweetie, you don't get it. Yes, I don't quite get along with werewolves—"

Before he could finish, my mom raised an eyebrow at him and said, "Don't get along? Lucas, you hate them."

I smiled.

"Bella, let me continue. Geez, as I was saying, I don't care if he's a wolf, vampire, hybrid, or human. You're my baby girl, and just seeing you grow up so fast makes me think you don't need us anymore."

I was shocked to hear what he just said. I was always daddy's little girl, even though I was more than a hundred years old. I gave my parents a big smile as I tried to prevent the tears threatening to escape my eyelids.

"Mom, Dad, you guys will always be number one in my heart. No one will ever replace you."

Then the thought came into my mind: *What will I do with Aiden?*

"It's just I'm confused on what to do. Aiden is my mate, but he is mortal. I don't want to lose another important person in my life," I whispered, looking at my lap as I played with my fingers nervously. My voice cracked in the end.

My mom took my hand in hers and smiled at me sadly. I'm pretty sure she knows who I was talking about.

"What does your heart want? I know you're afraid of what's coming, but sometimes you just have to stop worrying about the future and live the present. Take a couple of risks and have fun with your life. I just want to tell you that being with your mate is one of the best things in life."

When she said the last part, she looked at my dad. They were so much in love; it sometimes made me envy them.

I realized that what my mom said was right.

What does my heart want? I still don't know yet.

"Oh, and we have a little of bad news," Dad's worried voice broke off the moment.

Bad news? Splendid! Now what?

I looked at my dad so he could continue, but my mom beat him to it.

"Sweetie, Uncle Robert has gotten himself into an accident."

My mom paused as my eyes widened in surprise.

"He was out with a couple of friends when some wolves decided to attack. He is really injured, and not even his vampire powers can heal him," my mom continued.

I ran my hands over my face and through my hair. This must be so difficult for my mom to deal with. They were really close. After all of her family died, she had no one but him. Letting out a sigh of frustration, I looked back up at my parents.

"Me and your father decided that tomorrow morning we're going to go visit him and make sure he's okay."

What? Uncle Robert lived all the way in Japan!

"How long will you be gone? What about me? Can't I come with you?" I asked.

They're going to leave me here all alone in a pack with Aiden!

My dad shook his head then spoke, "Sweetie, we will be gone for probably three to four weeks, and Aiden won't allow us to take you with us for that long."

Dammit! Where is the overly protective father when I need him?

I sighed in defeat. I didn't want to stay here all alone, but I couldn't prevent my parents from going. They had to go.

I nodded my head understandingly.

"Okay, but you guys have to call me every day and tell me what happens," I said sternly, narrowing my eyes.

My parents nodded their heads.

Sometimes I feel like I'm the one who's parenting around.

❧

The day was pretty boring aside from the fact I witnessed someone being killed. I spent my afternoon with Marie. We were getting pretty close. She told me that she hasn't found her mate yet.

I know I never bring this up, but I gave up on finding my mate years ago. It's really rare for a vampire to find their mate. Living for so long had an effect on us. We usually don't get to meet them probably because they died years before we get the chance to meet them. The only possibility you can find your mate is if they're a vampire. If not, then your chances are very low.

I remembered the day Alice first met her mate. It was probably the best day of her life. They say being with your mate completes you. But how can you feel complete if you know that it's going to end? In a very, very terrible way.

Death.

I walked into Aiden's bedroom, still not accepting the fact that it's mine too.

The room was empty, so I decide to get changed and go to sleep. My parents are leaving early tomorrow to catch their flight, so I'll be waking up around six o'clock. I walked into the closet where I put my clothes in and grabbed the same clothes I wore yesterday.

After I came out of the bathroom, Aiden walked through the door looking all tired. It must have been a long day for him. I haven't seen him since this morning's event. Something inside me was telling me to let him sleep on the bed, but I ignored it.

Before I could tell him anything, he got on the bed and slept in a second.

He didn't even take off his own damn shoes!

I sighed in defeat as I walked over to the bed and took them off for him. I put an alarm on my phone so that I could wake up early, then I get under the cover. I make sure to leave enough distance between us. The last time I slept in the same bed with a guy was probably twenty years ago. I've been walking the single path for a while now, not wanting to get too attached to someone.

Aiden wrapped his arms around my waist and pulled me closer. If it weren't for his even breathing, I would have thought for sure he was awake. I tried to break free, but it's no use. Even in his sleep, he's stronger than me.

I guess it won't hurt if it's just for one night.

I closed my eyes as I felt myself drifting off. The last thought I had before sleep consumed me was how good it felt to be complete.

Chapter 7

Beep.

What's that noise?

Beep. Beep.

It's so loud.

Beep. Beep. Beep.

Ugh, can't it shut the hell up? I'm sleeping here.

I heard someone groan next to me. I felt so warm. Warmer than anything I've ever felt. I didn't want to get up.

Can't I just stay here forever?

I am not much of a morning person, but that didn't make me lazy. Nothing would ever make me stay in bed all day and not be productive. But now, well, I just wanted to stay like this forever.

It was so peaceful. My mind was fuzzy, and I felt as if I was on cloud nine. The smell of cinnamon and vanilla filled my nose as I breathed in and out.

It feels so perfect. I feel perfect.

Beep. Beep. Beep. Beep.

You know what! I change my mind.

I snapped my eyes open and groaned when I was met with light shining into my eyes. My head was lying on Aiden's chest. I looked up to see him sleeping, but every time the annoying sound would go on, he would groan in his sleep and mumble some unclear words.

What the hell is that sound?

I turned around to where the noise was coming from to see that it was my phone.

Shit. I totally forgot about today!

I got up and did a little happy dance when I was free from Aiden's tight grip. It took me a while to unwrap myself from him. He's just so clingy. I then rushed to the bathroom and took a quick shower.

Once I was done, I got dressed in jeans and a blouse. I left my hair down naturally and brushed my teeth. I got out of the bathroom, feeling all refreshed and ready for my day. I then was met with Aiden sitting on the bed as he rubbed the sleep out of his eyes and looking at me confused.

"Where are you going?" he asked in a sleepy voice.

I ignored the shivers that ran down my spine and answered his question, "My parents' flight is in two hours. They're leaving soon."

Aiden nodded his head, got up to get into the bathroom, and gave me a kiss on the forehead along the way.

I left the room after letting out a sigh and went downstairs to the dining room. I still got nervous when I'm around the pack members. Some knew that I was Aiden's mate, but not all did. Aiden and I hadn't discussed presenting me to the pack yet. And I was thankful for that. I needed a little more time.

I don't think I'm ready. I don't know if I ever will be.

When I made it to the last step, I saw my parents carrying their bags out the door. I made my way toward them to help.

Once they saw me, we gave each other a hug, and then they returned to what they were doing.

Half an hour later, my parents were ready to go, and Aiden was standing by my side. I hugged my parents and wished them good luck. Even though I wished they never had to go, I couldn't be immature. Uncle Robert needed them, and I had no right to prevent them from seeing him. I was sure going to miss them though. My mom and my dad told Aiden to look after me. I rolled my eyes.

I don't need Aiden to look after me. I'm two hundred years old!

They got into the car and drove to the airport. Aiden and I were standing outside of the pack house, and it was my first time being out here since I got here. Each person who would walk by would either give me a questioning or dirty look as if I was a rat with the plague. So Aiden had the nerves to wrap his arm around my waist. I gave him a glare as I tried to create some distance between us, but that only made him tighten his hold.

What will people say when they see us? Will they care that I'm a vampire?

"Come on, let's go get breakfast," Aiden started to drag me toward a car. He got into the driver's seat while I sat in the seat next to him.

"Where are we going?" I asked

He glanced at me then looked back at the road.

"I know this great restaurant. We're going there," he answered.

I nodded my head. I was pretty hungry. I was craving blood; the last time I drank some was the first day I got here.

"Can we stop somewhere after that so I could have a little blood?" I asked innocently as if I was asking about the weather.

He parked the car in front of a homely looking restaurant. He nodded his head at my question then got out of the door. I followed him inside, and right away I could tell why it's his favorite.

It had such a friendly looking vibe. Its walls were colored brown, and there were tables scattered everywhere. I could tell immediately that everyone here was happy and cheerful.

Aiden and I made our way to a small table and sat in front of each other. We ordered our breakfast. Mine consisted of a plate of pancakes while his had two strips of bacon and sunny eggs. As we waited, I bit my nails nervously as I tried not to let the strange looks of pack members get to me. Never in my life did I care about anyone's thoughts of me, yet now when I was sitting in front of their Alpha, things have changed.

I kept on staring at a clock that was hanging on a wall right across me. I listened to the tick-tock filling the silence between us which was awkward until Aiden broke it.

"You know, sooner or later you have to be presented to the pack. They deserve to know their Luna."

I knew this was coming. I was just hoping that it was later and not sooner.

It's not that I don't want to be the Luna or to have that responsibility. In fact, I do. Living for so long can teach you so many things and lessons in life. And you know what I learned? That sometimes getting attached to something can hurt in the end.

I guess you can say I would make a great Luna, but am I willing to take the risk? I know how this will end. Is it worth the pain?

My mind was saying no while my heart was screaming yes.

I wondered to myself why the moon goddess paired the most dangerous Alpha in America to a vampire. This would gain so much attention and would give everyone something to talk about.

I nodded my head at Aiden.

I can't fight fate. But could I change it?

The waitress—or should I say bimbo—came and handed us our food. I could tell that she was trying to gain the attention of Aiden by swinging her hips side to side and unbuttoning the first three buttons of her blouse. Stupid human!

Aiden wasn't even paying her a second glance, but she kept on persisting. She asked if he wanted a glass of water or something to drink with his food, pretending as if I wasn't there.

What's wrong with you, Stella? I mentally slapped myself.

Was I jealous?

No! Of course not. Why would I be jealous of a bimbo like her?

After many tries, she finally left. I sighed in relief. It took every ounce of me not to jump at her and drink her blood.

Speaking of blood, I really needed some.

"So should there be something you should tell me," Aiden asked.

I gave him a confused look and shook my head.

What on earth was he talking about?

"Come on, Stella. You know what I'm talking about. Who was he?"

He? Okay, now I'm confused.

"I have no idea what you're talking about," I said.

He ran his hand over his face and said, "The guy that's keeping you from living your life. Why are you holding back? Who was he to you?" he growled.

Oh, this again!

"There was no guy! For goodness' sake, why do you continue to jump to conclusions?" I asked.

He was quiet for a moment then asked, "What did you mean when you said you don't want history to repeat itself?"

I didn't answer, only shrugged my shoulders.

"I don't want to talk about it. Maybe when the time right comes," I whispered.

Aiden nodded his head, dropping the subject. I sighed in relief. I wasn't ready to tell him my fears and secrets. I wasn't ready to let him know how it felt to lose someone.

We dug into our food, both lost in our own silence. But this time, it wasn't awkward. It was comforting.

Once we were done with our food, we headed to the car and drove off to the woods. I didn't feel like drinking from a blood bag. No, I was craving something wild. I wanted to run after my prey as I see the life drain from its eyes. I wanted to sink my fangs into skin and taste flesh.

Aiden parked his car outside the woods.

"Let's go. You can have your snack while I go for a run. My wolf is begging to come out," he told me.

I nodded my head at him and started my hunt.

Aiden went behind a tree to strip out of his clothes and shift while I looked for a big juicy rabbit to feed on. I heard bones cracking which meant Aiden was shifting.

I felt a nose nuzzle on my back. I turned around to see Aiden's wolf looking at me with his big, beautiful, and mesmerizing blue eyes.

I kneeled down to pet him, running my hands through his beautiful gray fur. His wolf licked my face. I stepped back, allowing him to pass so he could run. But he lowered himself and sat on the ground.

I raised one eyebrow at him, not understanding what he's doing. He barked at me then turned around so his back was facing me.

Wait. Does he want me to ride his back?

I pointed at his back. "You want me to hop on?" I asked.

Aiden nodded his head.

I got on his back and wrapped my arms tightly around his neck. This was my permission for him to take off.

He ran faster than I doubted. The wind would hit my skin harder each time he picked up his speed. His fur was dancing in the air.

We passed by the trees in the blink of an eye. I could barely hear the birds sing. All I could hear was the sound of Aiden's paws hitting the ground.

This felt so good. I felt like I was flying.

I closed my eyes and took a moment to savor this feeling before it was too late. Before it came to an end.

For everything which has a beginning has an end.

Just like this life.

Just like love.

And just like Alice.

Chapter 8

A week had passed. A week since I arrived! A week since I found my mate, and a week of hiding in the bushes, staying in the dark as I savored the last moments I might ever have of being who I am. My final week of being free from everyone, for today will change everything.

This was the day I would be presented to the pack, and my nerves were acting up.

What if they don't like me?

Of course, they won't like me. I'm a freaking vampire! It will be a miracle if they actually like me. I'd be damned surprised if I even see someone smile at me.

I'd been talking with my parents every day since they left.

They had been encouraging me to follow my heart, but does my heart know what it wants?

Aiden and Liam had been very busy these past few days preparing for the ceremony. Marie took me shopping yesterday to buy the perfect dress to wear. I told her that was unnecessary because I had a few dresses of my own. She said that I have to wow the crowd.

I don't know if I can do that.

My self-confidence wasn't always like this. It's just my nerves were eating me up alive.

The ceremony would be held in the center of the pack at seven o'clock. It was three, and I just took a shower. Marie was going to do my hair and makeup. I thought it was too early, but Marie said we needed all the time we can get.

We'll see if she's right.

* * *

It was almost seven, and I was all ready to go. It took Marie about three hours to do my hair and makeup. Yes, three hours!

I never took that long. Through those three hours, I had to stay seated in the same position as she did her magic touch. She curled my hair and did my makeup.

I would explain what she put and how, but I don't know that shit. I'm not such a big fan of makeup. Yes, I would wear mascara and lipstick, but I always preferred plain. It's something I learned from Alice.

She always told me that beauty is what we were born with and not makeup. It was skin-deep. She was my motivation, and she boosted self-confidence.

I wore the black dress I bought yesterday. It ended mid-thigh. It wasn't too revealing, but the way it clung to my body screamed sexiness. At least, that was what Marie told me.

Every passing minute felt like an hour. I just wanted to get this over with. I couldn't help but feel excited and nervous at the same

waiting for us.

He was wearing a su.
his eyes rake over my body up and .
stare was so intense; it was making me
walked over to him, he wrapped his arms a.
brought his lips to mine.

These past few days, Aiden kept his distance .
and I appreciated it. He was giving me time to think abou.
whole situation. I have to admit that I did miss him, but I bet this
was his way of showing me that I needed him.

Do I?

I still cannot answer that question now but maybe soon.

The kiss was gentle and sweet, not like the last one. His soft yet hot lips were moving against mine, and the sparks returned. He brought me closer to him as he bit my lower lip. I was about to give him access when we heard a cough, bringing me back to reality.

I completely forgot there were people in the room. I saw Marie give me a teasing look while smirking. My cheeks were heating up in embarrassment, but Aiden seemed perfectly fine.

"Come on, let's go. The ceremony starts soon," Aiden said while dragging me out of the door and into his car.

This was the day my life would change. I still couldn't believe how this was happening.

How can I stay here knowing that there will be no happy ending? How can I sleep at night knowing that history will repeat itself? It certainly will.

No one can escape death.

Not even us vampires; it's just harder for us. A stake in the heart is all it takes to end it. And that's the problem. That's the only way. While we don't age, we get to watch our loved ones grow old and die. Is that really fair?

Sometimes I think this is some kind of punishment for us vampires for being bloodsuckers. The vampire reputation wasn't quite clean as it is today. We used to be the monsters everyone feared, the demons who roamed this earth at night. Now, well, we are just a myth.

As in every religion, race, country, or any group, you will find good vampires and bad vampires. Sometimes all it takes to ruin everyone is just one person. That's the problem with the world we live in. People start to criticize everyone they see for the mistake of one, and they forget to look at the bright side. They forget about the people who still have good in them.

That's something else Alice taught me. Being a vampire isn't always such a good thing when everyone used to fear you just because they've heard horrible stories of what you could do.

I stopped my thoughts from wandering off. Aiden drove to the center of the pack while holding my hand.

I still don't get how Aiden isn't worried about what's coming. Am I the only one who knows how this is going to end?

I took a deep breath and opened the window to relax my nerves.

Before I knew it, we arrived, and the place was full.

I bet everyone from the pack was here. Of course, they are. They are here to meet their new Luna. Their Luna who is a vampire. I just wonder if that's what they know.

As we got out of the car, I lifted my head up high. I did not want to seem like some kind of weakling. I wouldn't allow anyone to look down on me. If they did, then they would never look up at me their entire life. It's like what they say. First impression is everything.

Aiden walked to the stage with me in his arms. I was thankful he was holding me. I didn't want to trip in the middle of the stage and humiliate myself.

Yes, that happened before. It was somewhere in the eighteen hundreds. Alice and I were participating in a play, and while I was acting, I tripped and fell in front of everyone. Yeah, that wasn't such a good day.

As we got to the center of the stage, I could feel my heart beating so fast. Aiden was rubbing his hand up and down my back, trying to calm my nerves. And I think it worked. Aiden grabbed a microphone that was waiting on stage and began, "Good evening, everyone. We are here today to celebrate my mate's arrival. She will become your Luna. Every one of you should respect her as much as you respect me. So you better treat her kindly. And if I see any unmated male looking at her for more than two seconds, there will be punishments."

I mentally slapped myself. *Did he really have to say that last part?*

I stepped forward and took the microphone from Aiden's hand. As I said before, first impression counts. I couldn't really tell everyone that I mistakenly trespassed here and wanted to go home for I didn't want to be stuck with a mortal mate. No, instead, I put on a smile and showed everyone what Stella would say if she weren't immortal. What she would really say if she weren't afraid of losing someone so special.

"Hi, everyone. It's really nice to meet you guys. I hope to become a wonderful Luna in your eyes. I hope that my identity won't change the way you look at me. I am honored to lead you guys and become a part of your family."

I took a step back then my mouth fell open in surprise when everyone started to clap and cheer. *They actually like me!* Aiden's hands came around me and started to rub my arm.

"You did good." I heard him whisper but wasn't exactly paying attention. My attention was focused on the crowd in front of me.

How on earth did I make it here? I was only traveling the world with my parents a week ago. It just happened so fast. I hope the years won't come as fast as this did.

The night passed by in a blur. I spent my time learning the names of pack members who were interested in meeting their new vampire Luna. So far, I didn't meet anyone who hated me, but I could tell some she-wolves were glaring at me. I was leaning against a wall, having a moment to myself. Aiden was talking to Liam about some pack work. I couldn't wait until this night was over. All I wanted to do was get into bed and sleep.

A tap on my shoulder made me turn around. There was a tall, muscular guy smiling at me. He had black hair and blue eyes. I smiled back at him, not wanting to seem rude.

"How can I help you?" I asked.

He gave me his right hand to shake.

"It's a pleasure to meet you, Luna. My name's Ian. I'm your new bodyguard," he told me.

I lifted an eyebrow at him.

Bodyguard? Aiden didn't tell me anything about that. Why do I even have one? I mean I can take care of myself just fine.

I smiled at Ian and then said, "It's nice to meet you, Ian, but I have to go see Aiden."

He nodded his head understandingly as I excused myself.

Oh, Aiden's in so much trouble!

I walked through the crowd of people, trying not to get stopped every often. I looked for Aiden but saw him nowhere. That's when I spotted Liam. I quickly walked through the sea of people and over to him.

"Hey, Liam, do you know where Aiden is?" I asked.

He nodded his head. "Yeah, he went to his office to go grab some—"

Before he could continue, I thanked him and ran off to the pack house. Once I was there, I rushed into Aiden's office to see him looking for some papers. Before he could ask me what was wrong, I got to the point.

"Why do I have a bodyguard? I can take care of myself!" I said—well, kind of whined.

Aiden walked closer to me as his large frame towered over my small one.

"Stella, this isn't up for discussion. You're my mate and the Luna now, and I have many enemies, which means that you could be targeted. I'm not taking the risk. Ian is one of our best fighters, and he will follow you wherever you go," he said.

His tone told me that he was right—this was not up for discussion. But I didn't give up.

"Aiden, I'm a freaking vampire that lived for two hundred years. I can take care of myself," I yelled.

He didn't say anything, only shook his head and walked out of the door.

This is going to be harder than I thought.

Chapter 9

I think I'm about to lose my mind.

It's like having a second shadow.

It had been three days since the ceremony, three days since I met Ian, and it was driving me crazy. Wherever I went, Ian had to be there even if I just took one step outside the pack house.

I mean, it's not him. He seemed like a really nice guy. We had talked and got to know each other, and he's a really cool guy to hang out with. But I'm the kind of girl that does not like to have a second shadow. I needed my privacy and some alone time. But with a guard around, I couldn't have any of that.

I tried to convince Aiden to drop this I-need-a-guard act, but he was just so stubborn. He thought that since I was his mate, others would want to target me.

But come on, I'm a vampire! No one will want to mess with me. I might look small and delicate, but I'm not! I'm viscous and feisty. Believe it or not but I might have more enemies than Aiden does. But he won't listen to a single word I say. But don't worry, I have a plan.

If I can't convince him to drop this guard thing, then I will have to make him.

How?

Well, my dear friend, by using the power of flirting.

I smiled evilly to myself.

This is going to be great. I bet this will work one hundred percent. Here's my plan.

Flirt with Ian.

Aiden being his possessive Alpha self, he will obviously get jealous and fire him.

Then I can finally be free.

I just hope my plan doesn't backfire on me and get Ian into trouble. I don't want Aiden to rip him to shreds because I was flirting with him. I just want him to get mad enough to fire him.

I walked to the kitchen with Marie to grab a snack. When we got there, we saw Liam eating a bowl of cereal. I grabbed a bowl and the cereal box. It doesn't matter if it's the morning or not, I will eat cereal whenever I want.

"Hey, Stella, how's the Luna work coming up?" Liam asked as Marie sat next to him.

I shrugged my shoulders, not having an answer.

That's something else I have to talk about with Aiden. Yes, I know I didn't want to get too attached, but I also don't want to seem useless.

Aiden hasn't even given me anything to do. I mean, aren't I the Luna?

That is one of the things I hate to feel—uselessness.

It's a horrible feeling. To have others look down at you just because you aren't helpful. I remember in high school when I used to be in the choir. There was this girl named Katherine. Everyone looked down on her. She was the center of bullying in my class.

Why?

Because she couldn't sing, of course.

Everyone forgot about the amazing things she could do. She was full of talent, like dancing, writing, and drawing. But everyone chose to look only at her weak side. They judged her for her flaws, making her feel useless.

They forgot that no one's perfect because once they saw someone weaker than them, they felt better.

Which is why when we see someone succeed, we feel bad. When we learn not to love ourselves, we can never learn to love anyone else. Our happiness is someone else's suffering. And day by day that suffering takes over.

Once I was finished with my bowl of cereal, I made my way to the living room where I was sure Ian and Aiden were going be.

It's time to start my plan.

As I made my way downstairs, I saw Aiden talking with Ian.

Perfect timing.

I ran quickly down the stairs before I could lose that perfect moment. Then I stepped on something sharp. I tried to hold my balance but failed. I ended up falling forward.

This is going to hurt.

Before I could hit the ground, muscular arms wrapped themselves around me, preventing my fall. I could right away tell that it wasn't Aiden because I felt no sparks. I looked up to see Ian smiling at me. I didn't let that fall stop me.

I guess this will have to do.

"Oh, I'm so sorry, Ian. Thanks for saving me," I said as I put my hand on his chest. I smiled sweetly at him as I batted my eyelashes.

I was about to continue my act when Aiden pulled me out of Ian's arms and into his. I looked up to see him frowning. He looked pissed.

Well, that was easy. I didn't really have to do anything. I mean, you can't blame me when this is Aiden we're talking about.

"Ian, you may leave now," Aiden said.

Once Ian was out the door, Aiden pulled me closer to his chest, tightening his arms around me.

"I have to tell you something," Aiden said.

I nodded my head at him, hoping what I thought it might be.

"Ian won't be your bodyguard anymore. It was a bad idea. I'll have him do pack work."

Yes! Hello, freedom.

I did a little happy dance in my head because of my success.

I nodded my head eagerly at him. That wasn't even hard. I smiled smugly to myself.

"Great. I'll have Scott come over tomorrow."

Wait, what?

"Who?" I asked raising one eyebrow at him.

"Scott, as your new bodyguard," he said.

What! You've got to be kidding me. I get rid of one then comes another.

"But why? You already got rid of Ian. Why do you have to get me another guard?" I whined. This was ridiculous.

"I got rid of Ian because he was an unmated male. It was a mistake to bring him here. Scott is your new guard, and he is mated, so that won't be a problem. He will be here tomorrow. That's the end of discussion."

Great. Mr. Possessive is back.

I sighed in defeat.

That was useless. I swear Aiden is the most stubborn person I've ever met. He probably has the thickest skull in the world.

I rubbed my hands over my face, giving up.

"I have so much work to do so I have to go," Aiden said as he kissed my forehead then turned around to head out of the room.

"Wait!" I said suddenly, causing him to stop then look at me.

"Can I help with something? It's so boring to stay here all day," I asked.

Aiden smiled showing his bright white teeth.

"You want to help?" he asked.

I nodded my head.

He took my hand in his and dragged me out of the door.

"The orphanage is really busy today. There are coming couples from outside the pack to adopt some of the children. What do you say, want to help?"

I thought about it. I guess it is a good start. I wasn't actually expecting myself to work with a bunch of paperwork on the first try. Besides, I was new to all this. It wouldn't be that bad to meet new people. I nodded my head.

* * *

Half an hour later, I was standing in front of the orphanage. It seemed like a very homely place. It had a friendly vibe to it.

As I walk in, I saw kids around the age of seven to nine playing tag. I smiled at the sight. It was so adorable.

I walked into the room that had the word office on the door. There I saw a woman who looked to be in her mid-forties. She wore glasses and had blonde hair with little white strips. There were a couple of wrinkles on her face as she scribbled something on a piece of paper. Once she saw me, she got up immediately and stepped towards me.

"Luna, it's a pleasure to have you here. I'm Emily," she said as she shook my hand, and I smiled at her.

"The pleasure is all mine. I was wondering if I could help around here, maybe with the children."

It was her turn to smile at me.

"Of course, we could use all the help we can get."

She then took me out to the back where there was a playground. There were kids playing everywhere. A little girl came up to me and gave me a big toothless smile then ran away.

I know I might seem cold and heartless at times, but I'm not at all like that. I love kids and seeing them smile always makes my day. Seeing them smile reminded me of Alice. I think it was her playful and immature personality that I see in those kids.

Emily left so she could finish some paperwork while I play with the kids.

It had been ten minutes that I've been taking care of the children. One even fell and started to bleed, so I made sure to treat him before I left. I looked around to see all types of race, color, and religion. It's amazing to see so many children become friends despite their differences. They were all between five to twelve years old. I was chasing one child around when someone sitting on a bench alone caught my eye.

It was a little girl probably the age of seven to eight. She had brown wavy hair that came past her shoulders. But that's not what caught my attention. It was the way she was looking at the kids walking off with their new parents. There was something in her eyes.

Loneliness.

I stopped what I was doing and walked over to her with a smile on my face.

"Hi," I said then sat on the bench next to her.

"What a pretty girl you are. What's your name?" I asked.

Once she saw me, her eyes widened.

"Luna!" she sounded surprised. "My name's Sarah."

I nodded my head at her and thought of what I could probably say to make her like me. It was obvious she was shy and pretty lonely. I just had to approach her.

"What a pretty doll. Where did you get it from?" I asked as I pointed to the doll in her hand.

She smiled.

"Mommy gave it to me," she said—but it was more of a whisper.

My heart broke for her. It doesn't take a genius to know what happened to her mommy if she's here.

"So, Sarah, you want to play hide and seek?" I asked.

She nodded her head eagerly and got up from the bench.

I got up and walked to a tree to count. Once I was done, I searched the playground for her and found her hiding under a table.

"Found you!" I shouted.

When she saw me, she started to laugh, which was music to my ears.

Chapter 10

I ran as fast I could to keep up with the doctors. Tears were flowing from my eyes like a waterfall.

This can't be happening. Why did it have to happen now?

"Ma'am, you have to stay here while we check on the patient," the nurse told me, but I wasn't paying attention. All I could think of was how this day came so fast and how will this day end.

I walked away from the door and leaned against a wall. I slid down and sat on the ground. A sob escaped my throat as I recalled the scene all over again.

I don't think I'll ever be able to forget what I just witnessed.

Having someone you love disappear in your own hands hurts so much. I was scarred for life.

I heard the doctor shout to the nurse to get the oxygen tank.

This seems like a dream. No, make that a nightmare.

Alice was gone. And she's never coming back.

Jamie ran to me with tears in her eyes.

I engulfed her in a hug as we sobbed together.

Alice's death was a very difficult thing to accept, but I thought, *At least, she'll be with him again. Her mate Mason.* It's one of the reasons why she seemed like dying every day. Having your mate lying on his deathbed can kill you instantly. For years, it ate her up alive. It ate me up alive. How could I just stand there and not be able to help? What could I have done to stop this plague?

Nothing.

I couldn't do anything. We can't escape our fate.

Of course, I've tried million of times to get Alice to be turned into a vampire so she won't have to face death this easily. But she never gave in, especially not after her mate's death. She wanted to see him again.

She always told me that this was her destiny—to be a werewolf, not a hybrid.

The doctor came out of the door, and Jamie and I stood up. We were both anxiously waiting for the news that might ruin us or save us.

There's a chance that Alice will live through this, right?

She's a very strong woman who always finds solutions to her life problems.

But what if this time, death is her solution?

The doctor shook his head at us sadly and said, "We tried our best as much as we could. But we couldn't keep her alive. I'm sorry. May she rest in peace."

Once those words came out of his mouth, my life seemed to have ended.

I swore that I will never get too attached to anyone ever again.

Well, that's what I thought before I met him.

* * *

The sun was shining brightly into the room as I opened my eyes. Once reality hit me, I had no more room for sleep. Today was one of the days I dreaded the most: April 20.

The day Alice died.

I turned around to see Aiden's sleeping face. *This dude will never take a hint.* I gave up on making him sleep on the couch. If he did, he would just come back in the middle of the night.

I got up slowly, not wanting to wake him up, and made my way to the bathroom to get ready for the long day.

I was going to Ervin, a place not that far from here, just a couple hours away by car. It's where Alice and I went to high school. When I turned twenty, I had to start moving with my parents, but I made sure to keep in touch. We would FaceTime, and I made sure to see her once a week.

For years, I spent this day with Jimmy and visited Alice's grave with him. But Jimmy was already gone by this time.

People keep dying around me—Alice, Jamie, and all her children. What do you expect? Werewolves aren't immortal. They can't live as long as vampires.

I did my morning routine and wore a black dress. I got out of the bathroom to find Aiden looking at me with confused eyes.

"Where are you going?" he asked as he raked his eyes over my body up and down.

"Ervin," I simply said.

He lifted one of his eyebrows at me.

"Ervin? What are you going to be doing there?" he asked.

I shrugged my shoulders at him and said, "I have business to deal with."

He didn't look satisfied. That's when I remembered Scott, my guard.

"Oh, can you do me a favor and not make Scott follow me today?"

He shook his head at me.

"You're not going. Ervin is hours away. It can be dangerous to leave you alone," he said.

I shook my head furiously. That was a very important day. I've never once missed a year ever since Alice's death. I always made sure to visit her grave.

"No! You can't stop me. Today is really important, and I have to go," I said with a tone that meant it was the end of the discussion.

Aiden nodded.

Well, that was easy.

"Fine, but I'm going with you."

What?

Ugh, you've got to be kidding me. For once I just want Aiden to nod his head and agree. But no, he just had to be his stubborn Alpha self.

His tone was firm, and I couldn't argue with it. What was important was to visit Alice grave, even though I had an Alpha behind my trail. I nodded my head in defeat and looked at my watch.

"Get dressed. We leave in twenty minutes."

* * *

We had been driving Aiden's car for an hour and a half. I drank from the blood bag I brought with me as he kept throwing questions about where we are going and why. But I simply ignored him. He was going to find out soon anyway.

Once we got closer to the destination, I told him to stop at a flower shop I buy from every year. He only gave me a questioning look before I got out of the car and walked into the shop.

There, I was met with Alex, a werewolf who was the owner of the shop. He was about in his mid-forties and was a very happy man with a loving wife and two children.

Once he saw me, he came forward and gave me a hug.

"Sunshine, it's good to see you again. It's been ages. I was expecting you today," he said, and I heard a growl come from behind me.

I was pulled from Alex's arms and into Aiden's. I rolled my eyes at his possessive attitude. Always depend on Aiden to get jealous over anyone, especially a forty-year-old.

Alex gave me a confused look.

"You used to come here with Jimmy all the time, but I've never seen him before," he said.

I could feel Aiden's hold on me tighten when he heard Jimmy's name.

"Alex, this is Aiden, my mate," I mumbled.

Alex gave me a huge smile when he heard that I found my mate.

"Ah, that's wonderful. So what do you want? The usual?" Alex asked, and I nodded my head.

The whole time we were in the shop, Aiden was quiet. But I could tell he was sending death glares to Alex.

Once we were done, I said goodbye to Alex, and we got into the car with the flowers in my hands.

"Can you tell me what's going on! Who was he, and who's Jimmy? Why on earth do you have flowers with you? What's so important about today?" Aiden asked all in one breath.

"You'll find out soon. Just drive while I give you the directions," I said, and Aiden sighed in defeat.

Twenty minutes later, we made it to the graveyard. I got out of the car with Aiden following behind me. I made my way to Alice's and Mason's graves. Before Alice died, she told me that she wanted to be buried next to Mason. So that's what I did. Who am I to separate them even at death?

Once I was there, I sat next to Alice's grave while Aiden stood in front of me. I laid the flowers on Mason's and Alice's graves.

"Meet Alice, a special person to me. She was like my sister and best friend."

I paused.

Aiden didn't say anything. He just stood quietly.

"Alice and I went to high school here. She was a werewolf, and I'm a vampire, which meant we were supposed to hate each other, but it was a completely different story. She was my motivation in life and still is. She died many years ago and asked to be buried next to her mate," I said as I pointed to Mason's grave.

"Once she died, my world stopped. I felt like it was the end, and I promised myself never to get attached to someone ever again. I come here every year. Jimmy was her grandchild, but he died years ago too. Now it's just me. And I fear it will forever just be me."

I didn't know I was crying until Aiden sat next to me and pulled me into his arms. He wiped the tears from my cheek and brought my face to the crook of his neck as he patted my back.

"Let it out," he whispered, and that was all I needed to let it go.

Chapter 11

The birds were singing, and the trees were dancing with the wind. The sun was shining so bright that day I had to wear sunscreen. The leaves made crunching sounds as I stepped on them and made my way through the forest.

It had been two days since I went to visit Alice's grave, and I was really embarrassed to face Aiden. I knew I shouldn't be, but I couldn't help it. I tried to avoid him as much as possible by hanging out with Marie and sleeping in her room.

What does he think of me?

Probably some kind of weakling.

I talked with my parents every day, and yesterday they told me that they will have to stay with Uncle Robert for much longer. His health was fine. The bruises and injuries he got from the fight were healing. It was his mental health that worried my parents. They told me he lost a special human friend that was involved in the fight, and it was ruining him. I understood completely because I knew how it felt to lose someone special.

I made my way through the forest, swinging my picnic basket back and forth, while Sarah was ahead of me, chasing a butterfly while laughing. I asked Emily from the orphanage if I could take her out today, and she was more than delighted to accept.

We stopped near a lake and sat under a tree. I laid the blanket I brought on the green grass and put the basket on top of it.

Sarah sat on my lap as she took a sandwich from the basket and had a bite. I grabbed the book I stored in it and turned to the first page as I took a sip from the blood bag I brought with me.

The book was called *A Place Called Here*. I began to read it to Sarah, and she listened carefully. The past few times spent with her, I could tell she was a really wise girl even for her age. I grew attached to her the moment I laid eyes on her. Yes, cheesy, I know. When I told her to call me Stella instead of Luna, she came up with Stel.

As I read through the third page, Sarah grabbed a strand of my hair and twirled it with her fingers. It looked like she was lost in thought.

I bent the corner of the page, so later on, I would know where I stopped.

"A penny for your thoughts?" I asked.

She looked up at me with her mesmerizing big brown eyes which I could get lost in.

"Stel, do you sometimes feel like you don't belong?" she asked.

Woah.

This is what I meant when I called her wise. You don't usually hear an eight-year-old ask that.

I nodded my head at her.

"It's normal to feel out of place at times. You feel lonely and like everyone's against you," I said, and she nodded her head.

"But that doesn't mean that we don't truly belong. It just means that we have a different way of seeing things.

"We look at the thing as if it's giving the wrong impression, but that's not always the case. But our 'enemies' aren't always the bad ones. It's sometimes us. We put negative thoughts into our own minds, like 'They don't like me' or 'I don't belong here,' and we forget to learn how to love ourselves."

"Tell me, Sarah, what do you love about yourself?" I asked.

My question must have hit her by surprise because she took a while to think before she answered.

"I love the color of my hair," she said.

I nodded my head for her to continue.

"I also love the way my voice sounds when I sing. Mama used to say that all the time," she whispered the last part.

I gave her a hug, rested my chin on her head, and ran my hand through her hair.

I pointed to a bunch of birds flying above us.

"You see that bird that is behind all the other birds?" I asked.

Sarah nodded.

"He's behind not because he's the weakest or the slowest. He's behind because he's the wisest. While all the other birds are using up all their energy to fly the fastest, he's taking his time and saving his energy for later use. So when the time comes, he will be the one flying in the front."

Sarah looked up at me and spoke, "So what you're saying is that all things happen for a reason. That sooner or later it will become better?"

I smiled at her and nodded as I grabbed the book and continued where I left off.

* * *

After I had returned Sarah to the orphanage, we said our goodbyes, and I promised to come back again soon.

I made my way to the kitchen and saw Aiden eating an apple. I turned around hoping he would not notice me, but it was too late.

Once he saw me, he threw his apple away and rushed over to me. He grabbed my wrist, and I felt those sparks return as pulled me to his chest.

"Why are you avoiding me?" he growled.

I put on my best confused face and spoke, "What are you talking about? I'm not avoiding you."

He didn't look like he believed me. He cornered me against the counter with his arms around. He bit my earlobe, and shivers ran down my spine.

"Sunshine, you're being naughty today. First avoiding me, then lying. You should be punished."

Before I could say anything or realize what was happening, his lips touched mine.

This kiss was rough, no sweet and gentle one. I didn't want to get too into the kiss because we were in a public area and I didn't want to risk having someone come in and see us. But something also told me that I was lying to myself. I was afraid of getting attached all over again.

His lips fit mine perfectly. I couldn't resist it; my instinct took over, and my lips moved on their own accord.

A few moments later, Aiden bit my lip, asking for entrance, but I pulled away before he could ask for more and said, "You think of me as some kind of weakling, don't you?"

My question made Aiden chuckle.

"If it's about what happened two days ago, then you are wrong. I don't think of you as some kind of weakling," he said as he caressed my cheek.

"I think you are a very strong woman for what you've been through. It made you the woman you are today."

I nodded, letting his words overflow my mind. No one ever told this to me in my face. I guess I was just too shocked to deny his words.

Is this how he sees me? Strong?

He pulled away and grabbed my hand. He dragged me out of the kitchen and into the living room.

"Want to watch a movie?" Aiden asked.

It's been a while since I actually relaxed and watched a movie. I guess it wouldn't be that bad.

"Ya, sure, what're we watching?" I asked.

Aiden was looking through the cabinets, then he took out a CD and showed it to me. Once I saw what the movie was, I laughed real hard: *The Lion King.*

The big bad Alpha was going to watch *The Lion King.* Yeah, it's a great movie, but I couldn't imagine Aiden snuggling up in a blanket as he cried his eyes out. That was a sight I was willing to see.

"What? Why are you laughing? Is there something on my face?" Aiden asked.

I shook my head at him and sat on the couch, getting comfortable.

Aiden shrugged his shoulders then started the movie and sat next to me.

During the movie, I would check on Aiden to see if he was tearing up. But I finally gave up when nothing happened. He seemed to be really into the movie while I was dozing off. I'd seen this more than twenty times.

I don't remember when, but somewhere during the movie, I fell asleep.

* * *

I woke up to see the moon shining into the room. I was in bed with Aiden. I grabbed my phone and checked the time: 2:00 AM.

My throat felt dry, so I got up and headed to the kitchen to get a glass of water.

When I got there, I saw the lights on. I walked into the kitchen and found Liam stuffing a sandwich in his mouth.

"Well, somebody's hungry at a time like this," I teased as I grabbed a glass from the cabinet.

"Hey, I'm the Beta. I need all the energy I can get. Give me some credit," Liam said.

I laughed at his lame excuse and poured the water into the glass then took a sip.

"So how are things going on between you and Aiden?" Liam asked.

It took me a moment to answer his question. I didn't really know what to say.

Yes, I have been warming up to Aiden, but it's complicated.

"I don't really know. It's so confusing," I whispered.

"Because you're immortal and he isn't?" he asked.

I nodded my head.

"Aiden is a really confusing guy. Trust me, I know. All the years I've spent with him, he had always been the lone wolf. He grew up learning to be responsible because he is the heir of the pack. So that's why he's always so serious. But ever since you've arrived, he has been more cheerful. I don't think I've ever seen him smile at anyone other than me, Marie, and his parents."

The mention of his parents made me curious.

"Where are his parents? I mean, I haven't seen them," I said.

Liam took the last bite from his sandwich and spoke, "They're spending their anniversary in Paris. They left a day before you and your parents arrived. They will be coming back in two days."

Two days. I'm going to meet my mate's parents in two days. That's a very short time.

What if they don't like me because I'm a vampire? What if they make Aiden reject me?

All these possibilities were running through my head.

"Don't worry, Stella. I bet they'll love you," Liam said.

"Pft. Who said I was worrying?" I said as I made my way to the door. I was getting tired, and I wanted to go back to sleep.

Liam rolled his eyes at me as we made our way upstairs.

Before we walked our separate ways, Liam called out to me. I turned around to look at him when he said, "Give Aiden a chance. You've made him a better person."

And with that, he walked off and disappeared into the empty hallway, leaving me thinking about what he just said.

Chapter 12

Aiden

My eyes opened as the sunlight shined into the room. The birds were singing as they flew by the window. The smell of strawberry and chocolate filled my nose. I inhaled the heavenly scent. I look down to see Stella snuggling into my chest. I couldn't help but smile.

The very first moment I laid eyes on Stella I knew she was special. She was different. And she was strong.

I didn't want to get up. All I wanted to do was lay in bed all day as I watch Stella sleep, but I couldn't do that.

This was going to be a very busy day. My parents were coming that night, and the pack was holding a welcome home ceremony.

I remember when I told my parents that I found my mate. They didn't care that she was a vampire. I mean, yes, they were a little concerned about her immortality, but I told them that I didn't care if she ages or not as long as she's with me. Other than that they were so excited, especially my mom. She wanted to see my mate so badly. They told me that I had to take good care of Stella and treat her like a queen.

If only she can just give in. She's been resisting me since she first saw me. I know that she's worried about the future and what's coming, but sometimes you just got to live.

Of course, I've thought about some solutions with Stella about living my life with her as a vampire, but she shut me up almost immediately. She didn't want to go through the risk of turning me into one. She said that it's really dangerous and sometimes might not work. And if it did work, it would be difficult to handle with all the pain and craving for blood, which will make you go crazy.

Another reason was that my title as the Alpha of the most feared pack would only draw too much attention if I were a vampire. The elders would probably take away my ranking, for a vampire as an Alpha was never heard of.

These were Stella's words, not mine. I couldn't care less of what ranking I was or who I was to the pack. As long as I had Stella by my side, I wouldn't care.

I kissed Stella's forehead and got up to take a shower. Once I came out of the bathroom, Stella was still asleep. I made my way to the door quietly, not wanting to wake her up.

I walked to my office and opened my laptop as I sat down. I called Clarke, the third in command in this pack, and made sure everything was ready for the party. I didn't want anything ruining tonight because my parents will finally meet my mate.

Ten minutes later there was a knock on the door.

"Come in," I yelled.

Liam opened the door and walked right in. He had a worried face on, which got my guards up.

"Aiden, another two rouges were found hanging near the border," Liam said.

I sighed in annoyance.

We never really had a problem with rogues. They didn't dare cross the most dangerous pack in America. It's just lately they were found near our border seeming suspicious. I didn't send my guards to kill them because they weren't trespassing, I had them sent away far from the pack, but they just keep returning.

It's like they want something, and they won't leave me alone until they get it.

"What did you do?" I asked Liam.

"We had them sent away far from here. Again."

I ran my hands over my face and said, "Increase the guards around the border. If they step one foot into the pack, then don't hesitate to kill them."

Liam nodded his head at me then walked out of the door as I continued to work on a couple of papers.

Half an hour later, I got a call from my mom. Once I picked up the call, her cheerful voice boomed through the speaker.

"Aiden, how are you doing?" my mom asked.

"I'm fine, Mom. How are you? When does your flight take off?" I asked.

"Me and your father are already seated. We're waiting for the flight to take off in about five minutes. Just wanted to say hi before we take off."

I heard my father's voice in the background.

"Oh, and your dad asks if there is going to be any chicken wings when we get back," my mom asked playfully.

I laughed at my father's question. He always had a thing for chicken wings.

"Yes, Mom. I'll make sure there will be a lot," I said.

I said goodbye to my parents then hung up.

I looked at the time: 8:00 AM. My parents were going to arrive around eight to nine PM, so that gave us enough time to prepare. The ceremony was going to be held in the same place where Stella's ceremony was held, the center of the pack.

I continued working for another two hours until the clock struck ten. Stella must be up by now.

I got up and made my way towards our room. I saw Stella showered and all dressed.

Her scent was overflowing the room which was what I liked most. Ever since I saw her, my wolf wanted to mark her, but I had to control myself. I didn't want to do something that will make her hate me. I couldn't lose her after all those years of looking for her.

"Let's go have breakfast," I said and pulled her to my chest. I wrapped my arms around her waist, and we walked out the door. We got in the car, and I drove off to my favorite place to eat.

Half an hour later, we were seated at our table with our breakfast in front of us. I ordered scrambled eggs while Stella ordered toast. We were both eating in silence as I admired the way she was eating. Simply beautiful.

"So, Stella, tell me more about yourself. What do you like to do? How did you grow up? What's your favorite color? How many boys have you dated in the past?" I growled to myself when I asked that last part quickly. I didn't want Stella to have a history with any other man but me.

Stella rolled her eyes at me and said, "Well, I like to read and watch movies—you know, the usual. I grew up traveling with my parents, but the four years of high school I spent it in Ervin with Alice. My favorite color is red. It's the color of blood, and I don't remember how many guys I've dated. They're simply too many."

She smirked when she said the last part. I growl. My wolf wanted to find every guy she's ever dated and rip their heads from their body. She's mine and only mine, no one could have her.

"Are you a—"

Before I could continue, my question she interrupted me.

"A virgin? You really can't expect a two-hundred-year-old vampire to be one."

Her answer made me shake with rage. Just thinking of someone touching her in any way made me furious. No one was supposed to touch her but me.

I'm not mad at her for not saving herself for me because I didn't wait either. My first time was years ago with some girl I met in the club. I'm mad at the bastard who dared to touch her. If he were still alive, I would find him and rip him to shreds.

She put her hand over mine and said, "Are you okay? You're shaking." She sounded concerned.

I tried to calm my wolf down. I didn't want to scare Stella because of my wolf's self-control. I felt myself calm down by her touch as I took in a deep breath.

I nodded my head at her, reassuring her I was fine.

* * *

It's eight, and Stella and I were at the airport picking up my parents.

"How do they look like?" Stella asked as she looked around the place.

"Well, my dad is very tall and buff, while my mom is short and has brown hair that comes down to her shoulders," I answered.

Stella nodded her head as she looked around.

"Is that them?" she asked as she pointed to a couple.

I shook my head at her.

"Nope," I said then look around, trying to spot them.

"What about them?" she asked.

I turned my head to look at the direction she was pointing and saw my parents walking to us with big smiles on their faces.

Once they got to us, I opened my arms to hug my mom, but she completely ignored me and gave Stella a bone-crushing hug.

Well, I feel loved.

"Oh, it's wonderful to meet you, dear. How are you? Oh my god you're so pretty. Aiden, you've got a beautiful mate. Tell me, dear, has he been treating you well," my mom blabbed on.

Before Stella could answer any of her questions, my dad pulled my mom away and said, "Coraline, slow down. You're scaring the girl for Pete's sake. Stop bombarding her with your questions."

Stella giggled at my parent's attitude toward her.

"It's nice to meet you, Mr. and Mrs. Smith. And yes, Aiden has been treating me well," she said.

"Mom, Dad, it's good to see you," I said as I hugged them both.

"It's good to see you too, son—oh, and, hon, call me Coraline," my mom said.

She nodded her head then turned toward me, directing everyone's attention to me.

"We have a party starting in half an hour, so let's get home," I said.

* * *

The party started an hour ago, and Stella still wasn't out of her room. I was waiting downstairs in the living room, and it was packed with people who still hadn't gone.

I was wearing a suit while my parents were standing next to me. We were waiting for Stella so we can get going.

I heard a couple of whispers and gasps. I turned my face to the side to see Stella coming down the stairs.

My breath was caught in my throat the moment I laid eyes on her.

She looked gorgeous, so stunning.

She was wearing a red dress that hugged her body, showing off her curves. It came down to her mid-thigh as she wore those high heels.

I was raking my eyes over her body, wanting to remember every single thing about her, when I noticed some of the unmated males looking at her for more than two seconds.

I growled at them threateningly, and they turned their heads immediately. Once Stella was within arm's length, I wrapped my arms around her waist possessively and brought her closer to my chest.

This was going to be a difficult night, trying to keep the men away from her and trying to control my wolf.

Chapter 13

Stella

It was ten o'clock, and the party was nowhere to an end. The place was filled with decorations and yummy food to eat. When Aiden and I went to pick up his parents, I was so nervous and anxious that they wouldn't like me. But once I saw the look on their faces and the way his mom hugged me, I knew that they were good people. Ever since I came downstairs, Aiden hadn't left my side. Even when I wanted to grab a snack. He insisted on coming with me, which annoyed me a lot, but I decided not to say anything.

From all the juice I'd been drinking, I felt like my bladder was going to explode. I needed to go to the bathroom so bad. I took Aiden's arm from around my waist and put it to his side. Before I could take one step forward, Aiden grabbed my wrist.

"Where are you going?" Aiden asked.

"To the bathroom, I'll be right back," I answered, rolling me eyes. Aiden looked like he wanted to refuse but didn't say anything and nodded his head. I made my way to the bathroom and did my business.

Once I got out of the stall, I washed my hands and made my way to open the door when it opened from the outside.

A blonde appeared in front of me, wearing a black dress that was too revealing. It came right above her butt, and if she bent down, I bet it would be exposed.

She looked at me up and down like I was some kind of dead rat with the plague. I hated her already.

I mean, I'm not the kind of person to judge. I always make sure to get to know the person before I put any tags on them, but I could already feel such a bad vibe coming from her. I decided not to jump to conclusions and just ignored her as I walked out of the door, but something she said made me stop in my tracks.

"You don't deserve to be the Luna."

Excuse me?

"I'm sorry what did you say?" I asked, clenching my fist into a ball.

"You probably slept your way here, because I don't see any reason why the Alpha would want to be with you," she said as she put one of her hands on her hip.

I looked her up and down as I scrunched my nose.

"And how would you know that? What are you? The pack's slut? Probably, which is why you might assume that, but let me tell you something—not everyone's like you."

As I finished the last part, I lifted my head up high and turned around. But before clearly disappearing, I gave her the bird while she looked at me in shock and anger.

I got back to where Aiden was, and once he saw me, he wrapped his arm around my waist, bringing me closer to his chest.

"You took so long. Did something happen?" he asked, sounding concerned.

I shook my head at him and shrugged my shoulders.

I knew that sooner or later I would get a hater even if I was the Luna. I mean, there's a first for everything right. Especially if I'm a vampire. Not everyone was going to like me.

* * *

It had been hours, and the party was still going. I was getting really tired and sleepy. A bunch of people would come to me and greet me. I'm not sure how many names I heard and how many hands I shook.

I covered my mouth as I yawned and leaned against Aiden's chest for support. I felt my eyes closing through every passing second as sleep crept closer.

"Are you sleepy? Come on, let's go to bed," Aiden said, and I looked up to him.

"But what about the party? It's not over yet," I said.

"It's okay. I already told my parents I was leaving, and if they need anything, Liam is here," he said as he walked us to the car.

I don't remember when, but somewhere in the ride, I dozed off.

* * *

I woke up to find Aiden carrying me to our room. He walked in and set me on the bed, then he walked into the closet.

I went to the bathroom, changed into my pajamas, and went straight to bed.

As I closed my eyes, I felt the bed dip downward as Aiden got into the bed. He came closer to me and wrapped his arms around me, bringing me to his chest. I would have resisted him, but I was too sleepy to complain. The last thing I heard before dozing off was Aiden's steady breathing.

* * *

The birds singing woke me up from my sleep. I opened my eyes and saw that the sun was out, and it was shining so bright. I looked at the time to see it was ten o'clock. I turned around to see Aiden's spot empty. It was cold, telling me that he left a long time ago.

I got up, made my way to the closet, and grabbed a floral dress. I made my way to the bathroom, took a cold shower, and shaved my legs. I wore the dress and braided my hair.

As I made my way downstairs, I saw Marie in the kitchen eating cereal.

"Hey, immo, looking good. What's your plan for today?"

I shrugged my shoulders.

"I don't really know. I'm planning ongoing to the mall then visiting the orphanage," I answered as Marie nodded her head. I was planning on buying Sarah and the children their presents and a couple of things for them to wear. They all deserved it. I could tell that I was becoming attached to Sarah. She was becoming like the little sister I've never had.

I poured milk into my cereal and took a bite.

"Do you know where's Aiden?" I asked Marie.

She nodded her head at me and said,

"He has a meeting with the pack guards."

I nodded my head at her answer.

Once I finished my breakfast, I grabbed my bag and headed out the door. Of course, Scott was following me. I sighed in annoyance but decided to go with it.

I swear sometimes they act as if I were the queen of England.

I made it to the mall half an hour later with Scott following me not too far away. I went into the toys section and picked out a doll that Sarah would like. It had black hair that came down to its shoulders and was wearing jeans with a leather jacket. The other day, Sarah told me that she didn't like the girly dolls. Instead, she liked the ones that were different from the rest. I bought a bunch of other dolls for the girls there and toy cars for the boys with the money Aiden let me borrow.

After that, I went into the clothes aisle and picked out different dresses that had flowers on it and cute pink ballerina shoes for all the girls to wear. For the boys, I got hats and sports shoes for them to run and play in.

Once I was done, I decided to grab some coffee from a cafe and have a seat as I waited for my order to be ready. Scott was standing a few steps away from me, seeming so serious.

"Why don't you have a seat," I said as I pointed to the seat in front of me.

Scott looked at me then shook his head, not saying anything. Geez, why so serious?

I was starting to regret the stunt I did to get rid of Ian. At least, he wasn't so serious. He would smile and make jokes. I wonder if it was because he was mateless.

Once I got my coffee, I put all Sarah's things into a separate bag and headed out the mall with Scott on my trail.

By the time I made it to the orphanage, I was finished with my coffee, and it was around two PM.

When I opened the door, I saw Emily looking at me with shock when she saw all the bags I was holding.

"What are all these? Luna, you didn't have to," she said as she looked at me with a huge smile on her face.

"What are you talking about, Emily? The kids need something to brighten up their day," I said as I smiled back at her.

She pulled me into a big bone-crushing hug and said thank you so many times.

Once I made it to the back where all the children were playing, Emily called out to all of them to get their presents. They seemed so happy to open their toys and play with them. Not all girls took the dolls, some of them wanted the cars, which was fine with me. Seeing them smile made my day.

I took Sarah's separate bag and started to look for her. I found her sitting behind a tree reading a beginner's book. I crept behind her, wanting to surprise her.

"Surprise!" I yelled as I came in front of her and hugged her. She seemed happy to see me, but when she saw the bags in my hands, she looked confused.

"What's that?" she asked.

"Why don't you find out?" I said as I handed her the bags.

She took it from me and opened them. At first, she looked shocked, but that was soon replaced with happiness.

"Are these for me?" she asked excitedly.

I nodded my head, and she smiled widely at me. She jumped into my arms as I twirled her around.

"Thank you, thank you, thank you, Stel!" she said.

I put her down, and we both sat down behind the tree.

"What were you reading?" I asked.

"Green Eggs and Ham! It's my favorite," she answered.

I leaned my head against the tree and said, "Want to read it to me?"

She nodded her head excitedly as she turned to the first page.

Chapter 14

We drove past trees dancing in the wind. We could hear the birds sing. It was a really warm day, winter was finally over, and the sun was out. It was a beautiful day—too beautiful for my liking.

In cartoons, graveyard or funeral scenes are usually dark and rainy. Crows would fill the haunted place. As a child, I was scared of graveyards, because when I saw them on TV or read about them in books, they reminded me of death.

On this day, though, the graveyard where Alice was buried was anything but gloomy. It almost seemed cheerful.

But how can I be happy when this day haunts me every year?

My thoughts were broken when Jimmy parked the car in front of the floral shop we bought flowers from every year.

We walked in and bought the usual then got out.

Jimmy had been down lately because of his mother's death. He had two siblings, and he was the oldest. He was now in his mid-twenties. Jamie's death had been difficult for us. But at least, she was now with her mother again.

It took half an hour for us to get there. We got out of the car and headed to Mason's and Alice's graves.

"Stella, do you think Grandma is happy?" Jimmy asked as we sat next to the graves.

I smiled at him sadly. Jimmy and Alice were really close. He was closer to his grandmother than all his other siblings.

"Of course, she is, as long as she's with Mason," I answered as I put the flowers on their graves.

"She was always happier with Mason," I whispered more to myself.

Jimmy looked at me.

"Do you think you'll ever find your mate?" he questioned.

What he said hit me by surprise. I didn't always think about finding my mate because it's quite rare. I shrugged.

"I have no idea. Maybe when the time comes," I said.

Is having a mate really that important? I mean, sometimes I think that having a mate lifts off a weight from your shoulders. But how can you spend the rest of your life with a person you don't even know? What if they're a psychopath or a serial killer?

But seeing Alice happy with Mason made me realize that there's more to that.

But how could I know? I mean, I don't even have one.

I don't know if I want one.

Is there actually somebody out there is willing to do anything for me and will love me despite my flaws?

I might never know.

* * *

I was feeling hot—even sweating.

I opened my eyes and saw Aiden almost on top of me, hugging me so close to his chest. I tried to get him off me, but he was too strong.

I groaned. I needed a really cold shower.

"Aiden! Aiden, get up."

I tried to wake him up, but he only mumbled in his sleep.

I turned my head and looked for a glass of water to pour on him. But there was nothing. I sighed.

I had only one thing to do.

I inhaled deeply and counted to three.

One.

Two.

Three.

"Aaahhhhhhh," I screamed as loud as I could, making sure my mouth was right next to his ear.

Aiden got up immediately and looked around the room.

I could hear his heart beating so fast. I bet I scared the crap out of him. Again. I laughed so hard.

He turned to me and asked, "What the hell was that?"

I laughed harder until I remembered why I did that. I needed to take a cold shower.

"It's really hot today, and you were on top of me," I said as I got off the bed and made my way to the bathroom.

"And I need my personal space."

"But you really had to do that?" he asked.

I nodded my head.

"Yeah, you wouldn't get up. You're a really heavy sleeper," I answered.

He groaned as I got into the bathroom.

I stripped out of my clothes and got into the relaxing, cold water.

Twenty minutes later, I got out of the bathroom and found Marie examining something on the bed.

"What are you doing?" I asked her.

She turned to face me and smiled.

"Today we are going to the beach, and we need to find you a perfect bikini."

I walked over to her and saw several bikinis lying on the bed. They were all too revealing for me.

"Nope, I'm not wearing any of those. I'll just wear a one-piece," I said.

Marie shook her head.

"Not going to happen, immo. You are wearing one of these. Don't you want Aiden to be drooling when he sees you?" she said and grinned.

I raised an eyebrow, but I felt myself blush.

"You do realize that when he sees me in this, he won't let me leave," I spoke.

She grinned.

"Don't worry, immo. That's not going to happen. Now pick one," she said.

I sighed in annoyances.

Marie was a really stubborn girl.

I looked at all the pieces and picked a black bikini that was the least revealing.

"Who's coming with us?" I asked.

"Liam and Aiden. We are going to the beach near the pack, so there will be pack members and humans," she answered.

I nodded as I grabbed the bikini.

"When are we going?" I asked.

"In about an hour. Aiden and Liam went to buy some snacks from the supermarket. I'm going to make some sandwiches, and you should get dressed then come downstairs," Marie said as she walked through the door.

I walked into the closet and grabbed a pair of shorts and a t-shirt. I went to the bathroom and changed into the bikini.

Wow.

I looked good.

Not to brag, but I looked so sexy in this bikini.

I wore the shorts and the t-shirt and tied my hair into a high ponytail. Once I finished, I headed downstairs to help Marie. It was about eleven o'clock when Aiden and Liam arrived.

I grabbed the basket full of sandwiches and got in the car. Aiden was driving while Liam was sitting in the front seat. Marie and I sat in the back with the basket between us.

It took only ten minutes for us to get to the beach. It was packed. There were children playing in the water and teens playing volleyball in the sand.

Marie squealed.

"Girls, go find a spot for us to settle in. We'll carry the stuff," Aiden spoke.

Marie and I nodded, and we got out of the car. Once we found a perfect spot, Aiden laid the blanket on the sand, and Liam fixed the umbrella above us. Aiden and Liam took off their shirts and shorts, leaving them in their swimming trunks.

I tried hard not to stare at Aiden. He looked so sexy. I bet every girl in this beach was staring.

Something stirred in me, and I think it was jealousy. But I tried to ignore it.

Once I placed the basket on the ground, I took off my shirt and my shorts. I heard a loud growl coming from behind me. It was Aiden. He tried to cover me from the males who were passing by.

"What on earth are you doing wearing that?" he growled.

I shrugged. I knew his possessive side was taking over.

"Marie made me wear this," I said.

"Well, you had to listen to her. You aren't wearing that. Go change," he said.

I shook my head. I did not want him to boss me around.

"I'm pretty comfortable in this. I'm not changing. Besides, I don't have anything else."

Marie came to my side and wrapped her arm around my shoulder. She had changed into a light blue bikini.

"She's right, Aiden. Don't be so bossy, especially today. Let's just have some fun," Marie spoke.

Aiden shook his head.

"Fun? How do you expect me to have fun when every guy who passes by is looking at her," he growled.

I rolled my eyes. I seem to be doing that a lot lately. I looked around to see some guys staring at me, which was kind of uncomfortable.

"Oh, don't worry, Aiden. Just be by her side, and they won't dare to do a thing. I mean, you're pretty intimidating," Marie exclaimed, and I nodded. I didn't want Aiden going all Alpha on me, especially today. I just wanted to relax.

Aiden sighed and rubbed his hands over his face.

"Fine, but you're not leaving my side," he said as he pointed at me and grabbed my hand. He pulled me to his chest.

Our skins' contact made the sparks return.

"I swear if anyone looks at you, I won't hesitate to rip their heads off," he grumbled more to himself.

I only rolled my eyes.

If he actually meant it, then half the beach would be dead by now.

I sat on the blanket and grabbed the sunscreen from the bag that Marie brought. Marie and Liam decided to go swim while Aiden and I sat under the umbrella.

I started to put sunscreen on my arms and legs while Aiden watched. Surprisingly, I didn't feel uncomfortable under his gaze. When I got to my back, I had a difficult time trying to apply it.

"Here, let me do it," Aiden said.

I nodded and gave him the sunscreen. I lay down on my belly and rested my chin on my crossed arms.

Two seconds later, I felt Aiden's muscular hands rubbing my back. His touch made me shiver a bit. I think Aiden noticed because I heard him chuckle. His hands were roaming all over my back, leaving trails of sparks. His hands moved lower and lower my back, then come back up.

I think he was torturing me.

When he was done applying sunscreen, I got off my stomach and sat beside him. His arm wrapped around my bare waist, and he pulled me closer.

"You look so good in that. I just want me to see it and no one else," he said.

This made me blush.

I grabbed two sandwiches from the basket and gave one to him. He gladly took it from my hand and took a huge bite. I took my first bite and leaned my head on his chest. His hand rubbed my waist, sending shivers down my spine.

"Want to go swim?" he asked as he took the last bite from his sandwich. I nodded and put my unfinished sandwich in the basket.

I got up and walked to the water. Aiden pulled me to him.

I made sure not to go that deep.

Through all my two hundred years, the one thing I could never learn was swimming.

Even if we did go deep, I would make sure to stay close to Aiden. I still didn't tell him that couldn't swim. It's kind of embarrassing because mostly everybody knows how to swim.

Aiden splashed water at me, and I tried to walk away. But it's difficult to walk in water. Hearing his laughter was music to my ears. He wrapped his arms around my waist and twirled me around. I screamed and laughed.

Aiden put me down when Liam called for his help to carry something. He told me he would be right back and left.

I was splashing in the water when I felt something wrap around my leg. It felt like seaweed.

The waves pulled me farther away from the shore. I was getting too deep into the ocean. I started to panic when I couldn't feel the sand underneath me anymore. I tried to keep myself from going underwater but failed. Every time I surfaced for air, I was pulled back down. I splashed around, hoping anyone would notice me.

I felt myself being sucked deeper into the ocean, and I couldn't hold my breath any longer. My lungs felt like they were going to explode. Darkness crept closer as my eyes started to close. The last thing I saw before being engulfed by it was Aiden swimming toward me.

Chapter 15

My chest heaved as I tried to catch my breath. I was running as fast as I could through a dark forest. I could hear someone running behind me.

He's gaining on me.

I turned and headed deeper into the forest. I saw crows fly toward the full moon.

"Run!" a voice echoed through the air.

"Run! Don't let him find you!"

My legs moved faster at the strange voice's warning.

The leaves crunch below me as I ran for my life. The sound of paws hitting the ground made me run faster. I turn right hoping to lose whoever was chasing me.

Who was chasing me?

My steps slowed down when I saw something ahead of me.

How did I get here? I've never seen one so close to the pack.

A graveyard.

The strangest thing about it was that there was only one gravestone.

I walked closer to read what was written on it.

R.I.P. Lilly Claze

"Run!" the strange voice said once more.

But it was too late. A figure appeared from the shadows.

"Do it!" his powerful voice boomed through the empty graveyard.

I took a step back. He took a step forward.

"Do what?" My voice quivered.

He pointed at the gravestone and repeated.

"Do it!"

"No! Don't do it!" the strange voice said.

Don't do what? What the hell is going on?

But before I could ask, everything around me disappeared.

* * *

My eyes snapped open. My heart was beating so fast. Aiden, Marie, and Liam stared back at me worriedly.

What happened?

I then realized that we were still at the beach and I was lying on the sand.

"What happened?" I asked while getting up.

Aiden shook his head then carried me.

I felt too tired to argue with him, so I laid my head on his chest and closed my eyes.

"You don't remember, Stella? You were drowning," Marie spoke.

I knew this was something serious because this was the first time I heard Marie use my real name.

I looked up at Aiden and saw guilt in his eyes.

"Why didn't you tell me you didn't know how to swim? I swear if I knew, I wouldn't have left your side or asked you to swim with me in the first place," he said.

"It's not your fault. I didn't know this was going to happen. It's mine, not yours," I said.

He didn't say anything back. He only tightened his hold on me as he took me to the car with Liam and Marie walking by his side.

"We're leaving?" I asked.

Aiden looked at me as if I were crazy.

"You were drowning not ten minutes ago, and you want to stay? No way!" he said while shaking his head.

I sighed as he placed me in the back seat with Marie.

The drive home was short and quiet. Once we made it outside the pack house, Marie and Liam took out the things we brought while Aiden carried me again.

"I can walk. My legs aren't broken, you know," I said.

He simply ignored me.

He carried me into the pack house and upstairs to our room. He placed me on the bed, walked into the closet, and came out with a pair of sweatpants and a t-shirt. He put it on the bed next to me then walked into the bathroom. Two minutes later he came out.

"I've started your hot bath. Once you're done, wear these so you won't catch a cold," Aiden said.

I only nodded and walked to the bathroom with the clothes in my hand.

I stripped out of my clothes and got into the relaxing, hot water. I lay my head on the bathroom tile and sigh.

The crazy event that happened today kept playing over and over again in my mind.

* * *

It wasn't the first time.

Long way back, I think it was in my sophomore year of high school, Alice and I decided to have my sweet sixteen at the beach. We invited the whole school, and the party was huge. There were decorations everywhere and good food to eat. I made sure not to go too deep into the water. Only Alice knew that I couldn't swim. In the middle of the party, Alice decided to leave me alone in the water to go grab a bite.

One of the guys who were playing volleyball accidentally threw the ball in the water. It was getting farther out into the ocean by the second, so they asked me to go get it. I saw that it wasn't too far away, so I quickly moved my way through the water to get it.

I couldn't say no to them. If only Alice were there to help, she could have gone and got it.

But no, my stupid kindness got the best of me, and I ended up drowning on my sixteenth birthday.

I'm not sure why Alice even held the party there. I told her that it was probably a bad idea, but she didn't listen. She said that it had to be a great place where it will show the whole school how special I am.

Sure, like showing them how special I am in drowning.

I splashed around and screamed. Thankfully the guy who asked me to retrieve the ball noticed my struggle and immediately asked for help.

I don't remember what happened after that.

I woke up to the lifeguard giving me CPR. He was one hunk of a guy, by the way. The party ended early, and everyone went home.

Throughout two months, I was the-girl-that-couldn't-swim-and-had-to-be-saved at school until they ended up forgetting about it.

* * *

Ten minutes later, I got out of the tub and wore the clothes Aiden gave me. I got out of the bathroom and saw Marie sitting on the bed.

"Hey, are you okay?" Marie asked.

I nodded.

"Yeah, I'm fine. It's happened before. Don't worry about it. I'm a vampire, remember," I spoke.

She nodded.

"Let's go downstairs. Since we couldn't enjoy our time at the beach, Liam and Aiden decided to make dinner. Burgers are on the house!" She shouted the last part which made me laugh.

Marie and I made our way downstairs, and I swear I probably got stopped more than ten times by pack members asking if I was fine. I reassured them that I was okay and made my way to the kitchen.

There I saw Aiden and Liam grilling a lot of burgers.

"Who's going to eat all that? You know it's just the four of us, right?" I said.

"We are," Aiden and Liam said at the same time.

I raised an eyebrow.

"You both"—I pointed to them—"are going to eat all that. That's quite a lot."

Liam put his hand over his heart and pretended to look offended.

"Stella! We need all the energy we can get. We work our butt off for the pack. Give us some credit," Liam said.

I laughed at his lame excuse because it wasn't the first time he used it.

Marie and I grabbed our plates and put two burgers on each while Aiden and Liam were stuffing their faces burger after burger.

Men.

I looked around the room. Liam fought with Marie about who takes the last burger. Aiden held my hand while he ate. I could only feel one thing.

Complete.

I was starting to feel like home.

I just hope it lasts.

Chapter 16

I nodded my head, showing Emily that I was listening to all she was saying. She was telling me about the children who were getting adopted today. I was really excited. Those innocent and beautiful children were finally getting a home and brighter future.

Unfortunately, Sarah wasn't one of them.

I walked outside to see all the kids playing. Some were dressed properly for the adoption, while others were in their pajamas, looking like they just woke up. I walked over to the playing area and didn't see Sarah, so I went to our little place behind a big oak tree. And she wasn't there either.

I went up the third floor where her room was located. I walked through the empty hall and stared at pictures of the children hanging on the wall. The sound of my footsteps echoed throughout the hall.

When I got to Sarah's door, I heard a beautiful melody.

It was Sarah, and she was singing. Amazingly.

Mama, you'd be so proud,

The way I shine, wish that you could see me now.

Oh, great creature of the sea,

Please hold her voice for all of eternity.

And like a siren's lullaby

I know you always will

Return to me.

Return to me

On waves of ocean melody.

No magic can make you reappear.

But in the song of the whales, you are always here.

By the time she finished singing, a tear rolled down my cheek. My heart broke for this lonely little girl. All she wanted was her mother, a family, anyone to take care of here and love her.

I took a deep breath and knocked on the door then opened it. I peeked and saw her sitting on her bed while holding a photo frame. Her eyes were red, and her hair was messy. I could even see dried tear stains on her cheeks. I took a step into the room and closed the door behind me.

"Hey," I said softly.

I was trying not to show pity.

One thing I knew is that most people hate it when someone pities them. It makes them feel small, weak, and hopeless.

I walked over to her bed and sat down.

"You know, you have a beautiful voice. You're really talented," I said as I wiped the tears off her face.

My compliment made her smile, and I smile too. I just wanted her to be happy.

"You know, once you grow up and start going to middle school and high school, you can go to classes which can help you improve," I said as I remembered myself taking choir classes with Alice.

She nodded excitedly.

"So what do you want to be when you grow up?" I asked hoping to bring her cheer back.

It looked like she was thinking about it because she lifted her head, looking at the ceiling.

"I don't know. I want to be a singer, but I also want to be a teacher," she answered.

I nodded as I brushed a strand of hair behind her ear.

"Okay, if you become a teacher, what do you want to teach?" I asked.

She answered immediately.

"I want to be a choir teacher like Mommy!"

She smiled.

"I bet you'll be the best choir teacher ever," I told her.

I looked down at the frame she was holding. It was a picture of a woman that had brown hair tied into a ponytail. She had a wide smile on her face as she faced the camera. Next to her was a younger-looking Sarah. I took the frame from her hand and looked at it in awe.

"Oh my gosh, you look so cute," I said.

She blushed as she nodded her head.

"Your mother was a really lucky person to have you, Sarah. Know that you were loved, and you still are. I'm pretty sure she is looking down at you with pride," I said as I moved her on my lap.

"Mommy is gone," she whispered. Her eyes were getting watery.

"No, she isn't. Just because you can't see her, it doesn't mean she isn't here. She's been with you every step of the way, right here," I said as I pointed to her heart.

"Sometimes we lose hope in the things we used to believe in just because our eyes don't have the ability to see them anymore. The eyes are weaker than the heart. While your eyes can't see it, your heart can feel it," I said as I brought the photo frame to her heart.

This was enough for her to let it out. The tears in her eyes came down like a waterfall.

I brought her head to my chest as I patted her back.

"It's okay, it's okay. I'm pretty sure there's someone out there that will adopt you and love you as much as your mother did," I whispered to her.

She shook her head as she pulled her face from my chest.

"I don't want to be adopted! I feel like I'm..."

"Betraying your mother," I finished for her.

She nodded.

I put my hand under her chin and raised her head so she could look at me.

"Listen, sweetie, and listen clearly. Your mother wouldn't want you to be suffering and living in misery all alone. I'm pretty sure she would have wanted you to have a family and grow happily," I told her.

"Because if I were your mother, I would have wanted the same thing," I whispered the last part.

She smiled softly at me.

"You will become a great mother, Stel," Sarah said.

I smiled at her and hugged her tightly, knowing that the pain she's feeling about her mother's death may never leave.

It never leaves.

Because to this day, I'm still mourning Alice's death.

* * *

I walked into the pack house to see Marie running toward me. She looked excited for some reason. Once she approached me, she pulled my arm and dragged me upstairs.

"What's going on?" I asked.

"We are going to the mall," she said cheerfully as she pushed me into the room.

"Why?" I asked.

"Aiden's birthday is in three days, and he's turning twenty-five. We need to get him a present now," she answered.

His birthday in three days? God, what am I supposed to get him?

"Well, if you want, I could just go buy him a present while you give him something else, huh?"

She smiled at me smugly while wiggling her eyebrows.

I blushed at her comments knowing exactly what she meant but hid it with an eye roll. I then grabbed a pillow from the bed and threw it at her.

"No way!" I shouted.

She laughed as the pillow hit her face.

"Fine, fine, we'll just have to get him something else. Get dressed and meet me downstairs," she told me as she walked to the door.

But before she closed it, she popped her head back in and spoke, "Oh, and don't tell Aiden about this. It's a surprise."

I nodded my head and walked into the closet. I grabbed a dark blue dress with a pair of sandals and got dressed. I put on just mascara and left my hair down.

As I walked downstairs, I thought I bumped into a wall.

Wait. Since when was there a wall in the middle of the staircase?

I looked up to see that the wall was actually Aiden.

What does he take? Steroids?

"Where are you going?" he asked.

"To the mall with Marie," I answered.

"Why?" he asked.

"Oh, you know, the usual, to hunt down elephants," I said.

He only raised an eyebrow.

"Geez, we're only going to hang out. I'll be here around seven," I told him.

As I walked by him, he turned around and said, "Scott's going with you."

I sighed. Can't Marie and I just go and have some time to ourselves? But I knew Aiden wouldn't let me go if he didn't come, so I only nodded.

I walked into the living room to see Marie putting on her shoes.

"Good you're ready, immo. Let's get going," she said once she saw me.

I nodded and walked to the front door.

We got into the car as Scott got into his and followed right behind us. Twenty minutes later, Marie parked the car in front of the mall. We got out and walked to the entry while Scott followed not too far behind us. I was trying to figure out what Aiden would like.

Maybe Marie would know what to get him? She did know him since they were children.

"What would Aiden want?" I asked as we walked each store.

"I don't really know. He never really liked us getting him presents on his birthday. I would just buy him a t-shirt or sometimes a pair of shoes," she told me.

I sighed.

Well, I guess I'll just have to find something he'd like from out of my mind.

* * *

Two hours later, Marie and I were seated in the food court drinking from our sodas.

I felt satisfied! Like I've accomplished something.

It took me forever to find Aiden's present. I literally had to visit so many stores. I bet Scott was mentally begging me to go home.

It didn't take that long for Marie to buy Aiden a present which was a wristwatch.

I had the bag that contained his present next to me on the floor.

Marie was talking to Liam on the phone, discussing the party that will be held for Aiden. Marie told me that we couldn't do a surprise party because he would already be expecting one. They held a ceremony every year. I let my eyes wonder around. Scott was a couple tables away looking as serious as ever. I bet every human that passed by would think of him as a creep just standing there looking for any harm to come. When Marie got off the phone, I felt mine vibrate in my back pocket. I took it out and saw that it was my mom. I answered her call and put the phone on my ear.

"Hello," I said.

"Hey sweetie, how are you doing?" my mom asked.

"I'm doing fine. What about you? How's Uncle Robert?" I asked.

"He's getting better. We have a therapist come every three days to check up on him. Maybe by the end of the month, we will be back," she said cheerfully.

I smiled at her good news.

"Well, I can't wait to see you and Dad," I told her.

"I can't wait either, sweetie," my mom said.

We said our goodbyes and hung up.

I looked at Marie to see her texting then look up at me.

"Liam said Aiden is getting suspicious. Let's go home," she said as she picked up Aiden's present from the ground.

I got up, picked my bag up, and followed Marie out the food court with Scott following behind us.

I was really anxious for his birthday. I just hoped Aiden would like his present.

Chapter 17

Marie was decorating the place while I placed all the cupcakes on the table with some other pack members. She-wolves displayed a lot of yummy stuff they made for the party while Liam went to get the cake. Marie told me it was no ordinary cake. I heard it was going to be huge. This was April 24, Aiden's twenty-fifth birthday, and the whole pack had been busy since yesterday.

I hadn't seen Aiden since this morning. He woke up and went straight to his office to get some work done while I came here and helped the other pack wolves. The time was seven thirty, and Liam was late. Marie was getting really nervous, thinking something happened to the cake. I tried to assure her that Liam was probably just late because of traffic.

And you know what?

I was right.

Liam came in through the door with two men carrying a very huge cake.

"Why are you late you, nincompoop?" Marie asked Liam.

Wait. Did she just call him a nincompoop?

"My grandma is faster than you," she said.

Liam rolled his eyes.

"Relax, grumpy pants. We only got stuck in traffic," Liam said.

I looked at Marie with an I-told-you-so face.

Everyone stacked their presents on a table. There were many. I think it was useless to get him so much—I mean, he was the Alpha; he already had everything.

I held the small bag in my hand, wanting to give it to Aiden myself.

I was really nervous about giving it to him.

What if he doesn't like it?

I pushed the thought to the back of my mind, not wanting to think about it now. I turned my head to the side to see the doors open, and there came Aiden walking with his parents beside him. It looked like he was searching for something. Make that someone because once his eyes found me, it never left. He walked to the center of the stage, and his parents followed behind him. His dad came forward and took the microphone.

"Hello, everyone. Today is a very important day. We are here to celebrate my son and your Alpha's twenty-fifth birthday," he said then gave the microphone to Aiden.

"Hello, everybody. I want to thank you for the gifts and food. Also, thank you for coming and celebrating this day with me. Enjoy the party."

The crowd cheered and clapped.

I lost sight of Aiden for a couple of minutes. He was greeting a special guest. I heard that one of his best friends from an outside pack was there, but I didn't know the name.

Aiden soon made his way toward me, Marie, and Liam. We were standing near the food court because of Liam's big appetite.

I still don't know how he can stay in shape if he eats that much.

I wore a tight red dress, and my hair was curled. Meanwhile, Marie wore a white crop top and a black skirt, and her hair was braided.

Marie came to me three hours before the party. Three hours!

She said that she needed all the time to fix me up to look—I quote—presentable. I had to remind her to fix herself too because she was too distracted with me.

When Aiden reached us, he wrapped an arm around my waist and kissed my forehead.

"Aren't you going to wish me a happy birthday?" he teased.

I looked up at him and feigned confusion.

"Oh wait. It's your birthday today?" I asked.

"Ha, ha, very funny. Do I at least get a happy birthday kiss?" he asked.

I shook my head.

"You got so many presents today. I'm sure you won't need it," I teased.

He frowned, then swooped down and stole a kiss on my lip. His lips were sweet and warm. As his lips moved with mine, I felt the sparks return.

Someone coughing brought me back to reality. I put my hand on Aiden's chest and pushed him away. I looked around to see Liam giving me a smug look and Marie smiling at me teasingly.

The attention from other pack members made my cheeks heat up.

Stupid mate of mine!

An hour later, Aiden finished opening all his presents. I was reluctant to give him his present.

He got all kind of things from one million dollars to a new phone. The gift I got was nothing compared to those. I didn't think he would like it. I hid the bag behind my back, hoping Aiden wouldn't ask for it.

I walked away farther from the crowd and into the food court. I filled my cup with some juice and was going to take a sip of it when I saw the blonde bimbo that was in the bathroom the other day. She stuck her foot out and tripped me.

Oh no she didn't!

I closed my eyes, bracing for the fall, when strong arms wrapped around me. I knew that it wasn't Aiden because of the missing sparks. It was a really hot guy with blue eyes. He looked down at me with a smile on his face.

"Easy there. Are you okay?" he asked.

I nodded. That's when I saw that I spilled all my juice all over his suit.

"Thank you, but now I've spilled juice over your suit. I'm so sorry," I said embarrassed. I looked around for the bimbo who did this, but she was gone. The next time, I will not let her get away with this.

He chuckled.

"Don't worry about it. All it takes is to wash it off, and it's gone," he said.

"Then let's go wash it off before it dries," I said.

We walked to the nearest bathroom.

"This isn't necessary," he said.

I shook my head.

"My name's Stella. What's your name?" I asked.

"The name's Nate, and I know all about you," he said as we got to the bathroom door.

Okay? That's not creepy at all.

He must have noticed my uneasiness because he spoke.

"Relax. I'm not some kind of serial killer. I'm Aiden's best friend, and he tends to talk about you a lot," he said, reassuring me.

Oh.

I smiled at him as I opened the door and walked into the empty bathroom.

"You're best friends with Aiden? What pack are you from?" I asked Nate.

"I'm from Blue Moon pack," he said proudly.

My eyes widened in surprise. Blue Moon pack is known for their large territory. They are well-known.

Nate began to take off the top of his suit. My jaw dropped—well, not literally, but you get what I mean.

"Uh? W–what are you doing?" I stuttered. I felt myself blush.

Nate had a really nice body, not as nice as Aiden's but one to drool for. He had very muscular arms and a six-pack.

"Well, how do you expect me to wash off the stain while wearing it?" he said pointing to his suit.

He had a point.

"Okay, let me wash it. I'm the one who caused it anyway," I said.

I reached to take the piece of cloth, but he raised it high in the air, out of my reach.

"It's not your fault. I saw what the blonde did," he said and smiled teasingly.

"I don't know what's her problem. I never did anything to her," I said as I leaned against a sink while he began to wash his suit.

"It's obvious! She's jealous," he said as he glanced at me.

"What? Why would she be jealous of me?" I asked.

"You're so naïve. She's jealous because you're the Luna and Aiden's mate," he said in a matter-of-fact tone.

But before I could reply, the door slammed open, and a very angry Aiden walked in.

What happened now?

"Nate!" he growled once he noticed his best friend was half-naked.

Oh. That's why. It doesn't help that we are in an empty bathroom.

He stomped over to Nate and pushed him against the bathroom tile.

"Woah, woah, man, this isn't what you think," he said as he put his hands up in surrender. I ran toward them and tried to push Aiden before he hit his best friend.

"Not what I think?" he growled. "My best friend is in a bathroom half-naked with my mate! Can you tell me what I'm supposed to think of that?"

I noticed he was starting to shake, so I rubbed his arm to calm him down.

And it was working.

He let Nate go and pulled me to his chest. I grabbed the piece of clothing from the sink and showed it to Aiden.

"Relax. We weren't doing anything. I accidentally spilled juice over his suit, and we're washing it off before it dries," I told him.

What I said must have clicked in his mind because he was now calm and pensive. He looked at Nate and pointed a finger at his bare chest.

"Even though you're my best friend, I don't want you so close to my mate, especially if you're half naked," he said but didn't seem angry.

Nate smirked.

"Oh come on, she's really pretty," he teased.

Is he trying to get on Aiden's bad side?

"Nate!" he growled.

Nate's laughter was heard throughout the bathroom.

"Relax, bro, I was just kidding. I mean, yeah, she's pretty, but I know not to mess with you," he said and smiled as he patted Aiden's shoulder.

Aiden cracked a smile.

"Of course, you do. Don't you remember what happened the last time you messed with me?"

Aiden said.

It looked like Nate remembered something because I saw him cringe.

"Please don't remind me," Nate said.

Aiden looked down at me then at his watch.

"It's getting late. Let's go back to our room," he said.

I nodded and said goodbye to Nate and walked out of the bathroom.

When I got into the room, I put the bag on the counter and walked to the bathroom to change. I got into a baggy shirt and a pair of shorts then walked out the bathroom to find Aiden checking the bag.

I gasped in surprise and rushed over to him, took the bag from his hands, and hid it behind my back.

"What's that? My birthday present?" he asked and grinned as he took a step closer. I took a step backward and shook my head.

"Then what is it?" he asked as he got closer.

"Nothing," I told him as my back hit the wall.

"If it's nothing, then let me see it," he said as he took the bag from my hand.

"No!" I shouted.

He ignored me and took out a wrapped box. He read the paper attached to it which said 'Happy birthday, Aiden,' and smirked.

"If this isn't for me, then why does it have my name on it?" he asked and grinned.

I didn't say anything, just stood there quietly, not knowing what to say.

He started to unwrap the box, and I grew more anxious.

He is going to hate it. Compared to all the other presents he got, this is nothing.

He opened it and stared into what I got him.

"Is this..."

Chapter 18

"Is this a necklace?" he asked.

I mentally slapped myself.

"No, it isn't.

"It's called a bronze custom map key ring," I told him.

"You collect these. In each place you visit or go to, you get the map of its country and put it on a chain. I'm not sure if you like it, but I thought it was a nice gift because I've traveled everywhere and that's something useful to help you keep track of where you went," I whispered feeling embarrassed.

I looked at the ground, not wanting to see Aiden's reaction. This was definitely a bad idea! Why on earth did I think he would like a chain that goes around the neck? I must have been out of my mind when buying it. It's just I wanted something different and special so bad. After a few moments of silence, I was starting to ask myself why he wasn't saying anything. I tilted my head up to look at him and saw he was expressionless. He only stared at me.

Does he not like it?

I knew I shouldn't have gotten him that.

I took a step forward and snatched the chain from his hand.

"If you don't like it, then I'll just return it," I said.

It took him a moment to realize what I just did before he could react. I saw the corner of his lips twitch upward before he smiled smugly at me.

"What?" I asked.

"Why wouldn't I like it? Give it back," he said teasingly.

I shook my head.

"Why would you want it? You got a lot of great things today," I said.

"Because it's from you. I was waiting for your present the whole day. Now give it to me," he said as he snatched the chain from my hand.

He held it up to his face and was looking at it with awe.

What the heck is with this guy? I don't understand him at all.

He took a step closer to me then pulled me to his chest and wrapped his arms around my waist.

"Thank you," he said softly as he brought his face to the crook of my neck and inhaled my scent.

"Can I still have that happy birthday kiss?" he asked, moving his face from my neck and looking at me teasingly. I rolled my eyes. Before I could say a word, his lips met mine. The sparks never failed to surprise me every time we made skin contact. His lips fit mine perfectly as he moved them against mine slowly. This kiss wasn't aggressive; it was more of a sweet, tender kiss. His arms tightened around me, bringing me closer to his chest. I could feel my heart beating so fast against his chest. I think Aiden liked the effect he had on me because I could feel him smile against my lips.

My hands moved on their own up his chest and right into his hair. I grabbed a chunk of it as my back hit the wall behind us. His teeth bit my lower lip asking for entrance, and I opened before he could put his hand under my shirt like the last time.

His tongue entered my mouth and was moving with my tongue. His fingers were teasing my skin as they made their way up and down my arm. We were fighting for dominance. I finally won this time. I'm not sure if Aiden let me on purpose, but I took advantage of winning.

I moaned against his lips. He growled in satisfaction. A second later, he pulled away from me and moved me to the bed. I looked at him confused.

"We should stop. I don't think I would be able to control myself any longer," he told me.

I could see his eyes darken as he said that.

I nodded my head and got under the cover. I closed my eyes as I felt the bed tilt downward when he got in it, and he pulled me to his chest. I laid my head on his chest, and his hand played with my hair. His breath grew steady as sleep crept closer.

* * *

I woke up the next morning feeling cold. My hands were trying to find something—or should I say someone—to keep me warm. I opened my eyes and saw sunlight shining into the room. Aiden's part of the bed was cold. He must have woken up hours ago.

I got up and made my way to the closet, yawning. I looked at the time on my phone to see it was about nine. I then grabbed a t-shirt which had the words "I'm A Rebel" on it and a pair of skinny jeans, then headed to the bathroom. I stripped out of my clothes and got into the shower. After I was done, I wrapped a towel around my wet body and brushed my teeth. I dried my body before wearing my clothes and brushing my hair.

When I got out of the bathroom, I saw Marie sitting on the bed eating a granola bar as usual.

"Good morning, immo," she said with a full mouth.

I smiled at her, stepped forward, snatched the granola she was eating, and stuffed it in my mouth. It was so good.

"Hey, I was eating that!" Marie whined.

"Yeah, I know that," I said as I grabbed my phone from the counter.

She pouted at me then got off the bed.

"So what's the plan for today?" I asked.

Marie sighed at me.

"There is no plan for today, immo. I have lots of training today. Aiden is making the whole pack work their butts off today," she said.

I nodded.

"Well, can I come? It's been a while since I worked out," I said. I could feel myself getting excited about the thought of fighting.

Marie laughed.

"What?" I asked.

"You really think Aiden would let you fight? I think he would be too afraid of you getting hurt," she said as she wiped an imaginary tear from her cheek.

"Hey, I can fight too you know! I'm two hundred years old. I can take care of myself," I said, crossing my arms over my chest.

"I know you can, immo. That's why I'm here," she said smugly as she wrapped her arm around my shoulder.

"Let's go convince Aiden to let you train with us," she said as she dragged me out of the bedroom.

Marie and I walked outside for a few minutes. It was so relaxing just to hear the birds chirping as the trees danced with the wind.

Marie led me to a huge building that looked like a gym. I could feel my pulse quickening with the image of kicking butts.

As we walked inside, the smell of sweat hit me.

Marie was right. Aiden was going hard on the pack members today. I looked around to see some people working out while others fought each other as if they were the enemy.

We continued to walk until I saw Aiden fighting with Nate. Both had their shirts off as they tackled one another to the ground. Just by looking at Nate, I could tell he was an Alpha too.

He also had power radiating from him when I met him yesterday. But I could feel more power coming from Aiden. He looked stronger than Nate.

I don't know why I seem to like that.

I shook my head, ignored the thoughts, and walked closer to the room.

Aiden stopped what he was doing, sniffed the air, and turned his head to look at me. At first, he looked shocked to see me here.

Nate took this opportunity to tackle Aiden to the ground, catching Aiden by surprise.

I walked faster to them and helped Aiden get off the ground while Nate stood next to him, feeling proud of himself.

"Well, that was easy," Nate said more to himself.

"Don't get your hopes up. That won't happen again," Aiden told Nate.

Nate only shook his head and punched his arm playfully.

Aiden turned to look at me then at Marie.

"Why are you here?" he asked me.

"I want to train as well," I answered excitedly.

"No," Aiden said firmly.

I frowned.

Marie was right. This was not going to be easy.

"And why?" I asked, raising one of my eyebrows at him, and crossed my arms over my chest.

"Because you could get hurt. End of story," he said while shaking his head.

I felt myself getting angrier.

I'm two hundred years old! He's underestimating me.

"Oh, I'm not here to ask for permission. I'm training whether you like it or not," I told him then turned around and walked toward the center of the room where there was a mattress to fight on.

"Stella," Aiden growled warningly. He grabbed my arm and turned me around.

The surrounding wolves stared at us. They stopped what they were doing.

Great, we're attracting too much attention.

I pulled my arm away from Aiden and walked to the mattress. I started to do some stretches. I was wearing shorts with a baggy t-shirt. I changed before I got here. I couldn't train while wearing skinny jeans.

After a moment of silence, I looked around to see Aiden looking at me pissed while Marie and Nate looked entertained. Some other wolves were looking at me and waiting for me to fight back their Alpha.

"So who wants to challenge me?" I asked while looking around.

Aiden growled at the crowd threateningly.

Geez, why does he have to be so grumpy all the time? He should just let loose.

"No one is challenging you, Stella. So drop the act," Aiden said.

I only shook my head at him.

Something in the corner of my eye caught my attention. Or should I say someone? That bimbo from the bathroom yesterday.

I smirked to myself.

This was going to be fun.

"I'd like to challenge you," she said as she flipped her hair from her shoulders. She was wearing extremely tight leggings and a short tight shirt.

Yup, definitely a bimbo.

I grinned at the thought of tackling her to the ground and showing her who she was messing with.

I'm not such a violent person, but when you get on my bad side, then you pay the price.

"Kayla," Aiden growled at her.

So that's her name.

Kayla the pack slut. Yup, has a ring to it.

"Aiden, don't ruin the fun," I told him and pointed at him to go stand with Marie and Nate.

Nate mouthed me a "good luck."

I replied with a quick nod.

I turned around to see Kayla getting ready to pounce on me, but I was quick enough to step aside. She fell on her face beside me.

This is going to be too easy.

She got up immediately and tried to throw a punch at my face, but I blocked it with my hand. Once her fist made contact with my hand, I held it tightly and twisted her arm behind her back.

She hissed in pain.

While one hand was held behind her back, the other was trying to find my face. She wanted to scratch me with fake nails.

Who even wears fake nails while fighting?

Bimbos, of course.

This was getting too boring. I let her go so I could have a bit of fun. I needed some excitement.

I pushed her forward.

When she finally straightened herself, she turned around and looked at me dead in the eye. She looked angry.

This is going to be fun.

She jumped at me, and I landed on my back. I moved quickly and turned us around so that I was on top of her. She tried to pierce through my skin with her fingernails, but I grabbed her hands and put it over her head.

"Woah, woah, kitten, wouldn't want to break a nail, would you?" I asked.

She growled at me.

One thing I learned from Alice is that wolves hate to be called kittens or pups. It's an insult to them and tends to hurt their pride.

I got off her and put my hand on my hip.

I looked around to see Aiden looking at me with wide, shocked eyes. But the emotion in them was what caught my attention.

I saw pride and awe.

My thoughts were broken when I saw a shadow from behind me move quickly. But not fast enough. I was quicker. I turned around and used my leg to trip Kayla. She fell to the ground, humiliating herself.

"That was a low move, even for you," I said bitterly.

The surrounding crowd clapped and cheered. Nate and Marie were by my side smiling widely.

"You showed her," Nate told me. The talk we had yesterday came in my mind. He told me that she was doing this because of jealousy.

I wonder if there was something between her and Aiden. Were they together once? Or was it a onetime thing?

I tried to ignore those thoughts. My chest hurt for some reason as I thought about the possibilities.

Aiden was by my side for a second. He wrapped an arm around me and pulled me to his chest.

"Show is over. Go back to your training," Aiden told the crowd.

Some sighed before they went back to what they were doing.

"That was amazing," Aiden told me as he looked down at me.

"Still don't think I could take care of myself?" I asked looking up at him.

"It's not that I think you're weak. I know you can take care of yourself. It's just my wolf likes to think we're needed, and that's by protecting you."

His words left me speechless. Is that how he felt, wanting to be needed?

Marie pulled me away from Aiden and handed me a water bottle.

"Immo, that was amazing! You totally showed her who's boss." She squealed while shaking me. I felt like she was happier than me about my victory. I smiled at her and laughed.

I looked around to see Kayla walking outside of the gym. She looked super pissed.

Hey, she was the one to challenge me. I don't think she even put up a fight. It was too easy.

* * *

An hour later, Aiden, Marie, Liam, Nate and I were sitting at a table in McDonald's. We were waiting for our food.

After what happened in the gym, the boys became hungry and decided to have lunch early. I went back to my room and changed to what I wore this morning.

Finally ten minutes of Liam and Marie bickering, the food arrived. I swear that's all that Liam and Marie did—bicker.

Aiden handed me my tray and gave Nate his soda. I took two fries and stuffed them into my mouth, letting the salty taste hit my taste buds.

"So, Nate, how do you know Aiden?" I asked.

"We used to go to high school together," Aiden answered for him.

I nodded.

"You're an Alpha right?" I asked Nate.

He nodded proudly.

"For how long?" I asked. I could feel Aiden tense beside me.

It took him a moment to answer, like he was remembering something.

"I became Alpha when my father died when I was seventeen," he answered.

"Oh, I'm so sorry," I said but tried not to show any pity, especially not to an Alpha. Becoming Alpha in such a young age is something very difficult to handle, especially after a father's death.

"It's okay, it was a long time ago," Nate said and took a sip from his soda.

I could feel the pain coming from him when he brought up his father, even though he didn't show it.

Losing someone special to you can leave a dent in your heart. Whether you like it or not, it will remain there until the day you die.

Or in my case, for eternity.

Chapter 19

Aiden

The only sounds that I heard were the clock ticking and my fingers pressing on the keyboard. It had been hours since I've been here.

I looked at the clock and saw that it was almost three PM.

I got up sometime around seven and came straight here into my office. I had a pile of work to do. I had been so busy lately with Nate here in my territory ever since my birthday. Nate couldn't stay here for long. He had a pack to get to.

Even though he was my best friend, Alphas can't really be relaxed if they're not in their own territory. Their pack is their own responsibility. If something happens to it while they're gone, then it will be their fault, even though if the Beta is in charge. Nate told me that he would be leaving that night, so I had to get all these work done by the next few hours.

Another thing that had been keeping me busy was the strange rogue occurrence. For the past few weeks, they were noticed by the borders of our territory. I didn't know why but I was starting to get suspicious, thinking that this was probably not a coincidence.

I would send my guards to send them far away, but with every rogue gone, more would come back. They wouldn't step into my territory, but I had to make sure they weren't any harm.

Better safe than sorry.

Before yesterday, one even walked into my territory and tried to fight my guards. But one untrained wolf against four well-trained guards made it easy to take him down. I'm not sure why he decided to make that stupid move and risk his life, but he had to be killed.

I was not risking anything.

That's why I had all the grown wolves yesterday train their butts off. They have to be prepared for whatever was to come. Whether it would hit us by surprise or not, we would be able to take it down, whatever or whoever was a threat to us. I hadn't told anyone about it besides my guards and Liam because I was not sure if I should worry anyone with useless rogue news.

Maybe it was just coincidence, or maybe that rogue was just having a bad day. Whether it was that or not, no one was allowed to step foot into my pack without permission and then challenge my guards.

I was looking through all the papers on my desk and separating the papers I needed from the ones I didn't. I threw the useless ones into the trash while I stacked the useful ones. My stomach grumbled, so I decided to take a break and go have dinner with Stella. I smiled to myself when she came to my mind. I could feel her starting to warm up to me. I mean, yes, she was her stubborn self, and I couldn't help but love that about her. I loved the way she talked back to me and bossed me around. I also loved the way she scrunched her nose when she was disgusted. Or how caring she was toward others like Sarah and her deceased best friend.

What was her name? Oh yeah, Alice.

Her past was one thing that surprised me.

She's a very strong woman who's been through so much and is still standing to this day. I admire her determination.

I know that I love her, but I don't know if she knows that. I don't even know how this will end. But whatever happens, I want her to be by my side.

I can't tell her that I love her yet. I still have to get her to actually like me and accept me. I bet if her parents weren't all the way across the world, she would have left me weeks ago.

But I was not going to let that happen. I've been looking for her for years, and when I finally found her, I wasn't going to let her go so easily.

I closed my laptop and was about to get off my chair when somebody knocked on the door.

"Come in," I yelled.

The door opened, and I caught the smell of a perfume that I knew too well.

Kayla.

I sighed. This again.

I wouldn't say that Kayla was the pack slut. I would say she was more of a gold digger. She was a very spoiled and clingy she-wolf. She didn't stop until she got what she wants. What does she want?

Title, and what she wants is what Stella had. Being Luna.

There was nothing between her and me but only a couple of spoken words. Yet she persists.

I looked up from my desk to see she was wearing a very short skirt and a tight shirt.

Stella's victory over her came to my mind. Yes, I knew she was a very strong vampire, but I didn't want to risk her getting hurt. But when Kayla challenged her yesterday, I could only feel one thing.

Pride.

I was proud that Stella was my mate—a very strong and beautiful one.

I smiled when I thought about Stella, but Kayla must have thought that I was smiling at her because she twirled her hair with her fingers and batted her fake eyelashes. She walked closer to my desk while swaying her hips side to side.

The way she seemed so fake disgusted me.

Stella couldn't be compared to anyone. She was one of a kind. Special in so many ways.

"Kayla, as you can see I'm very busy, so if you have something to tell me, then get on with it," I told her seriously.

I didn't want her to think I would be so easy to get.

No, she had to respect her Luna and me.

"I was wondering if you'd like to go out for dinner. We could have some fun," she said while walking to my chair. She thought she was so seducing with her tight clothes and her face full of makeup.

I stood up, making sure that I had so much power radiating from me to show her that I'm only her Alpha—I will always be and nothing more.

"Ah yes, I was just about to take a break," I told her.

She smiled at me and was about to say something when I continued.

"Thanks for reminding me. I have to meet up with Stella. If that's what you're here for, then you may leave," I said as I walked to the door, pointing the way out.

Her smile immediately dropped from her face, and she looked pissed. It looked like she was fighting with herself to try more, but I gave her a dead look which shut her up.

She rushed out of my office and closed the door.

I sighed to myself. Finally, she's gone.

I looked at the time to see it was ten minutes past three, so I headed out of my office and made sure to lock it.

I went upstairs to my room and got changed into proper clothes. Stella wasn't in the room, so when I was done, I headed out to look for her because her phone was on the counter next to the bed.

I got to the kitchen and saw Liam and Marie once again bickering.

God, I wish they could go through one day without arguing.

"Guys," I said as I looked between them.

They didn't pay attention to me because they were too busy fighting over the last slice of pizza.

"Guys," I repeated but louder this time.

"Marie, I told you that's mine. You already ate three slices. I need it more than you, I'm the beta. Besides you're going to get fat if you don't stop eating," Liam blabbed on with the same excuse he uses all the time.

"I ate three slices? I ate two, and you took my third slice. I haven't eaten all day. You're the one who needs to stop eating. Nobody wants a fat Beta," Marie rambled on.

"Will you guys just shut up!" I yelled while rubbing my fingers on my temple.

Marie and Liam finally looked at me with startled faces.

"Woah, bro, what's wrong with you?" Liam asked while snatching the slice of pizza from Marie and shoving it up in his mouth.

Marie looked pissed but chose to ignore him.

"Aiden are you, okay?" Marie asked me.

I nodded.

"I'm fine. Just tell me did you see Stella. She left her phone in our room, and I don't know where she is," I told them.

Marie shook her head at me while Liam nodded his.

"I didn't see her," Marie said.

"But I did," Liam said as he ate with his mouth open.

Marie looked at him with disgust.

"She went out the door with Nate a couple minutes ago," he told me.

I didn't know why she would leave without telling me and why would she go somewhere with Nate.

Nate is my best friend. But when I remember the night of my birthday, I get pissed off. I don't like to think that some male was half-naked in a bathroom with my mate, even though he's my friend.

They only met a couple days ago, but they act as if they've known each other for ages.

"Where did they go?" I asked sounding irritated.

Liam shrugged his shoulders.

I sighed and walked out of the house. I looked around but didn't see Stella or Nate, so I started to sniff the air for their scents. Their smell was still in the air telling me that they didn't leave long ago.

I saw Scott and walked over to him.

Why isn't he with Stella? He's supposed to be guarding her.

"Alpha," Scott said and lowered his head.

"Where's Stella?" I asked. "Aren't you supposed to be with her?"

Scott looked confused.

"Alpha, you told Nate to tell me that I was taking the day off while Nate looks after her," he told me sounding confused.

My wolf was getting angrier by the minute.

Why would Nate tell him that and not tell me?

Where was he taking Stella?

I growled out loud.

My best friend better not be trying to steal what's mine.

"Where did they head off to?" I asked.

"I saw them walking toward Broadway Street," Scott said.

I didn't waste a second longer. I turned to my right and sprinted toward Broadway Street. As I walked really fast, I sniffed the air and smelled Stella's scent mixed with Nate's.

My wolf didn't like the fact Stella scent was mixed with another male besides me.

I followed their smell, and it lead me to a club.

Who would go to a club at a time like this? I don't even know why there is a bar open at daylight.

My wolf was getting restless; he wanted to surface.

Why did Nate bring my mate here?

He has some explaining to do.

I walked into the bar and was surprised to find it crowded. The place smelled of sweat and alcohol. I looked around but didn't see Stella or Nate. I walked closer to the bar and caught Stella's scent.

It was weak, but I followed it anyway.

A few minutes later, I finally found Nate and Stella dancing on the dance floor.

I felt a vein on my forehead pop. My wolf was begging me to let him surface. Stella was swaying her hips side to side while throwing her hand in the air. Nate was next to her shaking his body to the beat.

What the heck was going on?

I stomped to the dance floor and grabbed Stella's wrist.

"What the heck are you doing?" I growled.

Stella and Nate both stopped dancing when they saw me. I saw Stella's face turn from startled to shock to angry.

She pulled her wrist from my hold and took a step back.

"What do you want, Aiden?" she asked bitterly. "Can't you see we're trying to have fun?"

What the hell was going on?

I looked at Nate and saw him smirk at me.

"Nate! Mind explaining to me why you brought my mate here?" I growled at him.

He ignored my question and looked at his wrist.

"Oh, look at the time. It's getting late. I have to go," Nate said and sprinted to the exit.

"You're not wearing a watch, stupid," Stella yelled at him.

He only waved at her then walked out of the club.

Stella looked at me then walked to the bar and ordered a drink.

"Oh no you don't," I told her. "We're going home."

I grabbed her arm and dragged her outside to the car I linked Liam to get me.

"Oh no, I'm not," she yelled at me when we were outside.

"Why are you acting like this?" I growled. "First, you go to a bar with my best friend, and now you're acting as if I did something wrong."

"Maybe because you did!" she yelled back.

Her words shut me up.

What did I do? I don't remember doing anything bad.

"What are you talking about?" I asked.

She only walked past me.

I wasn't going to let her walk away. I grabbed her arm and dragged her into the car. I opened the door to the front seat and made her sit as she struggled against my hold.

"Let go of me, Aiden! I'm not going with you!" she yelled.

I ignored her and closed the door and got into the passenger seat. I made sure to lock all the doors before I took off. I drove for a couple of seconds, and the silence was already eating me alive. I sighed and parked the car outside the forest. I turned my head to my right to look at Stella, but she was too busy looking out the window, ignoring me.

"Can you just drive so I can just get out of here?" she said as she looked at the car.

"What were you doing with Nate?" I asked calmly, but I could hear my wolf's voice mixed with it. He was angry about the way Stella was treating us and how she was dancing with another male.

She looked at me with a bored expression.

"What else do you expect? What do people usually do at bars?" she said.

I lost it. My wolf took over, and I felt my canines surface from my gums.

"You are mine!" I yelled. "Don't you ever think you could leave me! You belong to me and only me."

But that wasn't the thing that made me wish I had more control over my wolf. It was the fact I grabbed her and sunk my teeth into her skin. I knew that I was going to regret this when I calmed down.

If Stella disliked me before because of something I did, then she was sure going to hate me now.

Chapter 20

Stella

A couple of hours earlier

I couldn't stop laughing at Nate. Tears formed in my eyes as I held my stomach with my hands. Nate and I were in the living room watching The Vampire Diaries when he decided to tell me funny stories about him and Aiden in high school.

"And that's how I ended up with a black eye," Nate told me and chuckled.

"I still can't believe you two did that. I can't imagine Aiden as the prankster type," I said between giggles.

While Nate told me stories of Aiden and his adventures, I couldn't help but compare the high school Aiden with the present Aiden. They seemed like two different people. Nate told me Aiden used to be a carefree and outgoing friend but not anymore. That all changed when he became Alpha. He had to learn to be responsible and serious to be able to lead a pack.

"Oh trust me, Aiden was known for being a prankster in senior year," Nate said.

I looked at the TV and saw the episode was ending, so I got off of the couch.

"I'm hungry. Want to go grab a bite?" I asked.

Nate nodded then got up.

"Let's go call Aiden. He's been working for hours," he told me.

I nodded and made my way out of the living room with Nate behind me. We walked in silence down the empty hall. I looked at the photos hanging on the dull wall. Aiden really needed to decorate this place. It screamed boring.

We made it to the end of the hall and were about to turn right to where Aiden's office was but someone bumped into me, and I stumbled backward. Luckily, Nate caught me before I fell.

I looked up to see a monster.

The most horrible creatures my eyes laid on.

It was disgusting.

Okay, fine. It was Kayla.

I scrunched my nose in disgust when I saw what she was wearing. I swear she could be a prostitute in those clothes.

When she noticed it was me, her face held hate and annoyance. I could see her eyes turn darker as she stared at me.

But after a few moments of silence, her hating face was gone and was replaced with a smirk.

She was looking at me smugly.

What the hell is wrong with her?

She fixed her hair that was over the place and pulled her bra strap that fell from her shoulder.

Ew. Don't tell me she was doing it in the hallway.

"Oh, didn't see you there," she said in a fake sweet tone.

"If I were you, I wouldn't go in there," she told me as she pointed to Aiden's office across the hall.

"He's changing right now," she continued.

Excuse me?

"I'm sorry. Would you like to say that again?" I hissed at her. She was trying to push my buttons.

"Don't you get it?" she said in a tone a person would use to talk to a baby.

"You're nothing. You actually think you're special? Well, let me tell you this. You're replaceable. Aiden is going to get bored of you sooner or later and throw you to the side like every other girl he's been with."

And with that, she left Nate and me staring in shock.

I really don't know what to think. She had the nerves to say that to my face. My brain is giving me a lecture about why I let my guard down. I still can't believe Aiden is sleeping around with other women while claiming to be my mate.

If I were smart enough, I would have gone to Aiden's office and get his point of view because who would believe a bimbo.

But I was too angry to even face him. If I did, I might have jumped to conclusions and hit him with all my force until I was satisfied.

Nate put his hand on my shoulder and tried to calm me down.

No one's supposed to mess with a vampire, especially me.

"Hey, maybe you should hear what Aiden has to say," Nate suggested.

I only shook my head.

"I don't want to right now. I think I'm about to have a headache. All I want to do is let loose," I said the last part more to myself.

"Let loose, aye?" Nate repeated.

I gave him a questioning look.

"Well, if that's what you want, then I know a perfect place that opens at a time like this," he said while wiggling his eyebrows and giving me a teasing smile.

I knew he was trying to make me feel better, so I smiled at him.

"Yeah, maybe that would be a good idea," I told him.

He wrapped an arm around my shoulder as we walked outside of the pack house. It's been a while since I've drunk and let loose. I think that's what I needed to forget about all my fears and problems.

As we took one step forward, I saw Scott making his way toward us.

Dammit! How am I supposed to have a bit of fun if I have a second shadow with me, or worse, goes tells Aiden?

Nate must've felt me tense because he patted my back and gave me a reassuring look.

"Oh, Scott, just the right person I was looking for," Nate said.

"Aiden wants me to tell you that I'll be taking care of Stella for the day while you take the day off," Nate lied.

Scott didn't look convinced at first but then nodded his head slowly before turning around and walking away.

I smirked at how Nate made that sound so believable.

"So where's the place you were talking about? I doubt there would be anyone at a time like this," I said as he walked with me down the sidewalk.

It was a really hot day today, and the sun was shining brightly.

"The place is right around the corner. A good friend of mine owns it, so you know what that means," he said while nudging my side with his elbow.

"Free passes?" I asked and smiled.

"Bingo!" he yelled cheerfully, and I laughed.

After a couple minutes of walking silently, we made it in front of an open club. I was actually surprised to find it crowded when we got in. Nate was right; it didn't take us much to get in.

The music was blasting loud as everybody danced to the beat. Nate and I made our way to the bar and ordered ourselves drinks.

"After this, let's go dance," Nate yelled over the music.

I nodded and started to look around the place.

I didn't really like crowded places like this where people get drunk and make out. But that didn't stop me from going there. It's been a while since I've actually gone to a bar. I would go with a couple of friends to hang out, but there was a time in my life when it became a daily thing for me.

To drown my sorrows in alcohol and forget about the guilt. To forget about my problems and what the future has in store.

The bartender finally arrived with our drinks and handed them to Nate and me. I took a sip, let the drink hit my taste buds, and I moaned in delight.

"Mmm. This is so good," I said as I looked at Nate.

He smiled at me then nodded his head before taking a sip from his drink.

"Yeah, it's my favorite," he said.

From the corner of my eyes, I saw a couple of girls checking Nate out. I smiled teasingly at him, and he gave me a look of confusion from him.

"What?" he asked.

"There are a couple of girls behind you checking you out," I said between giggles.

"Of course, they would. Who do you think I am? I wouldn't be surprised if I left this place with more than ten phone numbers," he said cockily.

I raised an eyebrow.

"Oh someone's cocky," I said.

"Well, if that's what you think, then fine. Let's make a bet," I said enthusiastically.

He looked at me then smiled evilly.

"When I get ten phone numbers or more before we leave, then you have to dye your hair pink," he told me.

I scrunched my nose in disgusted when the image of me with pink hair came to my mind. But I nodded anyway.

"If you get," I pointed out.

He only shook his finger at me and said, "Nope, when I get."

I rolled my eyes.

"Okay, and if you don't, then you have to tell Aiden you slept with me," I said smiling evilly.

Nate gasped.

"Are you trying to get me killed?" he whisper-yelled at me.

I laughed.

"Do you know what Aiden would do to me if I told him that? Why would you want me to?" he asked, pretending to be afraid.

"Because it would be so funny to see the look on his face," I said between giggles.

"Oh, so you're willing to risk your friend's life for your own satisfaction," he said while putting his hand over his heart, pretending to be hurt.

"Look, are you in or out?" I asked.

"Fine, I'm in. But only because I know I'll win," Nate said.

I was about to say some comeback, but my favorite song came on and blasted through the speakers.

"I love this song," I yelled over the music as I grabbed Nate's arm and pulled him up. "Let's dance."

"But how am I supposed to be getting numbers?" Nate asked.

"Oh hush. You can hit on the girls on the dance floor. Come on!"

We walked to the center where everyone was dancing. I put my hands in the air and swayed my hips side to side, moving with the beat. I felt free, like I was flying in the air where nobody could reach me. But suddenly I came crashing down to the ground when someone grabbed my wrist.

I felt the sparks return—which meant only one thing.

"What the heck are you doing?" a husky voice growled from beside me.

Nate and I stopped dancing. I looked up to see a very pissed and angry Aiden. I could feel my face move from shock to anger.

Who does he think he is?

He can play around with other girls, and I simply can't have some fun?

"What do you want, Aiden?" I asked bitterly. "Can't you see we're trying to have fun."

I could tell Aiden was shocked because of how I talked to him. He took his eyes off me and glared at Nate.

"Nate! Mind explaining to me why you brought my mate here?" he growled.

He ignored his question and looked at his wrist.

"Oh, look at the time. It's getting late. I have to go," Nate said and sprinted to the exit.

"You're not wearing a watch, stupid," I yelled at him.

He only waved at me then walked out of the club.

Well, looks like I won.

I looked at Aiden then walked over to the bar and ordered another drink. Before I could sit down, Aiden grabbed my arm, yanking me forward.

"Oh no you don't," he told me. "We're going home."

He dragged me outside the club and toward a car.

"Oh no, I'm not," I yelled at him. I wasn't going to let him boss me around.

"Why are you acting like this?" he growled. "First, you go to a bar with my best friend, and now you're acting as if I did something wrong."

"Maybe because you did!" I yelled back.

This shut him up. It looked like he was trying to remember something but failed.

"What are you talking about?" he asked.

Oh great, now he's denying.

I ignored him, not wanting to deal with his lies. I decided to walk home, but he grabbed my arm and dragging me into the car.

"Let go of me, Aiden! I'm not going with you!" I yelled.

He just shoved me into the car and made sure to lock all the doors. He got into the car and drove off.

I looked out the window, not wanting to face him.

Aiden parked the car outside a forest.

What the heck is he up to?

"Can you just drive so I can just get out of here?" I said.

"What were you doing with Nate?" he asked calmly, but I could hear his wolf's voice mixed with it. He seemed really angry and was losing his patience, which made him look scarier. Something in me told me not to mess with him while he's angry because he could do anything. But did I listen?

Nope, instead, I said the stupidest thing my mouth ever came up with.

"What else do you expect? What do people usually do at bars?" I said.

If only I could take that back because once those words came out of my mouth, I saw a vein pop on his forehead. He was shaking like crazy, and I knew his wolf was taking over.

"You are mine!" he yelled. "Don't you ever think you could leave me! You belong to me and only me."

And with that, he grabbed my shoulders and pulled me to him.

I felt his teeth sink into my skin the moment I made contact with his chest. A piercing scream came out of my mouth as I felt pain overwhelm where my shoulder and neck met.

He did not just do that!

I felt tears begin to form in my eyes, not because of the pain consuming me, but because now there was no way going back. I was trapped.

Trapped in a place I call destiny.

With no way out.

Chapter 21

I slapped Aiden across the face with all my force. I felt the tears run down my cheek as the new bite mark was throbbing in pain. My brain was barely processing what just happened.

How could Aiden do this to me?

Especially when I'm not ready. He's just applying more pressure on me.

Aiden didn't say anything. He seemed dazed, like he was thinking and like the slap didn't even affect him.

"How could you!" I yelled as I pushed him away from me and punched his hard chest. My fist hurt.

"Who gave you the right?" I yelled in his face. I was so angry. Yes, I know this was partly my fault for pissing him off, but when that usually happens to someone, they're supposed to shout it out, hit a wall, or something. He didn't have to mark me! He just took away everything I had with that one bite.

Now, I have to spend all my days knowing that I will watch history repeating itself. I'm going to live by his side for years watching him grow old and eventually die.

I felt my heart ache just at the thought. I couldn't stand to look at his face right now, not after what he just did. My shaking hands made their way to the button that released the seatbelt around me and unlocked the doors.

"Where are you going?" Aiden asked as he grabbed my arm. His voice was soft; I could hear the guilt in them. He probably feared I might never forgive him for what he's done.

But something in me told me that I would, eventually.

But right now, I refused. I needed some time alone, away from all the drama.

"Just leave me alone," I said as I pulled my arm from his grip and rushed out the door. My feet stepped on the grass underneath me, and I sprinted into the forest, leaving Aiden to think about what he'd just done.

The tears stopped, but my heartbeat didn't. It was beating so fast as I ran past the trees with my hair flowing with the wind. The forest was quiet as the sun shined down on the trees. The birds in the trees stopped singing, and the squirrels on the ground ran away as they saw me. The place was peaceful, helping me relax as I think. The sun was bright as it shined on my skin, not affecting me at all. Yes, you heard it. The sunlight doesn't affect us vampires, doesn't make our skin sparkle like in the movie *Twilight* or burn our skin like in all the fairytales.

Once I calmed my beating heart, I sat underneath a big oak tree and let my feelings overwhelm me. My mind was too focused on what just happened. My life flashed before my eyes.

I saw what I was going to go through, the same process I went through many years ago.

Get attached.

Live the moment as everyone tells me to.

Then regret it later on.

I put my head in my hands. I let the world around me shut down as I tried to forget and doze off.

Maybe I might be able to run away from all my problems.

But just like death, my destiny cannot be escaped.

Oh, sometimes I wonder to myself if the moon goddess hates me. Because it sure seems like it!

The sound of a branch breaking brought me out of my thoughts. I lifted my head from my hands as my ears perked up, trying to figure out where that sound came from. I noticed the birds that were on the trees flew away suddenly. I put my guard up.

I sniffed the air half expecting it to be Aiden, but I got no scent of his. Instead, there was a strange smell, a smell I didn't recognize. I got off the ground looking at my surroundings for any harm to come. The smell was still in the air, but there was no movement of any sort.

Maybe it was just my imagination. It could have been a squirrel.

But one thing was obvious.

The forest was quiet.

Too quiet.

I saw something move in the corner of my eye. But before I could make a run for it or process what was going on, I fell to the ground, hitting my head to a nearby tree. I hissed in pain. A dark brown wolf was on top of me. It was big, but not big enough to be an Alpha. Its canines were hanging out of its mouth looking awfully sharp. His eyes were what brought chills down my spine. And not the pleasurable kind of chill.

His eyes held so much darkness. It held danger, and it held death.

There was no life coming out of it.

He snapped his teeth at me threateningly.

I hiss as my eyes reddened. I let my fangs come out as I opened my mouth to show him who he was messing with.

I don't know what's his problem. But if it's a fight he wants, it's a fight he'll get.

I used as much strength I had to push him off me and quickly got to my feet. We were only a few steps away from each other, and every step he took forward, I would take one backward. My back hit a tree as the wolf growled at me. A second later, he launched at me quickly, but I was faster.

I got out of the way just in time before the wolf hit me. He crashed into a tree. I heard him growl in pain as his head made contact with the tree. Before he could turn around, I came from behind him and hooked my arm around his neck, choking him.

The wolf was struggling under me while trying to bite my arm. In one swift movement, I found myself flying into the air and then to the ground. I screamed, and my voice echoed through the forest.

The wolf jumped on me while I was in a weak state and started to bite my legs. One thing I noticed was that he wasn't going for the neck, which I was thankful for.

But why?

I struggled when he started to drag me from the ground, holding my legs.

What did this wolf want?

Before I could do anything else, the wolf was no longer on top of me. Instead, he was to my right on the ground while a huge gray wolf was on top of it growling viciously. Right away I knew who it was.

Aiden.

I was going to get up and help him, but I fell to the ground because of my injured leg. Blood kept spilling through the bites were, and my head throbbed in pain. I looked at the scene before my eyes and saw the brown wolf struggle underneath Aiden. But in one quick move, his teeth sunk into the wolf's neck. The brown wolf stopped moving.

Aiden left the lifeless body on the ground.

There was blood everywhere on the ground. My stomach growled. I know this wasn't the time to be hungry, but what can I do? I'm a vampire.

Aiden's wolf backed away from the dead body and came toward me. Once he reached me, he started to lick my wounded leg.

I sighed in relief.

Well, that was something.

I was speechless about what just happened.

Why was the wolf trying to harm me? Was it because I'm a vampire?

But that wouldn't make sense because if he wanted to harm me because I'm a vampire, then he would've wanted to kill me.

But that's not what the wolf's intentions were. Through the whole attack, the wolf was not aiming for my neck. My thoughts were broken when I noticed Aiden shift in front of me, displaying his gorgeous body.

I felt my cheeks heat up as I blushed in embarrassment. He must have noticed my reaction because I heard him chuckle lightly.

"What happened? Are you okay?" he asked as he checked for any other injuries.

When his hand touched the back of my head, I hissed in pain, and he to let go.

"Yeah, I'm fine, and I don't really know what just happened. He just attacked me out of nowhere," I answered.

He nodded at me before lifting his head, looking at the sky. His eyes weren't focused; he must've been linking someone. Once he was done, he gathered me in his arms and lifted me from the ground.

I winced at the sudden action.

He made his way through the forest and back to where we left the car. He was walking silently, and I could tell he was mad. I just didn't know if it was because of what just happened or because of earlier today.

Once we got there, he opened the car, sat me on the passenger seat, and went to the back of the car to grab something.

A few seconds later, he was back wearing shorts.

I noticed someone was running toward us. Once they got closer, I noticed it was Liam and some other guards I recognized.

"Are you guys okay?" Liam asked breathlessly.

"We're fine, but a rogue was here in our territory and even tried to attack Stella. Send guards to look over the area for anything suspicious. I also want to know how a rogue was able to sneak into my pack. Where were the guards when this happened?" Aiden growled out.

Yup, he was definitely mad.

Liam nodded his head and told guards to search the place.

"I don't know how, but I'll increase the number of wolves guarding the border," Liam said before walking away as he talked on his phone.

Aiden walked around the car and got into the driver seat. He started the engine and drove off in a direction opposite to the pack house.

"Where are we going?" I asked confused.

"Where do you expect? You're injured, and we need to check on it," he answered as he took his eye off the road and looked at me for a second.

* * *

Half an hour later, I was sitting on a chair in a hospital room with Aiden. Things had been awkward between us. We hadn't spoken to each other since we got here. I mean, what should I expect after what happened.

I just don't know if I'm able to be mad at him for so long. He's my mate.

But that still didn't give him the right to do that.

Through the whole ride here, I felt he was tense, as if any minute then I would break down because of what he did.

If I were going to forgive him, then he would have to earn it. I was going to make him work for my forgiveness; he had to get on his knees and beg.

I smiled evilly to myself when the thought came to my mind. Having the big bad Alpha get on his knees—oh, that's a sight I would want to see. I told myself that being mad at him wouldn't achieve anything; it's fate we're talking about. He was bound to do it sooner or later.

It's just I'm going to make him regret ever marking me without my permission.

The door opened, and a male doctor wearing a white lab coat came in holding some papers.

"Alpha, Luna," he said as he bowed his head in respect.

"Stella has an injured leg and a bruised head. I want you to check on her and see if everything is okay," Aiden told the doctor.

The doctor nodded and started to check my injuries. After a couple of minutes, he was done wrapping and cleaning them and went to check the papers he was holding before.

"Alpha, the Luna is fine, just has a bruised head that will heal by tomorrow. The same goes for the injuries on her leg," the doctor said. He bowed his head before leaving.

Aiden and I walked back to the car, and as we got in, he broke the silence.

"Next time you're not going anywhere without Scott. I'm also giving you an extra guard just in case," he said with a tone that told me this was not held up for discussion.

I sighed.

Great, more guards.

"You know that's unnecessary. This could have been a onetime thing. Besides, how many times do I have to tell you, I can take care of myself," I argued.

"Stella, I'm not risking it! Do you know how much you scared me when I heard you scream?" he said as his voice cracked in the end.

"Maybe that wouldn't have happened if you didn't mark me in the first place," I yelled.

This shut him up.

Through the rest of the ride, it looked like he was arguing with himself. I know he wasn't regretting about marking me; he just wished he could have had more control over his wolf and waited until I was ready.

That's something I will never understand about male wolves. Why do they have to be so protective and possessive? Especially Alphas. I heard that a Luna and an Alpha are both equal. They both get to say their opinions and speak their thoughts. The Alpha doesn't step over his mate, even though at times he might act like it, but they're not above them. They both have the right to make their decision and not be controlled around.

But why do I feel like I'm some kind of puppet when it comes to Aiden?

It's like he's choosing my life for me.

I noticed we were parked right outside of the pack house. I was about to open the door and head out when Aiden held my hand. I rolled my eyes.

"I'm sorry," he whispered, but it was loud enough for me to hear.

"I'm so sorry, Stella. You know I would never want to hurt you."

He paused.

"It's just when I saw you with Nate in a bar, my wolf lost it and wanted to claim you as his," he continued.

"But that doesn't give you the right to force me into being yours. Don't I get a say in all this? Aren't we supposed to be equal?" I asked as my voice rose.

"We are," Aiden said.

I shook my head.

"Then how come I don't feel like it? All I feel is like I'm your puppet, being controlled around, and you expect me to stay quiet while you control my life. Tell me. Why do I feel like you're making all the decisions for me? Why do I feel so useless when I'm with you? Huh. Why?" I yelled as my voice cracked in the end.

He only looked at me with sad eyes.

I opened the door and got out as I ran into the pack house. I didn't want to go into my room because Aiden might be there. So I made my way to Marie's room, hoping she could give me the comfort I needed.

I knocked on her door, and when she opened it, she gasped. She pulled me into her room and looked at my marked neck with wide eyes. At first, she seemed excited and happy, but when she saw my expression, it all went away.

"What happened?" she asked as she sat me on her bed.

"Aiden marked me earlier today without my permission, and I don't know what to do," I said as I rubbed my hands over my face, sounding frustrated.

"Wait, why would he do that?" she asked.

"Because earlier today, I saw Kayla coming out of his office, and it looked like they did it."

I paused, making sure she knew what I meant.

"So Nate took me to a bar to forget about it, and when Aiden found out, his wolf took over," I blabbed on.

"Wait, did you just say that there was a bar open at a time like this?" Marie asked.

I mentally slapped myself.

"Is that all that you heard?" I asked.

She shook her head while smiling softly.

"Oh, sweetie, tell me did you get Aiden's point of view on this?" she asked.

I looked down at my lap while shaking my head.

"Stella, I've known Aiden for years, and let me tell you, he's a very loyal person. Yes, I know that doesn't give him the right to mark you, but maybe you should ask him what actually happened. Besides, you can't really believe such a slut like Kayla," she said as she scrunched her nose in disgust.

I let her words sink into my brain. She was right. I should get his view on this, but that doesn't change the fact he marked me when I was not ready.

"Are you saying I should forgive him?" I asked.

"Hell no!" she shouted while shaking her head sassily.

"You need to get him on his knees, girl, and beg," she told me while snapping her fingers with more sass.

I laughed at her enthusiasm. This was what I needed, someone like Marie to help me forget about all my problems.

"Hey, would you mind if I slept here tonight?" I asked nervously.

Her eyes widened as she shook her head. She got up on her bed and jumped up and down.

"Yes! We're having girls' night!" she yelled.

"I have to get sleeping bags, chocolate, three bags of chips, bottles of soda, and the whole collection of the *Twilight* series," she told me while sprinting out the door.

I stayed behind laughing.

* * *

It was about nine o'clock, and Marie and I were making our way outside the pack to say goodbye to Nate who was leaving for his pack.

I thought a lot about what Marie said, and I decided to ask Aiden what happened but not to forgive him completely.

Once we were outside, the cold breeze as hit our skin, forming goosebumps. I saw Nate, Liam, and Aiden standing next to Nate's car. Once they noticed us, I could see Aiden growing tense in my presence.

Nate hugged Liam and Marie goodbye. He then came forward to hug me, and I could see Aiden grow tense even more when he wrapped his hands around my shoulders. Oh, but he didn't dare say anything after what happened today.

Nate was about to pull away before I whispered in his ear.

"Oh no, you don't. You're not leaving yet. You lost that bet remember?" I said as I smiled evilly at him.

His face held nervousness.

"Oh come on. Can't I do it over text, when I'm all the way in my pack, where Aiden can't harm me?" he whispered, but I only shook my head.

He sighed and rubbed his face with his hands. I heard him mutter something that sounded like, "You're trying to get me killed."

He then walked over to Aiden chuckling nervously. He gave him a hug and patted his shoulder.

"Bro, I'm going to miss you. You know we are best friends, and we don't try to kill each other—haha, yeah, well...I slept with Stella," he said the last part so fast and rushed to his car.

"What!" Aiden yelled.

And that's when I lost it. I fell to the ground laughing hysterically as Aiden ran after a screaming Nate as if he was going to kill his friend.

"Bro! Bro, I'm kidding. I swear I'm kidding. Please don't kill me. God, I swear I would never mess with you," he said breathlessly while hiding behind his car.

Liam and Marie were also laughing with me as they took in the scene. My stomach was starting to hurt as tears formed in my eyes.

This was only the beginning. I was going to make Aiden fall to his knees.

Chapter 22

Hoo.

I scrunched my nose at that sound.

Hoo hoo.

Is that an owl?

My question was answered when I heard it again.

Hoo.

What is it doing hanging around the bedroom window? Gosh, how am I supposed to sleep with all that noise?

I stretched my arm to grab anything to cuddle with—a blanket, a pillow, or even Aiden.

But I felt nothing. Not even the mattress underneath me.

My eyes snapped open, half expecting to be met with the sunlight, but it was the exact opposite. The place was dark; there was only one source of light.

The full moon.

I looked around to see that I wasn't in my bedroom at all. Not even in the pack house. I was in a graveyard. Again.

But how did I get here?

I started to panic. I was never too fond of graveyards. They scare the crap out of me, with the creepy vibe and the clouds taking over the sky. I looked around and saw that there was, in fact, nothing in the sky. It was clear, not one star, only the full moon shining brightly. I got up from the hard rock floor, dusting the dirt off me. I looked around for any exit. Any way to get out of here. But there looked to be no way out. I could see miles and miles of the same dull and scary place.

I was startled when a crow flew toward me while squawking at me. It was about to hit my head but instead flew over it when I ducked down. I stumbled backward before gaining my balance. I looked up to see that the crow was gone.

Weird.

I heard a dripping noise. Like when a sink is not closed all the way and drops of water are falling. I looked around but saw no sink, no source of water anywhere. There was an ache in my arm which I just noticed now. I was too busy worrying about how I got here to even notice.

I looked down to find my answer.

There was blood dripping from my right arm and to the ground. It was no simple cut; it was bleeding severely. I was surprised that I was still standing with the amount of blood I lost.

But how did this happen?

I was so confused as my panic increased.

Am I in hell? But how did I die? I don't remember anything. Why was my arm bleeding so bad? Who caused it?

My thoughts were broken when I heard leaves crunching from behind me. I snapped my head toward the sound, the sweat on my forehead increasing. I looked to see where the sound was coming from and gasped.

It looked like I was in the center of the graveyard, and around me were the dead.

In every direction, I was surrounded—I'm not even sure what to call them—mummies, zombies, or ghosts. But they surely weren't alive. I could tell just by looking at them. Their eyes held darkness, loneliness.

Death.

I took a step backward, feeling my heart beat quickly against my chest, but it was useless. They were everywhere.

Oh, if I wasn't dead before then, I am surely going to die now.

Someone from behind me grabbed my arm, turning me around.

"Pick me!" he yelled as he shook me.

"Make it me!"

What the heck is he talking about?

I yanked my arm from his grip and made a run for it. I pushed a person in front of me and ran past them as fast as I could with them yelling from behind me.

"No, pick me!" one yelled.

I ran past the gravestones, my hair flying in the wind. I saw not one but two crows flying above me. My injured arm wasn't helping; it only made it hurt to move.

"Please, you have to save me!" a woman's voice echoed through the air.

What did they want from me?

I forced my legs to move faster; I couldn't let them gain on me.

Who knows what they'll do?

"You have to do it!" a little girl said from behind me.

"Just make it me. I have to be the one!"

I turned my head around so I could see how far I was and saw that they weren't too far behind. The look in their eyes scared me, sending shivers down my spine. I felt the tears form behind my eyes, but I held them back, not wanting my vision to blur.

I couldn't stop now. I had to escape. I let the vampire in me take over, helping me run faster. But what surprised me was that through all this, my arm was still not healing. If I had lost the people who were after me, they would sure have found me because of my blood dripping everywhere.

My legs were becoming tired as I ran out of breath.

Is there no end to this?

My body stopped suddenly when I hit a hard wall, and I stumbled back. I looked up to see that it wasn't a wall. It was a hard chest. I moved my eyes up from the stranger's chest and to his face.

He looked so familiar. Like I've seen him before.

"Do it!" he ordered with a low scary voice.

Once those words came out of his mouth, I remembered where I saw him. I dreamed about this before.

"Do what?" I asked as my voice rose. I was getting tired of all this.

What is going on? I just want to go home.

"Do it!" he shouted pointing to a gravestone beside me.

I looked around and saw that the graveyard was empty; no one was in sight.

Wasn't it just filled with the dead trying to catch me a minute ago?

I looked at the gravestone he pointed at and saw what was written was the same thing I saw the last time.

R.I.P. Lilly Claze

* * *

My eyes snapped open as I was sweating with a fast-beating heart. I looked around frantically and sighed in relief when I saw I was still in Marie's room. I rubbed my hands over my face as I recalled the dream I just had. Or should I say nightmare?

I don't know what to think of it. Was it a coincidence that I saw the same person twice? Or did it mean something?

I didn't want to think about it, so I decided to forget. I looked around and saw the sun was bright as the birds were chirping.

I looked at Marie sleeping next to me and smirked when I saw her mouth open. Drool came out of her mouth and hit her pillow. Her bed was big enough to fit the both of us.

It had been three days since the incident, three days since I've been sleeping here, and three days since I started avoiding Aiden.

I wasn't avoiding him because I was mad. Yes, I was still ticked about what he did to me, but I was mostly doing it to drive him nuts. I know when someone has been away from their mate, it drives them crazy.

And that was my motive.

Through these past three days, I had been sleeping here with Marie. We stayed up all night long, watching movies or just talking. I didn't even see Aiden; I was trying my best to avoid him. But today I knew that I had to face him sooner or later.

We had to talk about what happened. Marie kept persisting that I get his side of the story. Now, you might be wondering, Big deal. Why is she worried about him sleeping with other women when she's trying to resist him?

Well, let me tell you. How does it feel to have someone snatch you away and force you to live a life you weren't expecting, telling you that you belonged to them and the next thing you know is he's sleeping around? And you get the feeling as if he can do things you cannot, which makes you feel inferior to him.

Which is what I felt when I saw Kayla coming out of his office.

I looked at Marie and heard her mumble something in her sleep about beating Liam up because he stole her cookie—I don't know, it was vague.

Wanting to tease her a bit, I grabbed the old, cold slice of pizza on the counter. I smiled evilly at myself as I lowered the soggy pizza into her opened mouth.

At first, nothing happened, but after a few moments of silence, Marie shot up from her bed spitting the pizza out of her mouth. I laughed out loud, tears forming in my eyes. She looked around the room until she saw me next to her. She gave me a deathly glare and grabbed a pillow from behind her.

"That was so not nice, immo!" she yelled as she hit me with the pillow with so much force, I fell off the bed.

I lay on the ground still laughing as Marie hit me several times with the pillow, looking like a zombie because she just woke up.

"Gosh, I'm sorry," I said between giggles.

"It's just you should have seen the look on your face. It was hilarious."

I breathed out, feeling my stomach ache because of how much I laughed as she hit me one last time.

"Haha, yes, very funny, immo. You know what, you should be a prankster because you love to mess with people, or a clown because you're a joker," she said as she walked to her closet and into the bathroom, but before she closed the door, she stuck out her tongue.

* * *

An hour later, I was all dressed up ready to start my day. My mind would occasionally drift off to the dream I had but wouldn't over think it. My mind was mostly set on confronting Aiden.

I skipped down the stairs as I hummed a tune. You know that annoying feeling you get when you know a part of a song but forgot from where it was or how it goes? Yeah, that's what I was feeling.

I walked into the kitchen humming, and I grabbed a box of cereal and poured it into a bowl then added milk. As I sat down, Liam came in yawning with lazy eyes. It looked like he didn't even wash his face.

I scrunched my nose at the thought as I stared at him pour his own cereal with only one eye open.

"How are you eating if you're barely awake?" I asked with my mouth full.

He sat down in front of me glancing at me then back at his bowl.

"Food is my number one priority in the morning," he said lazily.

I rolled my eyes. I don't get how he isn't fat with the way he eats.

Once I was done with my breakfast, I put the bowl in the sink and headed to Aiden's office. With every step I took, I felt my heart beat faster. I was anxious about what Aiden was going to say.

A couple seconds later, I was standing in front of his door thinking if this was a good idea.

Haha, yeah...maybe it isn't.

I stepped back and was about to turn around and leave when the door to his office opened.

Shit.

"Stella." Aiden sounded surprised.

When I looked at his face, I gasped softly. He looked horrible, as if he hasn't slept in days. He had black bags under his red eyes and wrinkles on his forehead that made him look much older than he really was. It looked like he hadn't shaved in days with the hair on his face.

"Uh, um, hi," I said.

"What are you doing here?" he asked with a hint of hope in his voice.

I sighed knowing we had to talk.

"Can we talk?" I asked.

He nodded his head eagerly as he opened the door wider for me to come in. I walked into his office and sat on one of the chairs in front of his desk, while Aiden sat in his seat.

"What do you want to talk about?" he asked.

"Well, you remember the day you marked me?" I asked.

My question made him cringe. I could tell he was regretting doing it without my permission.

He nodded his head.

"Well, before Nate and I went to the bar, we decided to go to your office so we could go have dinner together."

I paused. Aiden nodded his head telling me to continue.

"So we were walking toward your office when we saw Kayla coming out of it, and she looked pretty messy like...Well, you know what I mean," I said quickly.

He looked at me with a confused expression.

"What are you talking about?" he asked, and I got angry.

Is he denying what he did?

"You know what I'm talking about, Aiden. You really expect me to sit around while you have fun with other women?" I said as my voice rose.

When I said that, he seemed to understand what I meant earlier.

"Oh, ugh, God, Stella, you misunderstood. Nothing happened between Kayla and me," he said as he ran his hands through his messy hair.

"She just came to my office to ask if we could go out, but I declined her offer saying I was going out with you, and she left. That's it," he said, but I could see his mouth twitch upward.

I sighed in relief.

Wait, why is he looking at me like that?

"What?" I asked.

"You were jealous, weren't you?" he asked.

My face turned red as a tomato, but I tried to keep my calm.

"Me? Pft, no, I just saw it as a sign of disrespect, that's all," I said, but I heard it come out softer than I wanted.

He raised an eyebrow and gave me a boyish smirk.

"Sure. Let's go with that if it helps you sleep at night."

Gosh, why does he have to be so annoying?

Chapter 23

This was the day my parents were finally coming back. I was really excited to see them. It had been about a month since they left to go check on my mom's uncle after his attack. He had been doing well. His injuries healed fast, but it was his mental health that was the problem. At first, he was broken because of his dead friend, and I understood how he felt.

He was going through the guilt of not being able to save his friend's life. Going through so much sorrow and grief. Blaming himself for everything. Wishing he could have gone back in time and change fate.

Of course, he wasn't healed completely. No one can heal that fast from a tragic past. It takes time for a broken heart to be stitched back together.

My parents tried to stay as long as they could, which was about a month. But that was all they can do. They couldn't stay longer than that. It hurt them so much to watch a close friend suffer the loss of another friend.

You see the irony.

One person's tragedy is another person's sorrow, which can affect everyone around them. For when you truly have a pure heart, you start to focus on everyone else and not just yourself. Which means if your loved ones are happy, then you'll be happy as well. However, if tragedy strikes—even when it has nothing to do with you but with the ones you love—seeing them grieve every day is a nightmare.

Yes, they would still stay in touch as Uncle Robert attended therapy. I wish I could have gone to see him, but I couldn't even step one foot out of the pack house without Aiden hovering all over me.

Speaking of Aiden, things between him and me were now calm. We weren't fighting or arguing anymore. From time to time, he would try to apologize for what he did, but I would brush it off. I wasn't planning on forgetting about what he did. I was taking it slow so he could go through the days regretting what he did.

After we talked in his office, he begged me to sleep in his room. Literally, he got on his knees saying he couldn't sleep without me by his side. Okay, fine, maybe I was exaggerating. It wasn't that much, but he was pleading with sad eyes. This was, of course, what I was looking for, so I agreed to go back to his room.

Besides, I didn't want to bother Marie any longer. Even when she told me she didn't mind, I still felt like I was intruding. Three nights were enough.

Also, because I felt bad about the bags under his eyes. But, hey, he was asking for it!

I was in the kitchen helping some she-wolves with lunch. My parents were going to be there in about ten minutes. Their flight landed hours ago, and Liam and Aiden went to the airport to escort them here. They left around one PM, and it was past three now.

I was taking the food out of the oven when Marie came into the kitchen.

Or should I say running?

"Immo! Immo!"

I turned around and looked at her with confusion.

"Yes?" I asked.

"When will Liam and Aiden get back?" she asked quickly.

"Um, maybe in a minute or two. Why?" I asked.

She sprinted to the cupboards while cursing to herself.

"Dang it! It took me forever to find it, and now I'm late!" she said as she took out a glass cup and a small red bottle from her pocket.

"Um, Marie, what are you doing?" I asked as she poured Pepsi into the glass and put it on the tray with the others.

She looked at me and smiled evilly.

"Well, my dear friend, let me tell you a little secret. This is a special hot sauce made from India," she said as she pointed to the small bottle.

"A special friend gave it to me, and I'm going to put it in Liam's favorite glass that he always uses," she told me as she poured the hot sauce into his Pepsi laughing evilly.

I raised an eyebrow.

"And why would you do that?" I asked confused.

She looked at me and frowned when she seemed to remember something.

"Liam stole my granola bar yesterday," she said and pouted.

I couldn't hold my laughter.

"Really? Just because of that?" I asked.

She nodded.

"You're so immature. When will you guys stop fighting?" I asked.

She rolled her eyes.

"When Liam stops stealing," she said.

Once she said that, the door bell rang. I rushed out of the kitchen as my heartbeat increased. I went to the living room and saw someone about to open the door.

"No, it's okay, I'll open it," I said and walked over to the door.

I opened the door and was greeted with my parent's happy smiles. Liam and Aiden stood next to them.

"Mom, Dad!" I said as I rushed to them and was eventually engulfed in their hug. They were holding me so tight, I could barely breathe. But I didn't say anything. It didn't really matter. All that mattered was that my parents were back.

"Stella! Sweetheart, we missed you so much," my mom said as she brushed my hair and looked at me from head to toe.

"Sweetie, you haven't been eating much? You look thinner," she said as my dad gave me a kiss on my forehead and I chuckled.

"No, Mom. I have been eating. You don't have to worry about me," I said as I hugged her again.

"Come on, let's go inside. I'm starving," Liam said.

Marie poked his stomach with her elbow, and Aiden slapped his head.

"Oh hush, don't be so rude. Let them first catch up," Marie told him.

"No, it's okay. We're pretty hungry too," my dad said as my mom nodded.

We got inside and sat on the table where the food was placed. Aiden sat next to me a bit too close for my liking. After all, I wanted to tease him, not to give him satisfaction. So I stared at Marie, and luckily, she understood what I was asking.

"Oh, um, immo, could we change seats so I could be farthest from the window? The wind is hurting my eyes," she lied.

I smirked and nodded. Aiden grew tense, but he didn't say anything and just sighed.

As I sat down, everyone started to eat while having a small conversation.

"So, Mom, Dad, how was your flight here?" I asked.

"It was really relaxing, not like when we traveled to Japan," my dad answered.

"We almost missed the flight because we got lost, and when we finally made it, we were seated next to a werewolf, which was not a big fan of vampires, by the way," my mom continued.

We were all laughing at some jokes my dad was telling when Liam took a sip from his soda and screamed.

"Oh my god! Hot! Hot! Hot! Hot! Ah!" he shouted as he ran to the kitchen.

Marie's face turned red as she tried to hold in her laughter.

Liam cursed and ran back immediately looking at Marie.

"There's no water in the fridge!" he shouted.

"Not even milk!"

Marie started to laugh really hard as tears fell from her eyes, while a panicking Liam sent death glares to her.

"Where did you hide all the water, you little mutt!" he sneered at her.

Aiden and my parents chuckle at their behavior.

"Marie, really? You even hid the water?" I asked in disbelief.

She nodded while smirking.

Liam looked at Aiden with a red face. I kind of felt bad for him.

"Bro, do something. I feel like my insides are burning!" he told him.

Aiden rolled his eyes and looked at Marie.

"Marie, just show him where you hid the water," he said, and Marie sighed.

"Gosh! You just had to ruin the fun," she said as she left the kitchen with Liam behind her.

"So, Aiden, I've noticed you've marked my daughter. I hope you've been treating her good. You wouldn't want to face my wrath, would you?" my dad threatened.

Oh if only he knew that Aiden marked me by force, he would surely kill the guy. Yes, I wanted him to regret what he did, but I didn't want him dead. That's why I didn't tell my parents.

Aiden seemed unaffected by my dad's threat, as if they were having a normal conversation.

"Don't worry, Mr. Parker. Your daughter is in good hands," Aiden said.

I rolled my eyes.

Sure I was.

"I'm glad to hear that, son. But if I find out you hurt her, I will not hesitate to snap your neck," my dad threatened once again.

"Lucas!" My mom gasped.

She looked at Aiden apologetically and smiled sweetly at him.

"Please don't mind him, dear. He's only looking out for his daughter," she said softly.

Aiden didn't say anything after that. He only nodded his head.

Once we were done with lunch, my parents headed toward their room to rest, while I sat in the living room with Aiden, Marie, and Liam. We were watching TV.

Well, Aiden and I were trying to watch TV, but Marie and Liam were fighting over the remote. They kept pressing on random buttons, changing the channels.

"Um, guys," I said.

"No! We're going to watch *The Vampire Diaries.* I made it to the part when Elena and Matt fell off the bridge!" Marie hissed as she took the remote from Liam's hand.

"Guys!" I said a little louder, but they simply ignored me.

"In your dreams! *Arrow* is on, and I'm not missing it!" Liam argued as he snatched the remote from her grip.

"You guys do know that there are other TVs in this house, right?" Aiden's husky voice boomed through the room, and that finally brought their attention to us.

"Yeah, I know, but I want to watch TV here," Marie whined while Liam rolled his eyes.

"Stop being such a baby and grow up," Liam told her as he changed the channel.

"Me? A baby? I'm sorry, but I wasn't the one crying earlier today," she said while she put her fingers on her chin, pretending to remember the event from today.

"W–what! I wasn't crying. It was just from the spiciness!" Liam argued, but I could tell he was embarrassed because there was a hint of pink on his cheek.

"You know what! All of you are babies. Just give me the damn remote!" I yelled at them and snatched the remote from Liam.

I sat down next to Aiden while changing the channels. It must have been a bad idea because he took this as a sign to hold my hand. At first, I was tense, but I then decided to tease him a bit. I sat closer to him while one of my hands ran up and down his chest. I could feel the sparks return. From the corner of my eye, I saw him staring at me and not at the TV. I heard him growl as I continued to run my hands over his chest, smirking to myself.

In one swift movement, he lifted me up and sat me on his lap. I gasped. I was straddling him, and his eyes darkened. Yup, that's all it took just to tease him. It was too easy.

In one sudden movement, I got up from the couch and gave the remote to Marie.

"On second thought, I'm going for a walk," I said, and I walked to the door feeling Aiden's glare bore a hole into the back of my head. But before I walked outside, I popped my head into the living room.

"Oh, and Elena dies and gets turned into a vampire," I told Marie.

She gasped as I walked out of the door smirking.

Chapter 24

I heard Marie screaming at me about spoiling a *Vampire Diaries* episode as I walked toward the sidewalk. I smirked even more. Aiden didn't say anything as I left the house. He was stunned.

Well, he better get used to that! I made a bet to myself that by the end of this week, Aiden will explode. And until then, I will not forget what he did.

Something in me told me that all this was utterly useless because I forgave him a long time ago, but I'm not one to back down. I just wanted to have a little fun, that's all. Sometimes I think I would make a great evil villain in a Disney movie. I mean, come on. I'm pretty badass! For example, instead of poisoning Snow White's apple, I'll just hit her head with a baseball bat. Simple.

Okay, fine. I'm not that evil. I do have a heart.

Well, a dead one though. But you get the point.

I walked toward the orphanage. I was getting pretty attached to that place and with the children—I mean, who wouldn't? They were all angels who tragically fell to the ground. Especially Sarah. She was like the little sister I never had. Seeing her made me want to hold her and protect her from any harm.

Her smile brightened up my day and had become my motivation to wake up in the morning. Seeing a child go through tragedy and still be able to stand on their feet is inspiring. It made me want to become stronger just like her.

She might have been a child, but she had the heart and the brain of a wise adult.

The orphanage wasn't that far away by car, but I didn't have a ride then, so I walked. And also, I wanted to take a relaxing walk so I could admire the natural scenery. I walked along the forest and listened to the birds sing.

Five minutes later, I was trying to think of other ways to annoy Aiden when I accidentally tripped over a stone. I stumbled forward trying to regain my balance but failed. I fell forward, but before my face could hit the ground, I stuck my hands out to cushion my fall. The fall didn't hurt because I was a vampire, but I could feel my knees throb. *That's probably going to leave a bruise until tomorrow.* I got off from the ground, cursing at myself for being clumsy as I dusted off all the dirt on my clothes.

I noticed my right palm had a scratch. It was bleeding but not that much, so I decided just to continue my walk to the orphanage. I looked around to see if anyone saw me being such a klutz. Luckily, there was no one.

I was about to head forward when I noticed a little girl holding a red balloon. She was staring straight at me with lonely eyes.

Shivers went down my spine for some unknown reason, so I decided to approach her and ask her what's wrong.

"Hey, are you okay?" I asked as I got near. I noticed her hair was braided in an old fashion way. I was puzzled by what she wore. She was wearing one of those dresses you would see in the nineteen seventies or eighties, which was weird. Whoever was raising her must have bad taste in fashion.

The little girl shook her head.

"No, I'm lost, and I don't know where Mommy is," she whispered.

I smiled at her and kneeled down to her level.

"How about you tell me where was the last time you've seen mommy, and I will help you find her," I told her, and she nodded.

"The last time we were in the building Crowman, in the city center," she said.

I never heard of that before. It must be somewhere around the city center, but where? Since we were close to the orphanage, I decided to take the girl with me to ask Emily if she knew it.

"I don't know where that is, but we could ask a friend. Come on, let's go," I said as I walked with the little girl.

I didn't even know her name.

"What's your name, sweetie?" I asked.

"Isabel" she whispered.

I nodded. Something about her was different. I don't know, but she had a strange vibe coming from her.

Finally, we made it to the orphanage, and I saw Emily standing right outside the door. We walked toward her, and when she saw me, she smiled widely.

"Ah, Luna it's great to have you here," she said cheerfully, and I smiled at her.

"Thank you. It's great to be here," I said.

"Um, can I ask you a question?" I asked.

Emily nodded.

"Uh, do you know where the Building of Crowman is? I've heard it's somewhere in the city center, but I don't know where," I told her.

It took a moment before she realized what I asked, and a look of confusion covered her face.

"Luna, that building has been gone for years," she said, and I raised an eyebrow.

"What do you mean?" I asked.

"I mean that yes, there used to be a building for ceremonies and meetings called the Building of Crowman, but sometime in the nineteen eighties, it fell to the ground because of an earthquake, killing hundreds of people," she answered.

I was shocked.

But why did Isabel tell me it was there?

"Why do you want to know?" Emily asked.

"Oh, because I found this lo—" I stopped halfway when I noticed that there was no one beside me.

Isabel was gone.

I turned around looking at my surroundings to find her, but she was nowhere. That was awfully strange. Where did she run off to?

"Luna, are you okay?" Emily asked.

"Yes, but did you see where Isabel went?" I asked.

"Who?" she asked.

"You know, the little girl that was beside me when I approached you. With the old fashion braid and funny looking dress," I said.

Emily's face was blank until it changed from a look of confusion to a look of concern.

"What do you mean? There was no one besides you when you came. You were alone," she told me.

What?

I was left speechless. *What was that all about?* I could have sworn I've just seen a little girl and was walking with her. I felt shivers run down my spine at the creepy thought of just meeting someone no one saw.

Who was she?

Did I just see a ghost?

Pft, no. That cannot be real. They don't exist.

Do they? If werewolves and vampires do, could they too?

I rubbed my hands over my face noticing that the scratch from earlier had healed and stopped bleeding.

"Are you sure about that?" I asked Emily.

She nodded.

"Certainly."

* * *

I was sitting under a tree with Sarah as she colored in her coloring book and hummed a tune. We were in the playground at the back of the orphanage. The place was really peaceful and relaxing.

I wish I could have enjoyed it. But my mind was still thinking about what happened earlier today.

I'm not sure if I should feel creeped out and scared about the situation.

Was it normal for a vampire to see a ghost? I don't think so. Never in my two hundred years have I met one. So today was a complete shocker.

"What are you thinking about?" Sarah asked as she closed her coloring book.

I smiled at her curiosity but didn't want to tell a child that I may or may not have seen a ghost, so I decided to change the subject.

"I was thinking about a really great movie I watched. Speaking of that, what's your favorite Disney movie?" I asked.

She smiled widely and sat closer to me.

"*Tangled*, of course!" she squealed.

I wasn't expecting that. I was thinking maybe *Cinderella* or *Sleeping Beauty* or *Snow White*.

"And why is that?" I asked.

It took a moment for her to answer.

"Because Rapunzel had a dream. Just like me," she whispered.

"She was taken from her family and lived her life as a lie, but that didn't stop her from accomplishing her dreams," she continued.

Woah, that was deep for a child. Other kids would just say that they liked it because the princess is pretty or they like the prince.

"Oh, and because Flynn Ryder is funny." Sarah giggled.

"What's your favorite Disney movie?" she asked me.

I thought about it.

"Mulan," I answered.

She scrunched her nose up, and she looked confused.

"Why?" she asked.

"Because Mulan had a dream too, you know. She didn't let others decide her fate and tell her who she was supposed to be. She created her fate by standing up for what she believed in and showed everyone who she really was—a hero," I told her.

She nodded.

"The moral of the story is to not judge anyone without getting to know them. Sometimes we're born with everyone expecting us to do a certain thing, but that doesn't mean we have to follow the path everyone is walking on. Just stand up for your dreams and what you believe in, and that will be enough to prove everyone wrong," I said.

* * *

I left the orphanage before it could get dark. Aiden had to be his annoying self and send Scott to take me home. He said he didn't want me walking all alone in the streets.

But I doubted anything would happen. This territory was quiet and safe. Other than the rogue attack that happened, nothing really happened here.

I walked toward the car Scott was in. One of the reasons I didn't really complain was I didn't feel like walking past the woods as the sun set, especially after today. I wouldn't want to run into a ghost again.

I just don't get why in all my two hundred years I haven't run into one until now.

Probably just a coincidence.

I got into the car, and Scott took off toward the pack house. I laid my head against the window as I looked at the passing buildings and trees. I was getting really tired, which was weird because the sun was only setting.

I yawned as I closed my eyes wanting to sleep a bit until we got there. But after a few minutes, the car stopped, and Scott's voice boomed through the car.

"Luna, we made it," he said, and I groaned. I opened my eyes and saw that we were parked in front of the pack house. I got out of the car and made my way inside.

I walked into the living room to see Marie crying on the couch. All my exhaustion suddenly went away, and I rushed to her.

"Marie! What's wrong?" I asked.

She sniffed as she grabbed a tissue and blew her nose. She pointed at the TV screen and cried out when one of her favorite characters died.

"Oh God, this is so sad!"

I rolled my eyes at her.

"Really? It's only a series. I thought there was something wrong," I said.

She looked at me with a stunned face.

"Only a series? Immo, this more than a series," she cried out.

Once those words came out of her mouth, Liam came into the living room and saw the situation. He slapped his forehead.

"Oh not this again!" he grumbled.

He walked forward and took the remote from her hand.

"This is why you don't watch TV. You get too emotional," he said as he changed the channel.

Marie got up from the couch and jumped on Liam's back when he wasn't looking.

"Give me back the damn remote, you jerkface!" she growled at him.

"Woah, woman, get off me!" Liam yelled.

"Damn, you're so heavy, you're breaking my back, ah!" he shouted.

I look at the both of them as they bickered.

Yup, they would definitely make a great couple.

Chapter 25

I was wide awake. There was no sleep in me. After I came back from the orphanage, I went straight to bed, which was a bad idea because it was still early. I opened my eyes and looked at the clock sitting on the table next to me. It was two AM. I rubbed my eyes, giving up. I turned around to see Aiden's sleeping face. He's looked so peaceful when he slept. Not like the possessive and grumpy Alpha he was. The wrinkles on his face were gone, which made him look younger. He was breathing evenly as his lips parted slightly.

I tried to get up, but I was held down by Aiden's strong muscular arms. I sighed as I rubbed my face.

Here goes nothing.

My hands moved down from his—very slowly, as I did not want to wake him up. If he did, he would probably not let me leave the room, so I made sure to be careful and quiet. I grabbed his right hand lying on my stomach and slowly took it off me and put it to his side. I stopped when he started to move and grumble under his breath.

I sighed in relief when he didn't wake up. I grabbed his other hand and carefully took it off me and put it to his side and got up. I tiptoed toward the door as quiet as a mouse. I looked back to make sure he was still asleep and reached for the door knob, twisting it slowly. I quickly but quietly got out of the room and shut the door.

I looked toward the empty dark hall. The only source of light was the moon shining through the window. I took quiet steps toward the kitchen, wanting to grab a drink for my dry throat. I made a turn to where the kitchen was, but I saw the door wide open with the lights on. There were sounds coming from there. I grabbed a vase next to me and tiptoed toward the door.

Yeah, you might think I'm exaggerating, but, hey, it could have been a thief stealing our food. Better safe than sorry. Once I got to the door, I lifted the vase over my head and was about to hit it on the intruder's head when they spoke.

"Ah, Luna, you scared me...Uh, why are you doing holding that?" Ian, my old bodyguard, spoke as he pointed to the vase in my hand. He was holding a spoon and eating cereal.

Cereal? Who eats cereal at a time like this?

Oh wait, I do.

"Uh, nothing. Haha. I thought there was an intruder," I said as I put the vase down.

"Well, there obviously isn't. If there was, then I would have taken care of it," he said cockily.

Sure.

He just said right that I scared him.

"Um, what are you doing eating at a time like this?" I asked as I walked over to the cupboard and took out a cup.

"I was hungry. I spent all day patrolling the border, and I just finished now," he told me.

I nodded my head as I poured water into the cup and took a big gulp.

"I see the Alpha has marked you," he said, looking at me weirdly And staring at my marked neck.

I nodded.

"Yeah, it actually came by surprise. I wasn't expecting it," I told him honestly as he put the now empty bowl in the sink and walked to the door.

"It's about time," he said before he disappeared.

Okay.

That wasn't weird at all.

Note the sarcasm.

After I was done gulping water, I made my way to the nearest bathroom and did my business. Once I was done, I walked to my room.

My room.

It sounds so strange coming out of my mouth. Me and Aiden sharing a room. I could feel myself warming up to him. Especially after he marked me. Yes, I was trying to get on his bad side these couple of days, but the mark on my neck was making it harder.

It was not helping at all.

I could feel Aiden's emotions, and he could feel mine. Every time he looked at the mark on my neck, he looked at it as if it was a masterpiece he just drew.

He looked at it with pride.

I opened the door slowly and shut the door when I was in the room. I walked over to the bed with a sleeping Aiden. I got on it and under the covers, laying my head on the soft pillow. Once I lay down, Aiden's arms immediately wrapped around my waist, bringing me to his bare chest. If it weren't for his steady breathing and his slowly beating heart, I would have thought he was awake. I laid my head on his chest, feeling the comfort around me. Forgetting about what the future has in store, I closed my eyes feeling safe in his arms.

* * *

I woke up to a shaking.

Was there an earthquake?

I shot my eyes open as panic rose in me but went away immediately when I saw the source of the shaking. There was no earthquake.

It was Marie.

What the hell is she doing?

"Wake up! Wake up! Wake up, immo! It's a bright day today, just waiting to be explored," she sang loudly in my ear, and I groaned into my pillow.

"Stop!" I yelled.

"Can't you see I have my eyes opened? Geez, woman, stop freakin' shaking me," I grumbled at her, and she giggled at me. I closed my eyes once again, ignoring her presence.

"Why are you waking me up so early? Go away, I want to sleep," I told her as I pulled the cover over my head.

There was a moment of silence. I sighed in relief knowing Marie left the room to let me sleep. Well, that was easy.

I was about to drift off to sleep once again when something cold hit my skin like a brick. I shot up and screamed in surprise.

"Ah! Oh my god, oh my god. So cold!" I yelled.

I looked up to see Marie wearing an evil grin as she held an empty bucket. Oh, she had the nerve! I looked around to see that the bed was soaking wet.

"What the hell!" I yelled.

"What was that for?"

Marie put the bucket on the ground and took the cover off me.

"That was for not waking up when I told you to," she said as she grabbed my hand and pulled me up.

"Really, was that necessary? I mean, just look at the bed now. It's wet," I told her as I realized that Aiden was not in the room. He must've left an hour before and was in his office.

She rolled her eyes.

"Oh, hush, it's going to dry. Anyway, go take a shower. We have a busy day today," she said as I lifted an eyebrow at her.

"What are we doing today?" I asked as I looked at the clock. I was surprised that it was twelve PM.

"Today is the day we make Aiden fall to his knees," Marie said and smirked evilly.

"Please do explain," I said and grinned.

"Well, Liam's friend invited Liam, Aiden, you and me to this special gathering where we will eat dinner and dance and chat. So what we'll do is pamper you up to attract every guy there. Then when Aiden asks you to dance, you'll decline but dance with all the other guys," she told me and chuckled.

I liked the idea. Sure, it was no evil plan, but, hey, this is Aiden we're talking about. This simple plan would drive him nuts. I nodded my head at her and rushed to the bathroom to take a shower.

Twenty minutes later, I came out of the bathroom in only a towel. I saw Marie putting makeup on the counter. There was a dress hidden under a cover, lying on the bed.

"Is that the dress?" I asked, taking a step toward it.

"Yes, it is, but you're not supposed to see it until we're done, so sit down," she said as she dragged me to sit on a chair.

"I'm going to do your makeup. We leave in three hours, so hold still so I can get this done in time," Marie told me.

"But what about you?" I asked.

"I'll do mine when I'm done with yours. Now, close your eyes so I can put this on," she said as she pulled out foundation from her bag.

* * *

"Ready to see the dress!" Marie squealed with excitement.

I nodded while smiling. It had been over two hours and a half, and Marie just finished with her makeup. She finished with mine an hour ago, and I was so excited to see the dress I was going to wear.

Marie walked over to the bed and counted to three before she took off the cover that was hiding the dress. I gasped in surprise. It was beautiful. It was a white dress that wasn't too long or short. It looked perfect.

I grabbed the dress and rushed to the closet to change into it. Once I came out, Marie gasped. The dress came down right to my mid-thigh and was hugging my body, showing off my curves. The dress wasn't slutty, but it was also revealing.

I loved it.

I was going to have so much fun teasing Aiden.

"Wow, immo, you look gorgeous. Aiden will be drooling," Marie squealed.

"Haha. Thanks, Marie. This is all your work," I told her.

She nodded. "True, true."

"Let's get this show on the road. Aiden and Liam are waiting for us downstairs," she said as she dragged me out of the room and downstairs. Once I stepped into the living room, I felt all eyes on me.

Aiden was standing by the door looking so sexy in a suit. His eyes were raking over my body, from head to toe. I felt the blood rush to my cheeks from all the attention. I tried to remind myself that I couldn't give in because this was to tease him and not give him the satisfaction.

"Come on, guys. Let's go before we're late," Liam said as he walked to the door with Marie to his side. I walked out the door behind Marie and Liam as Aiden walked beside me. It looked like he was about to tell me something, but Liam spoke.

"We are taking separate cars," he said.

I looked at Marie, knowing that Aiden was going to make me come with him, but she had a relaxed face on.

"Liam, you go in the car with Aiden. I'll be driving yours with Stella," she said.

Liam had an are-you-crazy look and shook his head.

"Are you mad, woman? I'm not letting you drive my car! We all know you're crazy on the road," he said.

"Oh shut up! I'm not that bad, and besides, it's either that or your brand new one," she argued.

Liam groaned as he ran his hands over his face.

"Ugh, why do you have to be so stubborn? Besides, I think Aiden would want to be with his mate," Liam said looking between Aiden and me.

Aiden nodded his head while I shook mine.

"Nope, I'm riding with Marie," I said as I wrapped an arm around her shoulder, trying to ignore his glare.

"Fine! But if I see one scratch on my baby, then you're dead," Liam threatened.

Marie nodded then walked over to his car with me following right behind her.

Chapter 26

I stepped out of the car when it was parked outside of a big mansion. It took us about half an hour to get here. It was that far away. Through the whole ride here, Marie was telling me what I was and wasn't supposed to do. Like for example, I wasn't supposed to dance with Aiden or sit next to him when eating. But what I was supposed to do was sit with some men there and make sure to flirt and smile.

Oh, this was going to be fun.

The time now was three forty, and the weather was hot. I closed the car door as Marie came out of hers. Aiden and Liam came out of the car that was parked next to ours. We started to walk toward the entrance.

"What is this gathering for?" I asked.

"John, the host of this gathering, is moving to London. He invited me and told me to bring my friends," Liam said.

"Oh, and he's human, so make sure to act as human as possible," he told us but mainly was looking at Marie.

"Understood," Marie said as she rolled her eyes.

I heard her mutter something under her breath, but it wasn't clear. We walked to the front door and were met with a couple of servants that greeted us and took our coats. A young man that was very handsome came out of the door with a huge smile on his face.

"Ah, Liam, it's great to see you! I'm glad you're here," the man whom I assumed was John said.

"I'm glad to be here, John. Oh, and these are my friends: Aiden, Marie, and Stella," Liam said as he introduced us to his friend. Once he saw us, he gave us a welcoming smile and shook our hands—well, Aiden's hand.

When he greeted Marie and me, he kissed our hands.

Geez, what a gentleman!

I could see Aiden tense from the corner of my eye because of his actions, which was not a surprise at all. This was what I was looking for. But what actually surprised me was when he kissed Marie's hand. As she blushed, I saw Liam tense along with Aiden.

Weird.

"Please do come in. Dinner's almost ready," John told us.

We walked into the large mansion and gasped—well, Marie and I.

The place was huge and beautiful from the inside. It looked all fancy with its modern pictures hanging on the wall and its unique furniture. Just by looking at this place, you could tell John was filthy rich.

John walked us to the second floor that had a dining room. As we walked through the door, I saw many people seated on chairs having conversations. But they all stopped what they were doing and turned to look at us.

I caught a couple people staring at me, but I simply ignored them.

"Everyone, this is Liam, a friend of mine. And these are his friend—Aiden, Marie, and Stella." They all smiled at us and greeted us as we walked to the table.

I was walking behind Aiden so I could see where he would sit. When he sat in a chair that had an empty seat next to it, I walked all the way to the end of the table where it was filled with men having a conversation. As I sat down, they paused and looked at me with smiles on their faces.

I gave them a small polite smile and waved to Marie to come sit next to me.

I glanced at Aiden who looked pissed. He was scowling but didn't dare say a word as he glared at me. I averted my eyes from him and looked at Marie who just sat next to me.

"You think it's working?" she asked.

I glanced at Aiden again who was now glaring at the guys sitting next to me. I smirked to myself.

"Definitely."

After a few minutes, maids came into the room holding trays and trays of food. They looked so good, but do you know what would be better? If I had a glass filled with blood next to it. A few moments later, everyone started to dig in. I turned my head to my right when someone spoke. It was the guy next to me who had brown hair and hazel eyes, with a smile that was so bright.

"Hi, my name is Luis," he said as he stretched his hand out for me to shake. I smiled at him politely and shook his hand.

I smirked evilly to myself when I felt Aiden's eyes burn holes through my head.

"Hi, my name's Stella," I said in a flirty tone.

This was too easy.

"What brings you here, Stella? I don't think you're from here. I would certainly remember a face like yours," he said as he took a bite from his salad. I blushed at his compliment.

"Ha, thanks, and I came with a couple of friends. We aren't from this town," I said as I took a sip from my water.

Marie tapped my shoulder and came closer to my ear to whisper something.

"It looks like Aiden's about to break his plate," she whispered.

I looked over at him and saw he was sending death glares to Luis as he continued to cut his steak. I chuckled.

After about twenty minutes, everyone was done with their food, and desserts arrived. I chose a strawberry cheesecake, and Marie got a chocolate fudge cake. Luis and I were having a conversation about random things.

He was a pretty nice guy with good looks, but he was nothing compared to Aiden.

Dammit! I did it again.

I took a bite out of my cake and looked up to see Aiden talking with Liam. It looked like they were having a deep conversation. John's voice snapped me out of my state. I turned my head to face him like everyone else.

"Everyone, we will now make our way to the ballroom to dance," he said.

Everyone got up from their seat and walked out the door. I was about to take a step forward when someone grabbed my wrist, making the sparks return once again.

"Why are you doing this?" Aiden grumbled in my ear.

I plastered a fake smile and looked up to an annoyed Aiden.

"Doing what?" I asked sweetly.

"Ugh, don't play dumb, Stella." He groaned as he rubbed his face.

"Listen, I don't have time for this. We have to get to the ballroom," I said right before I exited the room. I caught up to Marie and walked beside her.

"Remember, immo, no dancing with Aiden," she told me.

I nodded and walked into the ballroom. It was huge, big enough for everyone to dance on, and had small tables on the side that was meant for drinking on. Servants were holding trays filled with champagne.

Marie and I walked to an empty table and looked around. Aiden and Liam walked to us, each holding two glasses of champagne. Liam handed one to Marie while Aiden handed one to me.

"You sure you didn't poison this?" I teased as I took a sip.

Aiden put his hand over his heart, pretending to be hurt.

"Babe, I don't need to poison you. If I wanted to get rid of you, all I need is garlic," he said.

I rolled my eyes. Everybody knows that garlic doesn't affect vampires. It's only a myth.

I looked to my left and saw that Marie and Liam were no longer beside us but instead dancing across the room.

"Want to dance?" Aiden asked.

As if Marie heard what he asked from across the room, she gave me the stinky eye, shaking her head furiously at me. I wanted to laugh at the confused look on Liam's face.

"Nope," I simply said.

It took so much to say no to Aiden. All I wanted to do was dance with him all day long as I looked into his blue eyes.

But he had to work for that.

Aiden had a disappointed look on his face. After a few moments of silence, he turned around and walked off to a table filled with women. He had a flirty smile on his face as he talked with one of the girls who had blonde hair. He took her hand and led her to the dance floor.

Oh, when I get my ha—

Ugh, calm down, Stella. You're supposed to be tormenting him, not the other way around.

I took a deep breath and looked around for any single guys in the room. I saw Luis from earlier sipping on his champagne all alone. I took this perfect moment when Aiden was staring at me as he danced with a bimbo, and I walked over to Luis, swaying my hips side to side.

"Hey, want to dance?" I asked.

He gave me a charming smile when he saw me.

"Aren't I supposed to ask you to dance, not the other way around?" he said and grinned.

"Yeah, well, I saw you standing all alone and thought maybe you could use some company," I told him as I batted my eyelashes. He smirked at me and nodded before we walked to the dance floor. All this time Aiden was glaring at us.

Through the first song, we danced and talked. I even laughed at some of his jokes. Each time I looked over to Aiden, he would either be glaring at Luis as if he wanted to rip him to shreds or look at the bimbo he was dancing with in disgust as she ran her filthy hands up and down his chest.

The first song was over, and I was about to walk back to the table when a random person asked me to dance with him.

This went on for the whole night—people asking to dance with me as Aiden tried to kill them with his eyes.

* * *

"Oh my god! That was hilarious. You should have seen the look on his face when Bob kissed your cheek," Marie said and laughed as tears formed in her eyes.

We were in Liam's car, driving back home. It was very late when we left John's place. And it took Marie forever to convince Liam again to let us drive in his car. Marie was telling me how Aiden reacted when each guy approached me.

She said it took him everything not to come up and snatch me from their arms and into his. I thought that tonight was enough of teasing him.

He got what he deserved.

A few minutes later, Marie parked next to Aiden's car outside of the pack house. As we got outside of the car, Liam came running to us.

Or should I say his car?

"Oh, baby! Did they hurt you?" he cried out as he inspected his car for any scratches.

"I swear I will never let someone crazy drive you ever again," he promised.

Marie rolled her eyes and poked Liam's stomach with her elbow.

"You're lucky I was going slow. Next time, I won't hesitate to race with random cars on the road," she told him.

"Why you little—"

Before Liam could finish, Aiden and I decided to go up to our room, not wanting to witness Marie and Liam tackle themselves onto the ground as they scratched their faces off.

I went into the closet and grabbed the clothes I was going to sleep with and headed to the bathroom. I stripped out of my dress and wore a t-shirt and a pair of shorts. Then I brushed my hair and put it up into a bun and washed off all my makeup.

I came out of the bathroom and saw Aiden sitting on the bed facing me. Once he saw me, he got up and straightened his back.

"Listen, Stella."

He paused.

I raised an eyebrow.

"I'm sorry," he said.

"I'm so sorry for marking you without your permission. I'm so sorry for treating you like you're below me. I'm so sorry for making you feel useless. I never meant to hurt you. It's just sometimes I lose control over my wolf. All he wants to do is show the world to whom you belong to. It took me everything I had not to shred those guys you danced with to pieces. And I know it's no excuse, but I want you to know that you mean everything to me and I would never hurt you," he continued.

By the time he finished, he was standing right in front of me but didn't touch me. I saw his hand twitch, wanting to wrap his arms around me, but he was too afraid.

Afraid that I might reject him or his apology. But I knew better.

I nodded and gave him a small smile.

"I forgive you. Just don't do anything like that ever again," I said.

"Stella, I know it's no excuse, but I—" Aiden stopped talking when he realized what I just said. The wrinkles on his forehead went away immediately; the same went for his frown.

My eyes were blind from the light when I saw him smiling. Not just any smile, but a wide happy one, when you feel like you can die as a happy person.

His arms automatically wrapped around my waist and pulled me to his chest. His hold was so tight, as if he never wanted to let me go. He put his head in the crook of my neck, inhaling my scent. I relaxed into his hold, loving the way I fit perfectly in his arms.

Chapter 27

I walked through town as Scott continued to follow from behind me. I looked at the map on my phone in confusion. The smell of food and flowers from bakeries and floral shops around me filled my nose. It was a really hot day. The sun shined over everyone on the street. I was wearing a white skirt and a simple crop shirt that didn't stand out. I was trying to find an Italian restaurant my parents told me to go to.

Sometimes I get carried away in eating and mess up my clothes, so maybe wearing white wasn't such a good idea.

They called me earlier, telling me that they wanted to have dinner together and catch up since they were away for a long while. But they left without me, and I had to find it myself. I tried to ask Scott, but he said he had never visited an Italian restaurant before.

Geez, what does this guy do with his life? He's all too serious. I don't think I've ever seen him smile at anybody.

I've seen Aiden smile more than him.

I closed my phone, giving up, and decided to ask the people around me. It never fails to surprise me how much people greet me on the streets and try to give me stuff for free. I always refuse to take anything without a price.

I was no different from anyone else in this town.

Except for the fact I was Luna.

And a vampire.

And mated with a very annoying and possessive Alpha.

But you get the point.

I saw a she-wolf that looked like she was in her mid-forties walking by, holding her head down in respect once she saw me.

"Um, excuse me," I said, trying to get her attention, and it worked.

Her head snapped up, and she smiled at me nervously.

"Luna! It's a pleasure to meet you," she said happily, and I smiled at her.

"Thanks, um, I was wondering if you know any Italian restaurant that's called Red Bella around here?" I asked.

It took her a moment to answer. It seemed like she was in shock because I spoke with her.

"Uh, yes, Luna, I do know where that is. Please follow me," she said.

We took off toward the end of the street and then turned left. A few moments later, we were in front of a big building that had the writing *Red Bella* in huge red letters. It gave off a very fancy vibe. I didn't really like this kind of places. Not with the whole dressing up fancy and eating expensive food. I preferred those homely, cozy places that had a friendly vibe. I didn't care about the food.

In the end, it was just food. No matter where you eat it or how much it cost.

I turned to face the lady who helped me find this place.

"Thank you so much for helping me," I said as I shook her hand.

"It was a pleasure, Luna," she said before walking away.

I turned back around to face the building. It looked like one of those types of restaurants where you have to make reservations months before.

I wonder how I will get in.

I walked to the front door and opened it, letting the fresh smell of Italian food run through my nose. My stomach growled in hunger. I walked up to a guy behind a counter who was writing on some paper. Before I could say anything, he looked up and saw me.

"Luna, welcome, welcome. Your table's waiting," he said.

Well, that was easy.

But God this was starting to get annoying—how much I get called Luna. Sometimes I think that maybe my name was Luna and not Stella. But I guess I have to get used to it.

I walked behind the guy deeper into the restaurant, becoming the center of attention. I rolled my eyes at how easy it was to grab everyone's attention in this pack. As we walked further, I could see my parents sitting and talking at a table. As I got nearer, they turned their heads and noticed me, giving me warm smiles. I walked to their table as the guy went back to what he was doing.

"Mom, Dad," I said as I hugged them.

"Stella, sweetie, sit down," my mom said and smiled brightly. I grabbed a chair next to my dad and sat down.

"Did you guys order?" I asked.

Both my mom and my dad shook their heads.

"No, we were waiting for you," my dad said.

We grabbed the menus and looked at what we were going to eat. We all decided to settle on pasta and called the waiter to order our food. As we waited, my parents told me about their trip to Japan—how they got lost and how my dad got them into trouble.

"So instead of taking us to the hospital where Uncle Robert was. Mr. Smartypants right here took us to a random school. I tried to convince him to ask for directions, but I swear he never listens," my mom blabbed as she pointed to my annoyed father.

Why isn't that surprising?

"Bella! Gosh, how many times do I have to tell you that it wasn't my fault? The sign said clearly that we were going in the right direction," my father defended himself.

My mom pinched his arm.

"You don't even read Japanese, Lucas!" my mom pointed out.

"I do too! And, geez, why do you have to be so violent, woman," he said while rubbing his arm where she pinched him.

Man, I missed these two.

"So what did you do while we were gone?" my dad asked.

I still find it surprising that my dad was able to leave me here with a pack he didn't know and traveled all the way across the world. But I wasn't complaining. I knew that they were forced to do it. They had to travel and visit Uncle Robert. It's just knowing my father, he's very protective. Yes, he did threaten Aiden, but I was expecting him to tell Aiden that I was coming with them, whether Aiden liked it or not.

Maybe it was the mate bond.

He probably knew how hard it was to be away from one's mate. And he knew he had to accept it, even though it was hard for him.

"Nothing, really. I got presented to the pack and just hung out with Marie and Liam," I said, not mentioning the part where I ran off to the woods because Aiden forcefully marked me and ran into a rogue.

They would surely freak out.

Finally, the waiter came with our delicious looking food. I grabbed a fork and took a bite from the pasta. I moaned, savoring how good it tasted. I was about to take a second bite when I heard windows breaking.

Screaming and growling were heard from behind me. I whipped my head toward the sudden commotion and gasped in surprise.

There was a big brown wolf in the center of the room, and broken glass was scattered across the ground. He was growling, and the women screamed and rushed out with their scared children in their arms.

What the hell was going on?

I could smell the wolf and tell that he was definitely a rogue. Something was up. A rogue wasn't that brave to trespass a pack and attack all alone. Unless they're stupid. The strong looking males, along with a couple of young she-wolves that were in the restaurant, stood straight, confronting the wolf. Some even came to stand near our table.

My dad took a step forward to help as Scott came rushing into the room.

Another two rogues hit us by surprise as they took down the people who were standing in their way. I saw the three wolves sniff the air before snapping their heads toward me.

I stood tall and proud, but I'm pretty sure I almost had a mini heart attack when they all looked at me like I was their prey. One of them even launched at me, but Scott was quick and brought him to the ground, shifting to his wolf.

My dad rushed over to the wolves that were brought down by the rogue to help them. My mom tugged on my shoulder, snapping my gaze from the rogues and to her.

"Stella, let's get you out of here," my mom said worriedly.

I shook my head at her. There was no way I was leaving with everyone to fight here. Isn't this what being Luna is about? To help your pack members whenever they need it and stand up for them.

"Mom, you go, but I'm not leaving," I told her.

She gave me a stern look.

"I have to help them. Besides, I'm pretty sure Scott contacted Aiden, and he will be here soon," I assured her.

I then turned my attention back to the attack and saw that one rogue was holding down one of the pack members that had shifted. I used my vampire speed and rushed over there to knock him off her.

I used all my force to push the rogue to a wall, releasing the she-wolf. I helped her get up but was then knocked to the ground. What surprised me was that the rogue did not go for my neck.

Which was the second time that had happened. Instead, he grabbed my shirt with his teeth and threw me over his back.

Wait, what?

I was in complete shock. I didn't notice that the wolf was heading toward the broken windows until Scott's brown wolf blocked him. I quickly got off the wolf but was blocked with the other two.

My mom helped the injured wolves get up, while my dad tackled one of the rogue wolves to the ground. The other two wolves were trying to get Scott out of the way, but they all stopped when they heard a vicious roar.

It was Aiden.

Aiden and a bunch of guards—probably fifteen—came through the door, surrounding all three rogues. Aiden looked mad. Or should I say furious?

"Take them to the dungeon. And I want them alive," Aiden ordered.

About seven guards dragged them out of the damaged restaurant as the others helped the injured wolves. Aiden came toward me inspecting me for any injuries.

"Are you okay? Did they hurt you?" he asked.

I wanted to roll my eyes at him so badly but didn't.

"I'm fine," I told him.

Scott came forward from behind Aiden who was completely naked.

"Didn't you see that?" Scott asked as he looked at my parents and me.

"They didn't attack the Luna but tried to take her with them," he pointed out.

My parents nodded with worry and confusion written all over their faces.

"What do you mean?" Aiden growled. "That they were here to get Stella?"

Scott nodded.

"It was just like the last time," I spoke, getting everyone's attention.

"They didn't go for my neck," I pointed out.

My dad came forward with an angry look.

"Wait, what did she mean when she said, 'like last time?'" His voice was low, and I could see his eyes redden from the anger.

"Did this happen before?" my dad asked, looking between Aiden and me.

I looked at the ground, nervous to answer his questions. But Aiden answered it for me.

"Yes, it happened before in the forest."

My mom's mouth fell open in surprise, but she didn't say anything. Meanwhile, my dad was trying to control his heavy breathing.

"And no one thought about telling me this?" my dad asked in a very demanding voice.

I took a step forward and put my right hand on his arm to calm him down.

"Dad, we didn't want to worry anyone. We simply thought it was a coincidence," I spoke.

My dad looked like he was going to speak, but my mom gave him the stinky eye, shutting him up.

"Lucas, this isn't the right time to talk about this. Leave it for later. Right now, let's just go home and clean up," my mom said.

We all nodded and walked out of the restaurant as Aiden held me tight against his chest. I just wanted to go home and forget this ever happened. Day by day, things have been becoming weirder—with being attacked twice by rogues, seeing ghosts, and having strange dreams.

It's like my life is one dramatic movie that never ends.

Chapter 28

"So care to explain?" my dad asked.

We were all sitting in the living room. My parents, Aiden, Scott, Liam, and Marie were all here. It had been about four hours since the attack, and we went home to clean up and rest for a while. I tried to sleep for a bit, but my mind was preoccupied with the thoughts and questions of that day's incident. Once Liam and Marie heard about what happened, they rushed over here.

I took a shower and wore some comfortable clothes and tied my hair into a high ponytail. I was now sitting on a couch in between Aiden and Marie.

"Well, the other day I was in the woods when a rogue attacked me. But the strange thing was that he didn't go for my neck," I told both my parents, avoiding why I was in the forest in the first place.

"And I didn't tell you guys because I thought it was some random attack and nothing really happened. Aiden came and took care of it," I finished.

"Some random attack? It was obvious that they tried to take you with them," my dad pointed out.

I rolled my eyes.

Why would they want me? It just doesn't make sense.

"I don't think that's true. What would they want with me?" I asked while looking at my parents and Aiden.

Aiden seemed stressed. He had been quiet since we've got here, and he kept running his hand through his messy hair. He wanted to know why the rogues attacked and how they got in the pack without anyone noticing them.

"I don't know, but until we find out, I'm going to increase your guards," Aiden said.

I sighed and rubbed my hands over my face.

"Is this necessary? All this could just be coincidence," I told him.

"Sweetie, I think he's right. We don't want to risk it," my mom said as my dad nodded.

"Fine," I muttered.

I looked out of the window, and it was getting dark. The full moon was shining brightly in the sky with no stars. I felt my stomach grumble in hunger. I didn't eat much for dinner because of the attack, only one bite of pasta, so I decided to get up and make myself a sandwich in the kitchen. As I got up, Marie got up with me, and we both walked to the kitchen. Once we got there, I opened the fridge and took out a bag of blood to sip on and bread and cheese so I could make a grilled cheese sandwich.

"Want some?" I asked Marie who was taking a sip from her orange juice.

She shook her head.

I grabbed a knife and started to slice the bread when I accidentally cut my finger. I hissed quietly in pain and went to the sink to wash the little scratch. I didn't want blood all over my food. Even though I'm a vampire, I don't drink my own blood. That's just nasty.

"Hey, immo, are you okay?" Marie asked.

I nodded.

"Yeah, just a cut," I told her then turned around and gasped.

There standing next to Marie was a guy with pale skin and bags under his eyes. He was looking straight at me. Shivers ran down my spine.

Who was he? How did he get in here?

What answered my question was what he was wearing— trousers that looked very old-fashioned, ripped, and dirty, and a brown shirt. His hair was parted in the middle.

Not again.

He was a ghost.

My heart started to pound against my chest as he took one step forward then reached his hand out to grab my shoulder. I stood still, not moving as if I was the prey in a lion's den.

Why were they appearing now? What did they want from me?

Was I being haunted?

"Immo, are you okay?" Marie asked.

But I wasn't paying attention to her. All my thoughts were at the stranger in front of me and what he said before disappearing into thin air.

"Pick me."

Once he was gone, I released a breath that I didn't even know I was holding.

What did he mean by that? It felt so familiar like I've heard it before.

Suddenly the memory of the dream I had the other day came to my mind. About the dead that were chasing me. They all said the same thing. But I still didn't know what that meant.

I looked down to my finger and realized that the cut was healed.

"Stella, are you okay?" Marie asked again. She was now in front of me with her hands on each of my shoulder.

I look up to her as I shook all the thoughts out of my head and gave her a smile.

"Uh, y–yeah, I'm fine," I told her, but she didn't seem convinced.

"It's just today's event tires me, and I'm still shocked about what happened. That's all."

It wasn't completely a lie; it was true.

She nodded before putting her cup in the sink and walking out of the kitchen. I sighed to myself as I stared at the spot where the ghost was once standing. I put the bread, cheese, and blood bag back into the fridge, not feeling hungry anymore.

All I wanted to do was sleep, even though it wasn't late. Maybe I might relax a bit.

* * *

"Stella," Marie called.

I rolled over so I had my face in my pillow.

"Stella." Her voice was louder.

I pulled the covers over my head, ignoring her.

"Stella, get up, or I swear I will not hesitate to get the bucket!" she yelled in my ear.

I immediately shot up when I heard her say the word *bucket*. I didn't want her to pour water all over me again. I gave Marie a sleepy glare.

"What do you want? Can't you see I'm trying to sleep?" I said as I rubbed my eyes. I turned my head and noticed Aiden wasn't beside me. He must have been working. I noticed that the sun was up and the birds were chirping.

"That's enough sleep, missy! You went to bed early last night, and you still haven't gotten up," she said as she pulled me off the bed.

Geez, sometimes I think she's my mother.

"Wait, what time is it?" I asked.

"It's twelve PM. Gosh, I thought you were dead or something," she said, and I rolled my eyes.

I wasn't expecting to sleep in that late.

"Anyway, go change. We aren't going to sulk around because of yesterday. We're going to be productive," she told me, and I groaned.

"Oh, come on! Can't we just stay in our pajamas all day and watch the entire series of *The Vampire Diaries* while stuffing our faces with Nutella," I whined, trying to convince her that being productive wasn't on my to-do list.

I saw her eyes soften at the thought. Did I mention that Marie was a big fan of *The Vampire Diaries* and Nutella?

She shook her head.

"Nope, ain't happening. As much as I would love to do that, you are going to march to Aiden's office and do some Luna work," she ordered.

I groaned again.

Where is the immature Marie when you need her? Oh yeah, I know. When Liam steals her food.

"Fine, whatever," I muttered and made my way to the closet. But before I went in, I turned to look at Marie.

"Then what are you doing today?" I asked.

She gave me a smirk.

"I have a date to get to," she told me.

My eyes widened in shock.

"Really?" I asked.

She nodded her head excitedly.

"With who?" I asked.

"You don't know him. We went to school together," she answered.

I smiled at her and told her good luck before walking into the closest.

I grabbed some clothes and went to the bathroom. I did my daily routine, took a shower, put mascara because I felt like it, and wore my clothes. I got out and decided to see if Aiden needed any help in his office.

I walked down the hallway and to his office door, knocking on it before going in. It was a mess in there. Papers were everywhere as Aiden was working on his laptop. He had bags under his eyes and very messy hair, probably from running his hands through them.

Once I closed the door, he noticed me.

"Stella, what are you doing here?" he asked.

"I thought I could help. After all, I'm not Luna for nothing," I told him as I walked to a couch in front of his desk and took a seat.

It looked like Aiden was too tired to refuse.

Did he even sleep?

You know what, since I've mentioned it, I don't remember Aiden coming to bed last night.

"Did you even get some sleep?" I asked.

He shook his head.

"Nope, I had so much work to do, especially with what happened yesterday." he grumbled more to himself.

"Don't beat yourself over it," I told him as I grabbed some papers I could work on.

What I said must have gotten him mad because I saw his eyes darken a bit.

"Don't beat myself over it? Stella, rogues are popping up everywhere, but that's not the problem," he said as his voice got louder.

"The problem is that they want you for some reason, and they've been coming into the pack, and I don't know how," he finished.

I sighed and rubbed my face.

"Gosh, I know, I know! But what would they want with me? I think you guys are just overreacting," I argued.

"It just doesn't make sense. A rogue attack happens, and you jump to conclusions. They just probably knew that I was your mate and wanted to piss you off," I told him.

He was silent and ran his hand through his hair.

"I'm still giving you more guards. I'm not risking anything," he told me.

I rolled my eyes.

I swear he never learns, but if it will help calm his nerves, then fine, whatever.

"If it helps you sleep at night," I muttered to myself.

"What did you say?" he asked.

"Uh, uh-oh, I said let's get started with these papers," I told him.

He gave me a glare before shaking his head at me then returning to what he was doing before.

* * *

Four hours and a lot of effort later, we were done with all the paperwork. It was four very boring long hours, and I thought I was going to pass out if I stayed in Aiden's office for another second. We spent the hours looking through applications for new pack members and checking on some papers Aiden will use for some future pack meetings. Also, we looked through some letters he received from other Alphas.

"Ugh, finally! I don't know how you can cope with that," I said as I stretched my arms and started to walk to the hall.

"You get used to it," Aiden said from behind me.

We walked to the living room and saw Liam sitting on the couch watching TV. I went to the kitchen to grab a snack. I found some chocolate chip cookies in the cabinet and walked back to the living room where Aiden and Liam were having a conversation.

I sat down and began to watch TV, but the front door slamming open caught my attention. Everyone in the room turned their heads to see Marie stomping toward us.

She was wearing a pretty white dress with her hair curled. She had on simple makeup that brought out the beauty of her face, but she looked angry for some reason.

Didn't she have a date today?

"You!"

She pointed at Liam.

She ran up to him, tackled him to the ground, and tried to scratch his face. Aiden got up immediately and pulled her off Liam, but she was too persistent.

"Let me at him!" she shouted as Aiden pulled her away from Liam.

"I swear, once I get my hands on you, Liam White, you're dead!" she screamed.

I rushed over to her.

"What's wrong?" I asked.

She glared at Liam who had a grin on his face.

"Wipe that grin off your face before I slap it off for you, punk!" she growled.

"Marie, calm down," I told her.

"Calm down? How can I calm down when he told Jack that I'm crazy!" she yelled as she sent death glares to Liam.

Jack must have been the guy who she was going on a date with.

I whipped my head toward Liam and gave him an are-you-crazy look.

"And why would you do that?" I asked.

He put his hands up in surrender.

"Hey, I was just stating the fact, didn't want the poor guy to get scared," he told us and grinned to himself.

"Really! You just had to do that? I freaking got stood up!" she yelled at him.

Marie used all her force to yank her arm out of Aiden's hold and tackle Liam to the ground once again. But this time, no one stopped her.

"That wasn't cool, dude," Aiden told Liam before walking out of the living room with me following behind him. I didn't want to witness a murder case.

Chapter 29

I looked around to see trees everywhere. They were in all types of sizes. Big and small, thin and thick. There were squirrels climbing on trunks and birds flying from one branch to another. I took a step forward as the wind hit my skin, causing me to shiver.

This place looks so familiar. Where have I seen it before?

I continued to walk through the forest. The only sounds come from singing birds and the cracking of leaves broken branches as I stepped on them. I couldn't remember how I got there. Everything was a blur. I saw something blue out in the distance, so I walked faster. It felt like I had been walking for hours, but it only took a few seconds. I walked past the last tree and stepped into a big beautiful meadow.

And in the center of it was a lake. Its water looked clean enough to swim in and was so clear that I could see the fish swimming in it.

Then I remembered the place and why it looked so familiar.

I used to come here with Alice many years ago. It felt like ages since I had last been here.

But why am I here? If I remember correctly, this is in the center of Ervin.

I walked toward the water and looked at my reflection. I looked like present myself, not my high school self.

So this cannot be a memory of some sort.

Something behind me caught my attention.

I turned around almost immediately and gasped. Tears formed in my eyes as I looked at the person standing in front of me.

This can't be. How can she be standing right in front of me?

Is this a dream?

No, it feels too real.

"Alice?"

My voice came out as a whisper.

She looked the same as ever, with her blue eyes shining as bright as the sky. And her short hair coming down to her neck. She gave me a big smile that showed her white teeth.

I felt a tear roll down my cheek.

"This can't be. How are you here?" I said, my voice shaking as I took a step toward her.

She ran up to me and gave me a bone-crushing hug. I wrapped my arms around her shoulder and hugged her back.

This feels so real. But it doesn't make sense.

We pulled away as tears ran down both our eyes.

"I missed you so much," she spoke.

"I miss you too, but how're you here? Is this a dream?" I asked as I pinched myself.

She shook her head immediately.

"No, it's not!" she said.

"Well, it's not real either, but this definitely isn't a dream," she told me.

I raised an eyebrow.

"What do you mean?" I asked. "If this isn't a dream but isn't real, then what is it?"

"What I mean is—when you wake up, don't doubt the things I'm going to say to you right now," she warned me.

I felt confused but nodded anyway.

"I don't have much time, Stella. You have to know what's going on over here," she said quickly.

"Going on where?" I asked.

"I don't have an exact name for that, but it's a place where the dead stays, and they want you to pick them," she told me.

I was getting confused more by the second.

"Alice, I have no idea what you're talking about," I told her. I noticed the wind was increasing, and the temperature was dropping as clouds filled the sky.

Crows were now flying above us, and the trees around us were disappearing.

"Listen, Stella, and I want you to listen closely," she said as she grabbed both my shoulders and looked straight into my eyes.

I nodded.

"You are different," she said quickly.

She glanced at her feet. They were gone. Alice was disappearing along with our surroundings.

"Alice! What's going on?" I asked her as panic took over me.

"Just listen to me!" she said.

"You're not normal, Stella! You're special, and you can do special things," she said, but now her knees were gone.

I felt the tears behind my eyes return. I didn't want to lose her again. I just saw her after all these years, and I certainly know that this wasn't a dream. I just wanted to hug her to death and tell her all the things that happened throughout the years. I wanted to ask her about Mason and see her blush when she talks about him.

I wanted to live the moment when everything was okay, and I felt complete.

"But he's after you! He wants her back, and he will do anything to have her back, even if it means by getting to you," Alice rambled.

What?

"Stella! Don't let him get to you!" she yelled. Now her stomach was gone, and she was fading.

I felt tears run down my cheeks as my vision blurred from the panic. I did not want to say goodbye.

"Don't let who get to me?" I asked.

Her face was the only thing left of her.

"The Alpha!" she yelled.

I took one step forward and went to grab her shoulder, but my hands went right through her as if she was a ghost.

"Alpha Ar—" Before she could continue, she disappeared. The only thing left was silence.

And my beating heart.

I fell to the ground and sobbed. I wasn't ready to say goodbye. I had so many questions I had to ask her, like what the hell is happening and who on earth wants me. But most of all, I just wanted my best friend back.

My mind was all over the place as I took in her words.

The ground beneath me began to shake and rumble. I got up and took one step forward but retreated when the ground started to crack. I walked backward, avoiding the cracks, but every second, they got bigger and bigger. The ground was now split into two, and I turned around and ran. I ran as fast as I can, hearing the ground crack from behind me. I looked behind me, which was a very bad idea because I ended up tripping on a stone.

I fell to the ground using my hands for support. I heard the cracking get closer until the next thing I knew I was falling.

* * *

My eyes shot open as my heartbeat quickened against my chest. I felt something wet running down my cheek and moved my hands to wipe it off. I looked at my surroundings and sighed in relief when I noticed I was in my room, in Aiden's arms.

I don't think I had ever been this happy to find myself in his arms.

I wiped the sweat off my face and rubbed the sleep out of my eyes.

What a nightmare.

The words that Alice told me were flowing through my head.

"What I mean is—when you wake up, don't doubt the things I'm going to say to you right now."

Should I keep her words in mind? I have no idea. These days, strange things are happening, and I don't know what to believe.

But it felt so real.

If Alice was right, then there is something awaiting. Something not good, not good at all. I should probably tell Aiden and the others about the strange dreams and the ghost. But I wonder if they are linked to each other, or to the rogue attacks.

What if they thought I was crazy?

I tried to get up but what do you know, Aiden had a strong grip on me. I sighed to myself and began to loosen his grip. Finally, once I was free—which took me a whole five minutes by the way—I got up and went to the bathroom.

I took a shower and brushed my teeth. I wore short jeans and a t-shirt I grabbed from the closet and tied my hair into a loose bun. I got out and saw that Aiden was still asleep, so I decided not to wake him up.

Today was one of those days where I wake up and find him beside me. He was usually working in his office by the time I woke up, so I didn't want to wake him up. He probably needed the sleep.

I walked out of the room and down the stairs to the kitchen.

I saw Liam eating his cereal with a black eye on his right. I grinned to myself, wanting to laugh so badly, but decided not to when I saw his annoyed face.

Is it bad that I thought he deserved it?

I mean, why would he try to ruin Marie's date in the first place?

"Oh my god! Liam, have you gotten into a fight?" I asked sarcastically and smirked.

"Haha, very funny, Stella. Why don't you be funny somewhere else today, huh?" he grumbled at me while sending me glares.

Geez, someone woke up on the wrong side of the bed today.

"Whatever," I muttered.

I walked to the fridge and took out a blood bag and started to sip on it. I leaned on the counter as Marie walked into the kitchen. She smiled smugly to herself when she saw Liam's black eye.

"Oh what a beautiful day," she sang as she walked toward the table where Liam was eating his breakfast.

"Oh my! Liam, have you gotten into a fight again?" Marie asked sarcastically as she put on a fake concerned look.

Liam glared at her. If looks could kill, then Marie would be ten feet underground. Liam stood up ignoring Marie's question as he put his empty bowl in the sink and walked out.

I could see Marie burning holes into the back of his head as he walked out of the door.

"He had it coming," she muttered to herself while shaking her head. She looked at me then smiled.

"Good morning, immo," Marie said as she walked to the fridge and took out milk for her cereal.

"Morning," I told her as I took another sip from the blood.

She looked at the blood bag in my hand and scrunched her nose in disgust.

"No offense, immo, but that's gross. Who drinks blood for breakfast?" she asked.

"Vampires do," I answered simply.

We both finished our breakfast and went to the living room to watch some TV. It was around twelve PM when Aiden finally came into the room looking as sexy as ever in his blue plain t-shirt and ripped jeans.

I barely see him dressed up this casual. I wonder why?

"Stella, go get dressed. We're going somewhere," he told me.

I raised an eyebrow.

"Where?" I asked.

"It's a surprise," he said.

Okay...

I got up and was about to walk out of the door when I heard Marie's teasing voice.

"Oh, Stella's got a date today."

I turned my head and glared at her before walking out of the room.

Is this a date? I mean, things between us are calm, but I never thought he would ask me to go on a date with him.

Or in this case, tell me.

Geez, what a gentleman. Note the sarcasm.

I went into the closet for the second time today and grabbed a simple floral blue dress. It wasn't fancy, but it wasn't plain. It was just right. My nerves were acting up.

I wonder where he is taking me.

I've been here for two months, and if I say that I didn't like Aiden, then it would be a lie. I feel myself getting closer and closer to him every day. It's just I try so hard to resist him and not give in, but it's so hard. When I look into those beautiful blue eyes, I get mesmerized. And his laughter is music to my ears.

There is no way of escaping fate, especially after he marked me.

The only thing I can do is prepare myself for the future.

Twenty minutes later, I had on my dress and simple makeup on my face. I walked down the stairs and heard Marie and Aiden teasing Liam.

"Oh, and Liam make sure not to ruin their date," Marie said.

"Yeah, you wouldn't want Stella to give you a black eye on the left," Aiden teased.

I walked into the room to find Aiden and Marie laughing as Liam ignored them, watching TV.

Well, trying to watch TV.

"Guys, cut him some slack," I said, grabbing all three of their attention.

Aiden looked at me with awe. His eyes were raking over my body from head to toe. He walked toward me, ignoring my statement, and wrapped his arms around my waist. He looked down at me, smiling.

"You look beautiful," he complimented me.

I smiled back at him.

"Thanks."

We walked out of the room and toward the front door before hearing Marie's voice.

"Make sure to use protection!" she yelled.

I slapped my forehead as the blood rushed to my cheeks. I heard Aiden chuckle as we walked out the door and to his car.

Fifteen minutes later, we were standing in front of an ice cream shop. I looked at Aiden with wide eyes.

"You brought me to an ice cream shop?" I asked, still not believing the sight I saw. I couldn't even imagine the big bad Alpha sitting down in a cute shop like this while eating ice cream.

Boy, that's a sight I would want to see.

Aiden never failed to surprise me.

"What? You don't like it?" he asked as worry covered his face.

I gave him an are-you-crazy look.

"Are you kidding me? I love it! Who doesn't like ice cream?" I asked him.

He smiled at me then took my hand in his. I could feel the sparks return as we walked toward the entry.

We ordered what we wanted. I, of course, took my favorite which was strawberry while Aiden took cookie dough. One thing I learned from him was that he hated strawberry ice cream. We sat at a small table facing each other as we picked up a conversation.

I put a scoop of ice cream in my mouth and moaned as the delicious taste hit my taste buds. I looked up to see Aiden staring at me with dark blue eyes.

"Save that sound for bed, sweetheart," he said and smirked.

I gasped at what he said and hit his shoulder playfully as I blushed for the second time today.

"That ain't happening," I told him.

He sighed to himself and laid his head on his hand.

"A guy can only dream," he said more to himself.

Before I could say anything, the shop door slammed open. There standing was the third in command, Clarke.

I never really talked to him; it's just I didn't see him around that much.

He ran up to us, and as he got closer, I could notice the grim look on his face.

This wasn't good.

"Alpha, Luna," he said quickly, and I could hear the nervousness in his voice.

"What's wrong?" Aiden asked, tensing.

Clarke looked worriedly at me and took a deep breath.

"Sarah, a little girl from the orphanage, has been attacked," he told us.

I gasped as I got up immediately.

No! This can't be. Why would anyone want to harm an innocent child? That is just sick!

"What happened?" I asked.

"She was found in the woods unconscious with her blood scattered everywhere," he informed us.

I felt my knees become weak as tears formed in my eyes.

"Who did it? And why?" Aiden asked as he helped me sit down.

"We don't know, but we found something written on a tree with her blood," he said.

My eyes widened at what he said.

I just hope she's fine.

"What did it say?" I asked.

He gulped and looked at Aiden and me with worried eyes.

"I think maybe you should take a look," he told us.

Chapter 30

We ran out of the ice cream shop and into Aiden's car. Aiden got into the driver's seat while I sat next to him and Clarke was in the back.

"Where is Sarah now and is she okay?" I asked Clarke.

"I don't really know about her condition yet, but she was sent to the hospital as soon as she was found," Clarke answered.

After we see what was written, I am immediately going to go visit Sarah and make sure she is okay. She has to be okay. I don't know what I will do if I lost someone else. It's as if the world is against me, taking away everyone I loved as I watched them disappear.

If that isn't bad enough, then I don't know what is.

"Aiden, can't you drive any faster?" I asked as my voice rose in panic, but I could hear it crack in the end. I felt a lump in my throat that wouldn't go away until I was sure Sarah was okay.

Aiden's knuckles were white as he gripped the steering wheel while sweat formed on his forehead.

"I'm trying! But this is as fast as I can get," he growled out.

I could see he was worried as well. Of course, he would be; he is the Alpha after all. Every Alpha would be concerned about his pack's well-being. Only a coward that was given the title for so many unknown reasons wouldn't care. I looked out the window to see us passing the trees with so much speed; I couldn't quite focus on them because they were a blur.

We were probably exceeding the speed limit. But I didn't care, for that was the last thing on my mind. It took me a while to notice that there were two wolves running next to the car, one on each side. I immediately recognized the wolf on the left as Liam but not the wolf to the right of the car. A few minutes of tension passed, which felt like hours, and we were finally in front of the woods. The same woods where I was attacked by the rogue, the day Aiden marked me.

I wonder what was Sarah doing in the woods all by herself?

Once the car came to a halt, I sprang out of the door and into the woods with Aiden and Clarke by my side. Liam and the other guard stayed behind just in case. Clarke led us deeper into the woods where trees were ruling their land as if they were the kings of nature.

"What was a little girl doing all alone in this part of the woods?" Aiden asked Clarke in a cold tone.

"We don't know, Alpha. But if she wakes up, then we'll ask her," Clarke said.

"If?" I asked as I pointed out what he had just said. I shook my head furiously.

"You mean when she wakes up," I told him. I looked at Aiden but saw no emotions from him, so I looked back at Clarke.

"She has to wake up!" I said as my voice rose.

Aiden came closer and wrapped his arms around me, bringing me to his chest. I breathed in his scent to calm me down as I counted to three.

"Where is the writing you were talking about?" Aiden asked Clarke.

Clarke looked at Aiden with worried eyes then back at me. They were staring at each other for a moment, and I realized they were mind-linking each other.

"What?" I asked while raising an eyebrow. I didn't like the fact they were mind-linking while I was here. It's like they were hiding something from me.

Aiden gulped then looked at me.

"I'll be right back. You stay here, and don't move," he told me.

I crossed my arms over my chest and gave him a confused look.

"Why?" I asked.

He ran his hand over his face and through his hair. I could tell he was nervous.

"Just do what I say, and stay put," he ordered.

I opened my mouth to protest, but before I could say anything, Clarke and Aiden took off, sprinting past the trees and deeper into the woods.

I looked around, observing my surrounding, taking in the view. I tapped my feet on the ground as I bit my lip. I started to pace back and forth as I ran my hand through my hair impatiently.

Why did Aiden want me to stay behind?

It's like he didn't want me to see what was written.

I thought about it and came to the conclusion that I was not going to stay put. I had to see what was written. *The faster I see, the quicker I check on Sarah.*

I sprinted toward the path where Clarke and Aiden ran, and I sniffed the air, trying to catch their scent. It was a bit difficult because I couldn't smell as good as werewolves, but since they weren't here too long ago, I caught their scent.

I followed it as I perked my ears up, trying to hear anything from Aiden or Clarke. A few moments later, I heard Aiden growl loudly, making the ground shake.

This definitely wasn't good.

I picked up my pace and ran faster. I heard Aiden's beating heart from a mile away. I passed a couple of trees and saw Clarke looking at an angry Aiden with concern in his eyes.

What got him so worked up about?

Aiden's tensed shoulders were moving up and down as he tried to control his wolf and his anger. None of them noticed me when I walked up to them, for they were too distracted on whatever they were looking at. I walked forward to see what was causing all this commotion when Aiden sniffed the air and snapped his head toward me.

"Stella!" Aiden growled.

"I told you not to come here."

Aiden's voice was mixed with his wolf. I had to see what was written if it was bad to the point where Aiden's wolf wanted control. I walked closer to where Aiden was standing, but when I was about to peek over his shoulder, he pushed me back.

"We're going home," Aiden said firmly, but I could tell he was furious.

Aiden and Clarke were both by my side in a second and started to drag me away from the writing, which was eating me up alive. Their behavior only made me want to see it even more. I yanked my arm from Aiden's grip and shook my head.

"I want to see what was written!" I told him stubbornly.

Aiden growled at me as he shook his head.

"No, you won't. I'll tell you later. Right now, let's go check on Sarah," he said.

His words almost convinced me. I really wanted to make sure Sarah was okay, but as much as I wanted to do that, I couldn't leave until I got a glimpse of what was written.

"I'm not leaving until I see what got you so angry," I said, but this time, I didn't give him the chance to answer. I sprinted past Aiden and toward a big oak tree. I heard Aiden and Clarke call out my name, but I simply ignored them.

My feet came to a halt when I saw what was getting Aiden so worked up about. My eyes widened, and the color drained out of my already pale face as sweat formed on my forehead. I just stood there staring at the writing. Aiden and Clarke were by my side in an instant, trying to get my attention, but I was consumed by the questions—how, when, who, and why.

I was so confused, and the longer I stared, the more afraid and insecure I felt.

Aiden grabbed my arm and started to drag me away from the scene once again. This time, I let him, because right now, I had no energy to fight back. It's like the world closed on me, and time was passing by slowly as I glanced back at the sight that caused shivers to run down my spine.

And not the good type.

There, on the big oak tree, Sarah's blood was scattered everywhere. But what caused me to feel so creeped out was what was written in big red words.

I'm coming for you

My picture hung under it by a knife, and my face was circled as the target.

Chapter 31

I played with my fingers nervously as silence took over the car. Aiden drove us to the hospital where Sarah was. I tried to clear my mind that was being bombarded with questions and thoughts of the recent events. And the dream I had about Alice wasn't helping at all. Neither did the sound of Aiden's heavy breathing and the sight of his white knuckles gripping the steering wheel as he tried to calm his raging wolf.

Every time I closed my eyes, I saw the scene over and over again. It's like it was glued to my mind with superglue that will make it impossible to get rid of. What angered me more was the sight of Sarah's blood everywhere. My fist clenched as the desire to rip the person who did it overcame me. I would not forgive them for laying hands on her. I imagined sucking every ounce of their blood just to satiate my anger.

What kind of cruel person would ever do this to a child, just to spread a message?

Oh yeah, a sick, psychotic person would.

If I am correct, an Alpha is behind all this. Before Alice disappeared in my strange dream, she said something about an Alpha. But he will be difficult to find. I mean, it can be anyone, from any state or country. Whoever it is, I am certain of one thing, and that is to tell Aiden about everything. Who knows what will happen next? So Aiden and I have to be ready for what's coming. And I can't endanger our pack as I hide behind the bushes.

I glanced at Aiden with worried eyes.

I just hope he believes me and doesn't think I'm crazy.

When we were alone in the car, I took the chance to tell him the strange things that had been happening to me lately. Clarke was left behind with some other pack wolves to clean up the scene.

"Can you stop the car?" I asked.

He glanced at me, then sighed before pulling over to the side. He turned around to face me, and I saw emotion flowing behind his beautiful ocean eyes. I opened my mouth to say something but was interrupted when he grabbed my hands in his.

"I know, Stella, that wasn't a sight you'd want to see," he started as he looked straight into my soul.

"And I'm sorry about Sarah. I will do everything I can to keep her alive," he told me as I felt his grip tighten.

"But I promise you, as long as I'm alive, I will not let anyone lay a finger on you. I will not rest until I find out who did this and why they want you. You're everything to me, and knowing that this happened only angers my wolf and me to the point where I want you to be in my sight all the time," he admitted.

"And I know that this bothers you, but I'm just afraid of losing you. And I will not risk that ever! So please believe me when I say that you don't have to be afraid because you will forever be safe with me!"

By the end of Aiden's little speech, he pulled me over to his lap and calmed himself down by inhaling my scent. He tightened his hold on my waist, And the heat rose to my cheeks as his words sunk into my brain.

I had no idea he cared about me this much.

I wrapped my arms around his neck and closed the space between us. I felt so safe in his arms. I believed everything Aiden just said, and I don't know why, but when he said he would protect me, I knew from the beginning he would. I rubbed my hands up and down his arm to calm him down, which worked.

I pulled away only a little when I remembered why I made him stop the car. I gulped and took a deep breath, trying to relax my nerves.

"Aiden, there's something I have to tell you," I said.

At first, he didn't pay attention to what I said. He was too busy kissing the skin on my neck to my jaw, all the way to his mark, which made me shiver in pleasure. For a second there, I almost let out a moan, but I held it back because this wasn't the right time.

I grabbed the back of Aiden's head and pushed it back gently so that I was looking into his blue eyes.

"There's something important you have to know," I said.

He raised an eyebrow curiously and nodded slowly.

"Just don't think I'm crazy, okay?" I blurted out.

He narrowed his eyes, and I could see a smirk forming on his lips once I said that.

"Why on earth would I think you're crazy?" he asked.

"Just don't," I said stubbornly.

Aiden only nodded after rolling his eyes.

I took a deep breath then started, "I've been having these weird dreams for a while now."

While I spoke, I looked at my lap and played with my fingers nervously. But I briefly glanced at Aiden to see his reaction. And you know what I saw?

A smirk.

"Don't tell me you've been having wet dreams about me already," he told me with a hint of amusement.

My eyes widened, and I slapped his shoulder lightly.

"No! I'm being serious," I said.

It seemed like my serious tone snapped him out of it as he remembered the situation we were in.

"I've been having strange dreams about the dead," I told him.

He raised an eyebrow at me.

"The dead?" he repeated.

I nodded.

"And at first, I thought it was just a coincidence, but in every dream, I would see the same person, and he would tell me to do the same thing."

"What would he tell you?" he asked.

"Do it," I said.

There was a moment of silence until Aiden spoke.

"That's all?" he asked.

"That's all," I said while nodding my head.

"But there's more. You see, before all this happened, I had a strange dream about Alice, my deceased best friend," I reminded him.

"And she told me that was no normal dream, and that I'm special, and that she came to warn me about someone," I told him.

"Warn you about who?" Aiden asked.

I shrugged my shoulder, not quite having an answer for that.

"I'm not sure. She disappeared before she could clearly tell me, but I do know it's an Alpha," I said.

"So you're saying that an Alpha could be behind all this?" he asked.

I nodded.

"You don't believe me, do you?" I asked.

He shook his head immediately.

"Love, of course, I do. I would believe anything you say," he said firmly as he hugged me closer to him.

I felt myself blush. It was like some weight was lifted off my shoulders when I finally got that out of my chest, but then I've realized something.

"Oh, and I forgot about something else to ask," I said.

Aiden nodded his head, wanting me to ask.

"Is your pack haunted?" I asked.

Aiden looked down at me with a confused look.

"Love, just because you've been having strange dreams, it doesn't mean our pack is haunted," he said.

I rolled my eyes but felt butterflies in my stomach when he said *our pack*. I pushed them away because right now wasn't the time for that.

"I don't mean that," I said.

"What I mean is that lately I've been seeing ghosts too, and I don't know why," I told him.

"So what you're saying is that you've been having strange dreams about the dead and seeing ghosts," he said.

"Don't think I'm crazy!" I said as I hit his hard muscular chest, which, of course, had no effect on him.

"Oh, I don't think you're crazy," he said.

"I think it's you who's being haunted," he said playfully.

I rolled my eyes and gave him a stern look.

"Wait, you're being serious?" he asked.

I gave him an annoyed look.

"Of course I am! And what I'm saying is that we don't know exactly who did this, but an Alpha could be behind it," I exclaimed.

Aiden growled when I mentioned today's accident and tightened his grip on me.

"Whether it's an Alpha or not, I'd rather die than let anyone lay a finger on you," he said.

I hugged him closer as I ran my hand through his soft hair as we lay our foreheads against each other's, finding safety in each other's presence.

"And that's a promise."

* * *

Aiden and I stood right outside the hospital door, and I gulped nervously. It seemed as if we had been standing there for hours, just trying to calm down our nerves. I could feel sweat form on my forehead, and the same goes for my hand, which was holding Aiden's.

It's like I was glued to the floor; my legs were paralyzed as I stared through the glass door and saw nurses and doctors rushing to their patients who were being taken away.

What if Sarah wasn't okay?

What if she never woke up?

I would never forgive myself if anything happened to her because it's all my fault this happened. It's all my fault she's here in the first place.

I couldn't bring myself to walk through the door and look her at the face.

What if she blamed me for everything? I really can't blame her. I would blame myself too.

Aiden tugged on my hand, snapping me out of my thoughts. I glanced up at him to see him staring at me with concern in his eyes.

"Hey, everything's going to be fine, love," he said as he ran his hands up and down my back.

I nodded and walked inside the hospital with Aiden by my side. We asked the doctor where Sarah was and headed there immediately.

As we walked down the hall, I saw many rooms. And behind every door was a story. One is maybe a tragic loss, or just a normal check up. The possibilities were endless, leaving me thinking about how life could hit us when we least expect it.

As we approached, the corner where Sarah's room was, I saw a tired Marie and a couple of she-wolves, along with some guards, outside Sarah's room. I rushed toward Marie and gave her a hug. We pulled away after a moment of silence.

"Stella, I'm so sorry for what happened, but I want you to know that you'll be safe with Aiden," she said as she glanced at him who was standing right behind me.

"Wait, how do you know what happened?" I asked while raising an eyebrow.

"Liam told me," she answered.

I nodded then looked at the door nervously then back to Marie.

"How is she?" I asked.

Marie gave me a sad smile.

"For a second, we thought we lost her, but it's a good thing she was found before it was too late," she told me, and I let out a breath I didn't know I was holding.

"Why are you all waiting outside?" I asked.

"The doctor won't allow more than one visitor," Marie answered.

I nodded my head and told Aiden I was going to check up on her, then approached the door and opened it slowly.

I peeked in and saw Sarah sleeping on a hospital bed with machines around her. I closed the door and grabbed a chair. Once I sat down next to her, I grabbed her small hand in mine and kissed it.

"Oh, Sarah, I'm so sorry," I whispered as I rubbed circles around her hand.

"I never wanted this to happen. All I wanted was for you to be happy and find a family. Not to end up here."

My voice cracked in the end as my vision blurred because of unshed tears. I pushed a strand of her hair away from her face and tucked it behind her ear then kissed her head.

"Please wake up," I whispered.

As if those words were the magic words to wake her from slumber, Sarah's eyes opened. My eyes widened, and my mouth fell open.

"Sarah!" I spoke.

She seemed confused as she took in her surrounding, her eyes darting from one place to another. She opened her mouth to speak but closed them. Assuming it's because of her dry throat, I got up from my seat and ran out the door.

"Guys! Sarah's awake. Call the doctor." I yelled.

Everyone's heads snapped toward me, and the she-wolves who were sitting down went to call the doctor as Marie grabbed a glass of water, walked into the room, and handed it to Sarah. The girl gladly took it and gulped it down.

A moment later, the doctor walked in with a couple of nurses behind her. She bowed her head at Aiden and me then smiled at Sarah.

"You know, you are a very strong girl," she told her, and Sarah smiled.

"And a very lucky one too," she said then turned to Aiden and me.

"Alpha, Luna," she greeted us.

Aiden nodded while I gave her a small smile.

"How is she?" I asked, referring to Sarah.

"She lost a lot of blood but is very lucky to make it out alive. She will need to stay here for a couple of days so we can make sure she's okay," the doctor informed us.

I nodded, sighed in relief, and walked over to Sarah's bed. Her face was pale, and she looked tired. I hugged her as I ran my hand through her hair.

"How are you feeling?" I asked her.

She shrugged her shoulders and looked up at me.

"I feel a bit tired," she answered.

I nodded my head and faced everyone who was standing around her bed.

"Didn't you hear her? She feels tired, so out we go," I told them.

I kissed Sarah's forehead and walked out with the others to give her some time to rest. But when I was about to close the door, I heard her soft voice call out for me. I popped my head back into the room.

"Can you stay for a bit?" she asked.

I gave her a warm smile and nodded my head. I sat on the chair I was previously on.

"Don't look at me like that," she said.

I raised an eyebrow and gave her a confused look.

"Look at you like what?" I asked.

"Like you're guilty of what happened to me and want to apologize," she told me.

I averted my eyes to my lap and nodded slowly.

"Maybe it's because I do," I said softly.

"Stella," she said firmly.

I looked up at her and saw her tapping the space next to her on the bed. I got up and sat next to her as she laid her head on my chest while she played with my hair.

"Do you know why I was out in the woods?" she asked me.

I looked down at her and shook my head.

"Mommy used to bring me there all the time, and we would have picnics there, eating and laughing at the silliest things," she told me.

"And every time I go there, I feel her presence, Stella. I go there to seek comfort. Because ever since she left, I've been feeling lonely," she whispered the last part as she looked at me with glassy eyes.

I patted her head, trying to comfort her, and I hugged her closer to me.

"But you know what? That all changed when you came into my life. You helped me see the light again and return my smile. So please don't blame yourself. If anything, I should thank you," she said.

Her words made me smile.

"It's you who I want to thank," I said as I got off the bed and kissed her forehead.

"Now, you should rest. I'll be back when you wake up," I reassured her then walked out of the room, feeling much better than I was before.

Chapter 32

I walked down the hallway holding the tray of food for Sarah to feast on. It had been two days since she arrived here in the hospital, and finally, they were letting her out today. The past two days had been pretty boring. I spent it here with Sarah, not wanting to leave her side. There were many times when Aiden tried to convince me to go home and rest, but I couldn't.

I was afraid.

Call me paranoid, call me whatever you want. It's just I didn't want to leave Sarah alone after what happened.

What if they came back and did more damage than there already is? I couldn't stand the thought of that. Yes, I know there were guards guarding the door, but still, that was not enough to calm my nerves.

Other than that, Sarah had been getting better. Her injuries were all healed, thanks to her being a werewolf, but it took her more than a day to get better because of her young age. Also, Aiden increased my guards; having two or three wasn't enough for him. Usually, I would complain and try to convince him not to be so protective, but I knew better than that now.

Especially after what happened. It was clearly shown that I was a target and whoever was behind this wanted me for some unknown reason. So if I were in Aiden's place, I'd be scared too.

Once I opened the door to Sarah's room, instead of seeing Marie and Liam watching over Sarah like they were supposed to, I was met with them bickering in low voices beside a sleeping Sarah. I walked closer to them and put the tray down, but they still didn't notice my presence because they were too busy glaring at each other.

"Liam! I'll say it one more time, and you will agree with me before I rip your face off," Marie warned.

"The egg came first!" she said firmly.

Liam didn't look like he was taken aback by her threat as he shook his head at her.

"Marie! Everyone knows that the chicken came first. It's obvious," he told her.

Marie shook her head at him furiously.

"How on earth did the chicken come without an egg? That's just nonsense," she said.

"Well, who on earth laid the egg? A chicken, of course," Liam argued.

"Maybe it wasn't a chicken. It could have been a dinosaur that mutated," Marie exclaimed.

Liam looked at her as if she grew two heads.

"Where on earth did you get that crazy theory from? That's ridiculous!" he told her.

"I got it from my brain, which I use! Not like you. If you think that the chicken came first, that is absurd," she said.

"It's not absurd! What's absurd is your crazy theory about how the chicken evolved."

"Is not!"

"Is too."

"Is not."

"Is t—"

Before Liam could finish his sentence, I grabbed the magazine that was sitting on the counter and rolled it up, then hit it on the back of his head as I sent Marie a warning glare.

"Will you two grow up!" I told them.

"You guys are literally arguing about what came first while Sarah's asleep," I whispered-yelled as I pointed to the bed next to them.

"You guys are the most immature people I've ever met. Now, if you don't mind, take this somewhere else," I said as I pointed to the door.

Liam was rubbing the back of his head where I hit him, while Marie was trying to bury him six feet underground with her death glares. They both walked toward the door and opened it, but before they closed it, I called out their names.

"Oh yeah, and Liam's right. The chicken came first," I said.

* * *

I gave the last remaining bag to Aiden and helped Sarah off the bed. The time was now around eight PM, and we would have gotten her home sooner if it wasn't for Liam's thick skull. You see, after I kicked Marie and Liam out of Sarah's room, Liam decided to take Marie to some college library, which they presumed had the answer to what came first: the chicken or the egg. I doubted they would find it.

And I was right.

After they were done wasting their time, Liam's car broke down, and they were miles away from the pack. Aiden had to use his car to pick them up. And being the possessive and protective Alpha he is, he didn't want me taking Sarah home all alone. Even though I would have guards escorting me there, he still wanted to be with me. So I had to wait in Sarah's room with a bunch of new guards, along with Scott, until they came back.

I turned my head to my left and saw Marie creating holes in the back of Liam's head with her eyes, while Liam looked away from her annoyed. I walked beside Aiden while holding Sarah's hand as she clung to me.

We weren't taking her to the orphanage yet. Aiden and I decided that it would be better if she stayed with us in the pack house for a while until things got better. I wished she could always stay, but it wasn't allowed until she became the age of eighteen or was adopted by someone who lived there.

We walked toward Aiden's car as guards surrounded us. No matter how many guards I had beside me, I wouldn't feel as safe as I would be if I were with Aiden. I guess it had to do with the mate bond. Knowing that he's there for me decreased the fear and panic inside me, making me feel much better.

Once we were all in the car, excluding all the guards who were taking their own car, Aiden began making his way to the pack house.

"So what's going to happen now?" Liam asked once Sarah fell asleep on Marie's lap who was sitting in the back seat beside Liam.

"Well, I called Nate. If you guys remember him, he was here on my birthday," Aiden reminded us.

"Oh, don't worry, dude. We totally remember him after what happened," Liam brought up the topic of when Aiden marked me by force.

Aiden rolled his eyes.

"Well, anyway, he said that if there will be an attack, then he will gladly stand by our side. So he's coming here tomorrow so we can discuss the patrol and what not," he said.

I smiled knowing that Nate will be here tomorrow. It felt like ages since I last saw him, and I knew I hadn't known him for long, but I felt like we already clicked the moment we met each other.

"What are you smiling about?" Aiden asked as he narrowed his eyes at me, giving me a suspicious look.

I rolled my eyes, knowing that he was jealous of the friendship I had with Nate. The last time his friend was here, things didn't go pretty.

"Nothing," I said.

I laid my head on the window as I stared at the trees we passed with enough speed to make it look like they were only paintings hanging on a wall. The stars were clear as crystal, while the moon hung in the sky. It looked as if it were hung by an invisible threat.

Time flew by, and before I knew it, we were in front of the pack house. We got out of the car as Liam carried a sleeping Sarah. Aiden took my hand and lead me to the door. Once we got in, Liam and Marie took Sarah to the room she would be staying in, while Aiden and I went to our room to sleep.

I yawned, as with every second, I became more tired. Once we were in our room, I grabbed a pair of shorts and a shirt for Aiden then went to the bathroom while he changed in the closet. I did my business then wiped off any remaining makeup I had and exited the bathroom to see Aiden in his boxers.

He sat on our bed as the covers fell to his waist. I blushed at the sight and felt his eyes rake over my body.

"You know my clothes look good on you," he said.

I rolled my eyes but then smiled and got into bed. We lay down next to each other as we stared into each other's eyes. Aiden tucked a strand of hair that was covering my eye then caressed my cheek.

"Don't be afraid of what tomorrow has in store," Aiden said as if he saw right through me and knew that secretly, deep down, I was afraid. His arms moved around my waist and pulled me closer to his bare chest.

"Sleep, my love," he said.

And with that, darkness crept closer and spread throughout my body as my eyelids became heavy and shut my vision as if they were curtains.

* * *

I ran toward my closet and grabbed a pair of short jeans and a crop top.

I'm pretty sure if someone saw me right now, they would think I was trying to break the world record of the fastest clothes changing.

As I tried to pull up the tight jeans, I stumbled and fell on my butt. I immediately got up, while cursing Aiden for not waking me up earlier, and wore my top. The time was around ten PM, and Nate was already in the pack's territory. I was supposed to wake up an hour ago, but it looked like Aiden didn't want to wake up his sleeping beauty.

Once I was done, I let my hair fall down naturally and ran down the stairs to see Aiden giving Nate a hug. I rushed up to them and stood next to Aiden with a wide smile. Once Nate noticed my presence, he pulled me over and gave me a bone-crushing hug. I hugged him back until I was pulled away by none other than Aiden.

"Hi, Nate," I said as I tried to ignore Aiden's possessiveness.

"Hey, Stella, it's good to see you again," Nate told me and smiled.

"It's good to see you too," I told him.

Nate was about to say something when Aiden cut in.

"Nate, you go wait in the living room while I have a word with Stella here," he said.

Nate narrowed his eyes, then looked at Aiden and me, and slowly nodded.

"Okay then. Stella, you're probably in deep shit, which I'm not surprised," Nate told me, and the smile on his face was replaced with a smirk.

I rolled my eyes then shook my head while chuckling.

Nate disappeared down the hall and into the living room.

I turned to look at Aiden and was surprised to see his eyes a dark shade of blue.

"What's wrong?" I asked.

"That's what's wrong," Aiden answered as he pointed at my clothes.

I looked down at them then looked back up at him while raising an eyebrow.

"What's wrong with what I'm wearing?" I asked.

"It's too revealing. That's what's wrong," he growled out.

I narrowed my eyes at him and put my hand on my hip.

"Are you seriously doing this right now?" I asked.

"Just go back upstairs and change into something else," he said, ignoring my statement.

I shook my head.

"No, I don't want to. It's hot outside," I argued.

"Then go change into a dress," he ordered me, but I simply shook my head.

"Aiden, you're my mate, not my father," I pointed out.

He took one step forward and was towering over me with his tall frame.

"Well, I'm your Alpha," he said.

"Are you seriously going to pull that card on me?" I asked.

Aiden nodded.

"I will if you don't get that sexy ass of yours up those stairs and into our closet, or so help me, Stella, I won't hesitate to carry you there myself," he warned me.

I growled in defeat and crossed my arms over my chest as I stomped up the stairs as if I were a child getting her toys taken away from her.

Stupid mate of mine.

Stupid, stupid, stupid.

I continued to curse at him as if those words would sink into his thick skull and remove the possessive side of him which would get annoying at times.

But deep down inside, I knew that I kind of liked it.

Chapter 33

Aiden

I watched as Stella stomped up the stairs as if she was a kid whose toys have been taken away. But little did she know the effect she had on me, with her smooth long legs that can attract any guy's attention and that sexy ass that moves from side to side when she walks.

Yes, I know she hates my possessive side, but what can I do? My wolf and I go crazy when we see others looking at her for more than two seconds.

No one can look at her but me because she's mine. She belongs to me, and I belong to her. That's how much I care for her.

Now, don't get me wrong. Stella is more than that. Her smile brightens up the whole room, and her confidence is a motivation I seek. I might seem like a lovestruck puppy, and it's true. She has me wrapped around her fingers, and she only has to snap them to make me do anything.

I would do anything to see that gorgeous smile and hear the beautiful sound of her laughter which makes me and my wolf satisfied. Knowing that someone is trying to take that away from me angers me. The moment I saw what was written on that tree, my wolf wanted to break free and find whoever wrote that and rip them to shreds. No one is going to lay a finger on my dear mate as long as I'm alive.

I smiled at the thought of her probably cursing at me for making her go change, as she scrunches her nose upward while her face reddens, which is a sight I would want to see. Not because I love to tick her off, but because I find that side of her that's sassy and confident adorable.

I was about to walk upstairs and take her into my arms, but Nate's presence in the other room stopped me. I took one last glance at the door Stella dashed into and walked down the hall to the living room. I opened the door to see Nate looking at some photo album my mom left on the shelf.

"Didn't your mom ever tell you that it's rude to snoop?" I asked with a hint of amusement in my voice.

Nate put the album down then looked at me with a grin.

"Oh, she did, but if you know me by now, then you'd know that I never did listen to her," he answered.

I nodded.

"Of course, you wouldn't. You were a troublemaker," I told him, and he shook his head and wiggled his finger at me.

"Ah, nu-uh, we were troublemakers." Nate corrected me, and I chuckled.

We both then walked over to the couch and sat down. We got serious in an instant, talking about ways we can back up each other if an attack of some sort happens.

And I hope doesn't. I don't want to risk my mate's life or my pack's. But if it does come, then I won't hesitate to fight back for my mate's sake.

Five minutes later, we were talking about the routes in my pack's territory when Stella walked into the room.

And can you guess what she was wearing this time?

She was wearing a dress, which I did tell her to wear. But when I said dress, I meant the ones that came down her waist loosely and above her knees. Not hugging her curves and too short for my liking.

I mean, it was so sexy on her, and I loved it. But only I can see her wear this, and no one else. If any guy saw her wearing this, then they sure will be captivated by her beauty, and I can't allow that.

I glared at her as she sent me an evil smirk, knowing that she was ticking me off. Of course, what did I think? That if I tell Stella to do something, then she will obey?

Pft, no. This is Stella we're talking about. She doesn't like to get bossed around and will fight until she wins.

Nate snapped me out of my thoughts when I heard him say. "Damn."

I growled and glared at him, but he seemed unaffected and only smirked at me. I got up and walked over to Stella.

"Why are you wearing that?" I growled, but I already knew why. It's to tick me off and show me that she won't let me boss her around.

"Because I want to. You did tell me to wear a dress," she said, acting all innocent.

I rubbed my face and opened my mouth to say something when Nate interrupted.

"Oh no, wait! Don't start yet. I still need to get the popcorn," he said as he got off the couch and dashed to the kitchen.

I really wanted to smack that smirk off his face but decided to ignore him and focus on my little mate over here who was trying to drive me crazy.

Knowing that if I make her go upstairs again, she might come down naked—which was a sight I wished to see but knew that couldn't happen because of Nate's presence. So I tried to calm myself down and control myself.

"Okay, fine. Stella, you win," I said.

"I won't be ordering you around, and what you wear is none of my business," I said.

Oh, but yeah, it is, my wolf growled, but I ignored him.

"But please, for me. Will you just go change into something that won't make me want to rip every guy's eyes out for staring at you?" I said.

Damn, I never knew I would say this. I guess I was right when I said that she's got me wrapped around her fingers.

Stella's face turned from smug to shock to surprise in only a couple of seconds. It seemed like she wasn't expecting me to say something like that.

"Wait. Aren't you going to argue back?" she asked.

I shook my head slowly then was surprised when she touched my forehead with the back of her hand.

"Are you okay? You aren't acting like yourself. Oh my god! You must be sick." she said as her eyes widened with concern.

"Nate, come here! We have to get the doctor. There's something really wrong with Aiden," she yelled, and then Nate came running from the kitchen with a bowl of popcorn in his hands.

"What did I miss?" he asked with a mouthful of popcorn.

Seriously?

I growled, annoyed by these two behaviors, and rubbed my face again.

"Guys! There's nothing wrong with me! Geez," I said.

"I'm perfectly fine," I grumbled out then looked at Stella's dress for like the hundredth time.

"Or at least I will be until I'm assured that I won't have to make someone blind today," I said as I gave Nate a warning glare when I noticed him staring at Stella's long legs. He only chuckled at my threat.

To my surprise, Stella slowly nodded and took a step back.

"Yeah, well, I was planning on hanging out with Marie today, so I'll get changed and just be going," she said then ran to the door.

Well, that went well.

I turned around and saw Nate pouting as he looked at the bowl of popcorn in his hands in disappointment.

"Aw man! I was looking forward to a bit of action and booty kicking," he said while putting the bowl of popcorn down.

I raised an eyebrow.

"Booty kicking?" I repeated then shook my head at him.

This guy is unbelievable.

After a minute or two, we both sat down in our previous places, took out some papers and maps of my pack, then got to business.

* * *

I walked up the stairs and toward Marie's room. It had been about two hours since I last saw Stella, and Nate and I were discussing the recent events and how they could be linked to the culprit. But unfortunately, we hadn't come up with anything. There were too many holes that were yet solved. For example, how were rogues able to come into my territory without being caught by my guards.

I went to the bathroom to do my business then when I came back, I found Nate gone. Knowing that Nate would have wandered off somewhere and gotten distracted, I decided to take a little break and see how my gorgeous mate was doing. I knocked on Marie's door and waited until she opened it. I greeted her then asked to see Stella.

Yes, I know it has only been two hours, but I missed her already. It's like she's my oxygen I needed to live. Okay, yes, that was kind of cliché, but who cares. I miss my mate, and I want her in my arms now.

"Stella isn't here. She left with Nate a couple minutes ago," Marie said.

Ugh, not again!

How come every time Nate visits, he always manages to steal Stella. I swear this dude will be the death of me.

I took a deep breath and ran my hand through my hair, trying to calm my wolf that was taking the worst of this situation, because the last time this happened, I ended up regretting letting it take over. I thanked Marie then walked off to find those two, but before I could disappear, I heard Marie's teasing voice.

"Oh, and Aiden, make sure you don't mark Stella for the second time. Yeah, that won't be necessary," she yelled, and I decided to ignore her.

Geez, what is it? Make Fun of Aiden Day?

I walked past a couple of rooms, following Stella's scent that was mixed with Nate's and found myself in front of the gaming room. I heard a couple of noises from behind the door and opened it quickly.

I was met with the sight of Nate and Stella yelling at each other while holding game controllers in their hands. They were playing Call of Duty while standing up, and it seemed like they still hadn't noticed me because they were both glaring at each other.

"We aren't even five minutes into the game, and you're already cheating," Stella accused Nate.

He then put his hand over his heart and feigned hurt.

"What! I can't believe you'd accuse me of that. I thought you'd know me better," he said, and Stella gave him a stern look.

"Oh, don't get all innocent on me. I saw what you did with my own eyes! You cheated!" she told him.

Nate put his hands up in the air in surrender and smirked.

"It's not called cheating. It's just playing with a higher intelligence. That's all," Nate defended himself.

Stella was about to say something, but I got their attention when I cleared my throat. Their heads snapped toward me, breaking them from their little argument.

"What's going on?" I asked calmly.

"Nothing, really. Just found out how much of a cheater Nate really is," Stella said as she put the controller down and walked toward me. I welcomed her with open arms and gladly pulled her to my chest.

These days I have felt like Stella has finally accepted me as her mate. Especially after what happened with all the strange events. They have only brought us closer to each other.

"Am not!" Nate defended himself.

"It's just I'm better than you in playing video games," he said, and Stella glared at him.

"You really want to test me?" she asked, but it felt more like a warning.

"Is that I challenge I hear?" Nate said as he put his finger behind his ear.

Stella nodded eagerly with a grin on her face.

Nate sat down on the floor, and Stella sat on my lap, and they began to play as if their lives depended on it.

Great, this isn't going to end anytime soon.

Chapter 34

Stella

I put on my sporting clothes and made my way to the bathroom. It had been a day since Nate's arrival, and he wasn't planning on leaving anytime soon. He might stay for a week or two. Aiden wanted him to be here just in case if we might need back up, and Nate said it himself that he wanted to help.

Nate finally convinced Aiden that it would be a good idea that I train with them and learn a couple of moves I don't know. Now, I didn't think it would be challenging because I am pretty good in defense, but Nate said that if I would be going against an Alpha, then there was only a small chance that I might win, because Alphas are stronger than normal vampires. So training with not one but two Alphas would teach me the right moves I needed. I grabbed a hair tie and put my hair up into a high ponytail then heard Marie's voice from outside my bedroom.

"Stella, will you hurry up? Nate and Aiden are both waiting downstairs," she yelled.

"Alright, alright, I'm coming," I yelled back then dashed toward the door and opened it to face Marie.

Marie was wearing a normal shirt and a pair of jeans, which meant she wasn't going to participate in today's training.

"So what are your plans for today?" I asked Marie as we walked along the hall and down the stairs.

"I don't know. I was thinking of going to the movies today with a couple of friends," she said.

I smiled and nodded. She deserved to go out a bit because the last couple of days, she had been stressed about my well-being. She needed to let loose and not stress herself over my problems. But I really did appreciate her concern. It's nice to know someone cares.

It had been a while since I actually felt like I had a real friend. Most people these days were all two-faced and backstabbers. In my whole life, I've only had a couple of people who stood by my side through the thickest and thinnest, and one of those people was Alice.

Once I was downstairs, I was met with Aiden and Nate in their sports clothes, which looked sexy as hell on them. I averted my eyes before they could notice I was checking them out. Aiden would probably tease me about his sexy looks or would growl at me for looking at anybody but him. I felt my stomach grumble and knew that I couldn't train without my breakfast because I needed the energy to fight.

An apple will do.

"Guys, I'll be right back," I said before running into the kitchen. I stopped in my tracks when I saw what was waiting for me there. I immediately wanted to run back to and forget about my breakfast. I scrunched my nose and cleared my throat so that both my parents would know about my presence and stop eating each other's faces. Witnessing my parents makeout in the kitchen was not a sight I'd want to see before I ate my breakfast.

"Break it up, you two," I said.

"Go get a room."

My parents pulled apart and seemed unaffected by my presence. My mom smiled at me while my dad seemed annoyed because I interrupted their little makeout session. My mom stepped forward and gave me a bone-crushing hug while my dad just kissed my forehead.

I know that they're concerned about me and my safety. They might not have been bringing up the subject of the rogue attacks or the accident with Sarah, but I know it's because they don't want me to be paranoid. They just want to see me happy. I can see the concern in their eyes; it's obvious.

"Just showing a little love and affection, kiddo," my dad said, and I smiled.

It's good to know that my parents are happy even though their past wasn't too bright. When they're there for each other, the dark disappears. It's sometimes strange calling them my parents when they look just about my age, and it still freaks me out to this day, but that is normal for us vampires.

I snapped out of my thoughts when my stomach growled again, reminding me why I was there in the first place. I grabbed an apple, washed it, and ate it in a record of sixty seconds. I threw the apple right away when Aiden walked into the kitchen.

"Oh, take your time, love. We got all day." Aiden's voice was mixed with sarcasm.

I rolled my eyes then drank a glass of water.

"Where do you think my energy comes from? Thin air?" I asked sarcastically, but he didn't answer, only grabbed my wrist and pulled me out of the kitchen in a hurry.

Nate, Aiden, and I walked down the road and toward the big gym where everyone trained. After a couple minutes of relaxing silence, we were in the gym. The place reeked of sweat as everyone was either exercising or fighting one another.

We walked into a room where it wasn't too crowded and had mattresses scattered on the floor. We spent the first couple minutes stretching and learning a couple of exercises that might be useful. Then finally Aiden stepped forward and straightened his back, clearly showing that he was ready to attack. I was going to try to fight Aiden first, then Nate. Then after that, they both were going to go against me.

Not fair, I know right. It was almost impossible to beat an Alpha, but two? Well, it's going to be challenging but not impossible. I'm Stella after all.

Mostly everyone in the room snapped their heads toward us, giving us their complete attention. They must have been curious on to who would win: their Alpha or their Luna? Well, there was only one way to find out.

I saw from the corner of my eye Aiden running toward me, but I dodged him and threw a kick to his side, which seemed to have no effect on him. Before I could make a move, Aiden pounced on me, bringing me to the ground, and brought his mouth to my ear.

"You're going to have to try much harder, love," he whispered.

I felt shivers run down my spine but ignored it. I used all my force to push him off me so that I was on top. I grabbed both his hands and was going to put them over his head when he grabbed my wrists and flipped me over his head, landing me on the hard ground.

We both got up immediately and threw punches at each other. I blocked Aiden's punch that was directed to my face by swapping it to the side quickly. I saw his eyes soften when I dodged it, probably grateful that I didn't get hurt. Then I threw a punch to his jaw, which I ended up regretting. His jaw was as hard as steel, and it left my fist throbbing in pain.

"Jesus Christ! What are you made of? Steel?" I hissed lowly so that nobody could hear me but only Aiden.

He then grabbed my arm, twisting it behind my back, and brought his mouth to my ear once again.

"Babe, that's called muscles," he pointed out, and I rolled my eyes. As he spoke, he made the mistake of loosening his hold on my arm, and I took this advantage to push him away, hooking my leg with his and jerking it forward, causing him to fall to the ground. I kneeled down so that our eyes were at the same level, then smirked.

"You're going to have to try much harder, love," I mimicked what he said earlier.

In one swift movement, he was off the ground and right in front of me, towering over me with his tall, intimidating frame. He then picked me up, carrying me on his shoulders as I squealed in surprise, then slammed me to the ground. Once again he hovered over me.

By now everyone was surrounding us in a circle, watching to see who would make the next move and win. Their eyes followed us as if their life depended on it, not wanting to miss a single thing. I had the urge to beat Aiden. I didn't want to go down, so I had to make the next move. And I did.

I hit him where the sun doesn't shine.

Unknown

I watched from the window at a far distance as Stella and her mate tackled each other on the ground, kicking and punching one another until one of them won. They seemed so determined to win and face whatever's coming.

Pathetic. Stella will have to do more than that to keep her safe from what's coming. Oh but she has no idea what she can do, and it's all Aiden's fault, which we should thank. Once he dug his canines into her skin, he immediately activated her powers.

That mark on her neck will lead to good things for us, my original Alpha and me. We have been waiting for this day to come, and when I heard that Aiden has found his mate who is a vampire, I told him immediately and kept my eyes on her just in case if she was the one.

And with no doubt, she is. It's just like what the legend says. And soon, we will get what we have been waiting for so many years. But I have to be patient. I cannot strike just yet, or I will mess things up. I have to wait until the time comes, and then I will take actions.

I smirked to myself at the thought.

They had no idea I was watching them. They had no idea that soon, very soon, he will strike.

At first, we used rogues to try to get her after we heard that she was marked. But after countless times of them failing, such useless creatures, he had decided to do it himself. All I have to do is lure her away from her precious mate. Which will be too easy. Why? Because they trust me.

Fools.

They should know not to trust anyone, for they don't know what could be behind that smile. I just wish there was another way. But after so many years of searching, after so many years of misery, you begin to rot, and when you see your chance, you take it. Snatch it as if you needed it to breathe. And that is what I'm doing. I need to accomplish my mission if I ever want to see her again. Because if I don't, then the Alpha will sure have my head.

I felt my phone vibrate in my pocket. Once I took it out, I opened it to see that it was a call from him. I looked around to see if anyone was there, and when the coast was clear, I backed up into the shadows and answered the call, bringing the phone to my ear.

"Hello," I said. There was a bit of shuffling in the background until I heard him answer.

"What is she doing now?" he asked, getting straight to the point. His voice was low; you could already hear the evil in it. I turned my eyes to see Stella fighting off her mate and his friend—what was his name? Oh yeah, Nate.

"She's training with two Alphas, trying to increase her defense abilities," I answered. I heard him chuckle from the end of the line.

"She can try all she wants, but she won't be able to defeat me," he said.

I nodded but then realized that he couldn't see me, so I spoke.

"True, true," I said.

"When will we strike?" I asked.

"Be patient. It isn't the time yet, but it will come soon. Just keep your eyes open and inform me whatever happens," he said then ended the call.

I went into my history and deleted the call I had with him then turned my phone off, putting it back into my pocket. I glanced back at the window and saw Aiden and Nate holding Stella as she tried to wiggle from their grip.

She doesn't even stand a chance.

I turned around before anyone could notice my intense stare and made my way out of the gym, smiling fakely to whoever greeted me.

They will never suspect a thing.

Chapter 35

Stella

I opened my eyes quickly when I heard the sound of water running. I took in my surroundings and realized I was in a dark place. A very dark place. The only source of light was the full moon shining above me.

I then noticed trees in the distance, shadowing the land with their mysterious looks. I realized that I was on the top of a mountain. I was about to take a step forward when I was held down by something strong. I looked down to see myself tied down to a chair with very strong ropes. I tried to free myself, but it was no use. The harder I tried, the more energy I wasted.

I got weaker and weaker through every attempt.

I gasped when I noticed the color red everywhere. My blood was running down the mountain like a flood. And it was a lot. The metallic smell filled the air and was replacing the smell of nature. That's when I noticed the throbbing pain in my right arm. I looked down to see a huge cut from my shoulder all the way to my wrist. It was gushing out so much blood; I was surprised I was still awake. I looked around panicking.

Where am I? How on earth did I get here?

It seems like I have been asking myself these questions constantly nowadays. But it's not like I could blame myself. My life as a normal vampire has flipped upside down ever since I've met Aiden. Half good, which I do have to admit, and half bad.

I looked back down at my arm, and my confusion just increased by the second when the injury wasn't healing.

That just doesn't make sense, the cut is at least supposed to be closing. But it isn't. It seems to be getting worse and worse.

Whispers from a distance caught my attention. I whipped my head up, looking around my surroundings, moving my head to see as much as I can, but I didn't see anyone. The voices seemed to be lonely and sad. I could hear the pleading in them, but it was only a buzz. They weren't too clear.

I could make up a couple things like "please," "save," and "help."

The temperature seemed to drop in an instant. The wind was moving faster and stronger as clouds took over the sky but didn't dare come near the full moon. The trees in the distance started to dance with the wind as the leaves said goodbye to one another and flew to wherever the current would take them.

It was like the light shining from the moon was directed at me, as if I was in the spotlight on stage. I saw something flash in the corner of my eyes, catching my attention once again. But when I turned my head to the side, it was gone.

Well, that's strange.

Suddenly, the smell of my mate's exotic smell hit me like a brick in the face. It was so near yet so far away. Aiden's smell was wrapping the air in its strong scent, giving it more meaning.

But there was something wrong.

His scent was mixed with something else. A smell I knew too well.

Blood.

Now, the reason I was panicking was that I could smell my mate but had no idea where he was and not because of the metallic smell mixed with his scent. Why you might ask? Because I was pretty sure the smell of blood was coming from me. It should be obvious because there was a waterfall of my b—

I stopped talking to myself when I noticed that my blood that was scattered around me a while ago was gone! The smell wasn't coming from me; it must be Aiden's blood!

Okay, now, I was panicking.

Unshed tears were forming behind my eyes, causing my vision to blur.

But no! I mustn't cry. If Aiden is hurt, then I have to be strong.

I looked around to see anything, any glimpse of him, any sign that he was here. And that's when I heard his voice calling out for me.

"Stella! Help me!" he cried out.

It sounded so painful. As if he had been trying to get to me since forever. The unshed tears were now running down my cheeks. Aiden was out there somewhere, and I couldn't reach him. A sob escaped my throat.

I have never felt this useless in my life.

"Aiden! Where are you?" I called out. I was now jumping in my seat, trying to get the chair to move, but it was no use. It took a moment for him to answer. He sounded so tired and out of breath. The grunts of pain were making it harder to bear.

"Stella! I just want to let you know that I lo—" He was cut off by his own scream of agony.

My wrists were probably bruised because of my reckless attempts to free myself.

"Aiden!" I cried. I couldn't stand the sound of his cry. It was so painful to hear. It's as if my own heart was being stabbed, tearing apart my soul. And with that, my sanity flew away into the night. I could only feel one thing.

Loneliness.

The whispers returned, but this time it wasn't some unknown voice. It sounded like Aiden, but different in a way. It wasn't the same voice that would tease me and call me love. It wasn't the serious and possessive Alpha I knew.

It was dark and full of misery.

It was the sound of death.

* * *

"Stella, wake up!" Aiden's voice was back. But this time, it was right in my ear. His voice was mixed with concern and panic. I opened my eyes only to be greeted by the light shining into our room as Aiden sat next to me.

Aiden reached out to wipe something wet off my cheek, and that's when I realized that I was crying. Aiden lifted me up and sat me on his lap. He rubbed my arm up and down trying to calm me as I hid my face in the crook of his neck.

I couldn't stop the tears that were running down my cheek. The dream felt so real, and I didn't know that I cared about Aiden so much.

I think I might even love him, but the memories of the dream were distracting me. Could I actually be capable of love?

The answer was yes! Yes, I do love Aiden. All this time I did; it's just I was too afraid to admit it.

Aiden was whispering comforting words into my ear, not questioning what the dream was about.

"It's okay, baby. It was only a nightmare," he reassured me.

It felt like hours, but actually, in reality, it was only minutes. I continued to sob as I drenched Aiden's shirt he surprisingly had on. Usually, he would sleep half-naked, showing his gorgeous chest—but that's not the point.

I felt myself calm down when he started to run his hand through my hair while leaving kisses on my temple. I released a breath I had no idea I was holding in and rubbed the sleep out of my eyes. I looked up at Aiden and smiled a small smile when I saw him looking at me in concern.

"You know you can talk to me, right?" Aiden said.

I looked up with sleepy eyes because I just woke up and nodded slowly. I wrapped my arms around his waist and kissed his lips.

"It was just another strange dream," I said. I didn't have the courage to tell him why I was crying. It hurt so bad, and now I know what they mean when they say, "You don't actually appreciate something until it's gone."

"Aiden," I said hesitantly. I knew what I had to say. I had to get everything off my chest and confess.

What if something happens, and I never get to tell Aiden how much I cared for him? What if I never got to tell him that I was in love with him? He would live the rest of his life thinking that I was rejecting him. One thing is for sure is that I have to tell him.

"Yes, love?" his voice came out soft, calming my racing nerves. I took a deep breath and gulped down my anxiety, reminding myself what I had to do before I chickened out.

"There's something I have to tell you," I told him.

He nodded, encouraging me to continue.

"Aiden, I lo—" Before I could continue my sentence, Liam and Ian, my old bodyguard who I purposely got removed, slammed the door open. You could see the panic written on both of their grim faces.

Aiden let out a growl.

"Can't I have a bit of privacy?" he growled out at both men standing in front of us.

"There's no time for privacy," Liam said firmly.

"What's wrong?" I asked, looking over Aiden who was blocking me from their view even though I had appropriate clothes on. No matter what the situation was, depend on Aiden's possessiveness to always be there.

"Rogues," Ian said.

"A lot of them."

I gasped as Aiden got off the bed, dragging me with him. He looked furious as he let the Alpha within him come to life. He then pushed me into the closet.

"Get changed so Ian could take you to the underground dungeons where the elders and children are being kept safe since Nate isn't here, while Liam and I go deal with this problem," he told me.

Nate left yesterday because his pack needed him. There were a couple of rogues hanging near the border, and he wanted to be there with his pack just in case something happened, but he promised to be back soon to check up on us.

I nodded then took his hand.

"Be careful," I said.

He nodded his head and kissed my lips, letting it linger there for a bit.

"We will finish the conversation we were having when I get back," he whispered huskily in my ear then ran out the door with Liam by his side.

I left Ian waiting for me outside my bedroom and changed clothes in less than sixty seconds and dashed out.

Ian bowed his head at me, showing his respect.

"The dungeon is this way, but we have to move quick," he spoke.

I nodded my head and followed Ian closely as we ran out of the pack house and into the woods.

Oh, why is my luck so bad? I didn't need a genius to figure out that the rogues are here for me. But why? And why now? I mean, I was just about to confess my feelings until they had to ruin everything.

I just hope Aiden will come back soon. I can't stand the thought of him hurt.

We quickened our pace and ran through the woods. I was expecting to hear growls or yells of pain, but for some reason, it was quiet.

Too quiet.

I stopped suddenly, causing Ian to stop with me, when I realized that we weren't even near the dungeon.

We were in the same place my parents, and I first found out that we crossed a pack. And it was very close to the border. I turned toward Ian in confusion.

This wasn't right.

"Why are we here?" I asked.

"We're supposed to be heading toward the dungeon," I said.

Something about Ian looked different. It wasn't his hair or his looks; it was his eyes. They were pitch-black, and you couldn't see any light in them.

Oh no.

I took a step back, causing him to step forward.

"You!" I said.

This was all a distraction! The rogues weren't here for me. They were here to distract Aiden and the guards.

I was about to scream for help when he grabbed my head and slammed it into a tree.

"It's a pity I had to do this," he said.

My head was throbbing in pain as I let out a painful scream. I fell to the ground while black spots were blurring my vision as everything around me started to turn. My ears were being assaulted by the painful clanging of bells, but before I was engulfed by the darkness, I heard Ian speak.

"But it's the only way."

Chapter 36

Aiden

I ran out of the pack house and into the woods with Liam by my side. I let my inner Alpha take over as my wolf guided me. He wanted out! He wanted to rip every single wolf who had been trespassing just so they could get their filthy hands on my precious mate. No one is going to lay a finger on her if that's the last thing I'll do.

I still don't know why they want Stella, but I'll have my men spare one life so I could extract some information from him. Some guards were running with Liam and me; our best fighters were with us. A couple of females and males.

Unfortunately, I couldn't bring Ian with me. Even though he may not be mated, he still is one of our best fighters, and I needed someone to be there for Stella, even though I know she could protect herself. My wolf just won't be relaxed until he knows she's safe. He won't take the risk, even though she might be a very strong vampire, I just needed someone to escort her to the dungeons so that I know nothing bad happened.

The wolves who were patrolling the border said that they were less than a mile into the pack. Which meant that we had to move fast, or else they could escape. I growled and let my wolf take over completely as Liam and the others shifted too.

Finally, when we made it there, we were all panting and tired, but I couldn't relax until I saw blood. Blood from the people who wanted to hurt Stella. Until I was satisfied, they weren't going to come back. But I stopped dead in my tracks when I saw the guards patrolling the border looking confused.

Where were all the rogues?

My wolf let out a furious growl and ran behind a tree to shift. I then grabbed a pair of shorts that were hiding behind a bush and wore it. I stomped from behind the tree and walked closer to the confused guards.

"Where are all the rogues?" I asked as I gave the guards a cold look.

The guard looked nervous when he spoke, "We don't know Alpha. There was a lot one minute then in just an instant, they retreated, and they were too many for us to actually fight back."

I let out a frustrated growl and hit the tree beside me.

I can't believe they let the rogues get away. They could have been useful. I could have found out who wanted Stella and why. But maybe I can find some clues if I look hard enough.

I turned to face a guard.

"Which direction did they go?" I asked.

He pointed to my left and wasting no time, I dashed past the trees and deeper into the woods. The air was filled with the scent of rogues as I ran faster and faster. Soon I found myself across the border by a couple steps. I knew I couldn't travel too far, for if something happened, then my pack would need me. I couldn't waste much time.

Then in just a split second, I smelled something odd. No one would have caught it if they weren't concentrating, but lucky for me, I'm an Alpha, so I was able to. And it wasn't the smell of rogues. It was the smell of power. Something strong and intimidating.

It was the smell of an Alpha.

My heart started to beat faster in my chest as I thought about an Alpha that could be the one behind all this near my territory.

Something bad is going to happen, and I just know it. I have to make sure Stella is okay and increase the patrol for the millionth time this month. I guess I'll just have to come back here next time to look for any clues.

I took a step back, trying to calm my raging wolf, and was about to run back when something shiny on the ground, near a bush, attracted my attention. I kneeled down and picked up a chain, which looked like a necklace. It looked very old and rusty, as if it has been kept for years. At the end of the chain was a heart-shaped lock. I tried to open it, but it was locked, so I put it in my pocket and ran back to where Liam and the others were.

Once I approached them, I saw the look of rage on Liam's face as he shouted orders to everyone around him. This got my guard up. I walked over to him, giving him a questioning look, and when he noticed my presence, he seemed to tense.

"What's wrong?" I asked.

He looked at me with worried eyes and placed his hand on my shoulder. He had a nervous vibe coming from him, and he spoke hesitantly.

"Aiden, I want you to take a deep breath and listen carefully to what I have to say," he said.

He didn't have to tell me what he was about to say because that was all he needed to say to let me know what was going on.

"Where is she?" I yelled.

I felt my breathing become faster as my chest heaved. My wolf wanted control.

"She better be okay or so help me I won't hesitate to rip someone's head off!" I shouted at everyone around me. I knew Liam had nothing to do with it because he was with me the whole time, but when I get my hands on Ian, oh something bad will happen.

That bastard was supposed to be protecting her! Why can't he just listen to one order! One freaking order!

I didn't realize I was shaking until Liam and the others were trying to calm me down, pulling me out of the forest. There were about five men who dragged me back to the pack house. I took a deep breath and listened to what Liam was saying.

"Aiden, you have to calm down! For Stella's sake," he said.

He's right. I can't go all ballistic right now. I have to be the Alpha I am and try to get my precious mate back. But there is something inside me nagging. My wolf is blaming me for which it has every right to be blamed. I promised her one thing. And that was to keep her safe, but I have failed to keep that promise. She is somewhere—who knows where? Probably suffering by the second.

What if she was being tortured? I will never forgive myself if something happened to her.

I'm a failure.

"Where is Ian?" I growled.

"We don't know, Alpha. She was supposed to be in the dungeon with the elders and children, but she wasn't found. Her last trace was in the woods near the border with Ian," one of the guards said.

Wait, but why was she so far into the woods?

Ian was supposed to take her to the dungeon which was somewhere near the pack house and not in the woods. Unless he purposely took her there.

Oh God!

Ian was the traitor!

So that's how rogues came into our territory without the guards knowing. He could have just lured them away while the rogues snuck in. Because Ian was one of the most trusted guards. Well, not anymore. I won't hesitate to kill him the next time I see him. But why? What was the purpose?

I started to shout orders around as I sent trackers to track her scent.

I have to get Stella back! Without her, I don't know what I'd do. She's everything to me, and I know this may seem cliché, but I can't live without her. She's my world.

I let everyone do their job and dragged Liam to my office. We had to move fast or else I might never see Stella again. I shook my head at those crazy thoughts as my wolf scolded me.

We will find her, and she will be safe, my wolf reassured me.

"What are we going to do now?" Liam asked.

I walked down the hall and took the keys out of my pocket to unlock my office door. The necklace I found earlier fell to the ground.

"What's that?" Liam asked as he picked it up from the ground.

"I don't know. I found it earlier, and I couldn't get it to open," I said.

Liam observed the necklace closely then moved his eyes from the heart-shaped lock to me.

"Where did you find this?" he asked.

"Somewhere near the border, why?" I asked.

"This could be a clue, and what might be inside it could give us some answers," he said as I saw a glint of hope in his eyes.

"Well, that's great and all, but how are we going to open it?" I pointed out.

Liam gave me a small smirk.

"Oh, not us, my friend, but there's someone I know who can," he said then dragged me upstairs.

We quickened our pace, walking faster, for every second counts. We stopped in front of Marie's door which slammed open immediately. By the look on her face, she knew what was going on.

I'm guessing Liam mind-linked her.

"We will find her," she said to me, but I felt like it was more to herself.

Liam nodded then walked into her room.

"Yes, we will, and maybe this might lead us to where she is," he said as he showed the necklace to Marie.

"But it's locked, and we need your help," I said desperately.

Marie took the chain in her hand and observed it for a second then snapped her fingers while giving us a confident smile.

"You can always count on a bobby pin to help," she muttered to herself then placed the chain on the counter next to her bed and started to look through her drawers. A moment later, she had a bobby pin in her hand and looked at us.

"This will need so much concentration, so please be quiet," she said.

We nodded obediently and stared for what seemed to be hours but actually minutes of her trying to unlock the lock.

Finally, we heard a clicking sound and rushed over to where she was standing. I gave Marie a thankful smile then took the chain into my hand and looked at both of them nervously.

What if this didn't have the answers?

What if I was wasting my time trying to unlock this while I could have been searching for Stella?

Well, there was one way to find out, and that was to open it. Marie and Liam stood next to me, peeking over my shoulders so they could see as well. With sweaty hands, I opened the lock. My mouth fell open as Marie gasped, and Liam gave me a surprised look.

The lock had a picture of a beautiful girl in it smiling, and on the bottom was her name.

Lilly Claze

Well, now we know where to look.

Chapter 37

Stella

I was moving. My body was shaking as it moved up and down. But I was numb, and my whole body felt weak. Everything was dark as I felt a throbbing pain in the back of my head. I wanted to moan in pain, but somehow I couldn't. It was like my lips were sealed.

And maybe they were because I felt a kind of fabric tied around my mouth.

I twitched my hand and was about to move it to take the fabric off, but it was held down by something strong. Something that stung my wrist whenever I tried to break free. That's when I heard some murmurs around me. They sounded so close yet so far away.

And reality struck me, causing me to finally open my eyes.

I remembered everything from the rogue attack to getting hit on my head by none other than Ian. I don't think I've ever had this much hatred toward someone. He deserves the golden medal of being a traitor. I then gathered as much energy I could get and used it to look at my surroundings.

I was in the back of a moving car, lying down on my side. I looked up to see two strangers, one driving and the other next to him as they talked about something I couldn't quite get. Something about moving into a pack after handing something over. By the smell of them, I could tell they were rogues. They both weren't paying attention to me as they focused on the road.

Where were they taking me?

What did they want from me and why rogues? I thought it was an Alpha that was behind all this. Unless these rogues were working for him in return for something.

I started to panic, but I knew I had to be strong so that I could make it out alive. I needed to get rid of these two so that I could hop out of this car and run back home. Thankfully, my feet weren't tied up, only my hands and mouth. I guess they weren't expecting me to wake up this early, which I do have to thank my vampire abilities for.

But before I could make a move, I have to break my hands free. Each time I pulled apart, it would apply more pain to my wrists.

What is this? I've heard about ropes especially made to weaken wolves, but never did I hear about ropes made for vampires.

I tried to cut the ropes by using my long nails or fangs. I successfully freed my mouth by dragging the piece of fabric down to my neck. But I couldn't do the same for my hands. Only a wolf could break me free because they were immune to this charm.

There was only one plan, which I wish I didn't have to do but it was the only choice. I had to do it, especially if I wanted to go back home into my mate's arms. I didn't really want to take anyone's life, but I had to remind myself that these people kidnapped me and who knows what could happen to me if I didn't fight back

This was a battle between life and death.

And I couldn't die! I don't know what would happen to Aiden if something happened to me. I didn't want him to feel the pain of losing someone; it just hurts too much.

I made sure to act quickly so that the rogues wouldn't see me move from the mirror. With my tied hands, I choked the rogue sitting in the passenger seat, pressing on his neck tightly.

The wolf driving noticed what was going on and started to swerve the car in different directions in panic. He was about to stop the car and attack me, but before he could do any of that, I let my inner vampire out. My fangs came out of my gums, and I sunk them into his neck.

So basically I was choking one wolf as I sucked the life out of the other.

Yay me!

He was screaming in pain as the other one tried to break free.

I kept sucking the blood out of the rogue, which was delicious by the way. I felt my energy come back as I swallowed every drop of blood. I made sure that both men were unconscious, or maybe dead. I jumped out of the car and looked around to see if anyone was following us. A car was coming toward my direction, so I dashed behind a bush and hid.

I peeked over and saw the car come to a stop as Ian and a bunch of other rogues came out of the car and ran to the one I was previously in. There was someone else sitting in the car, but I couldn't quite figure out who. All I knew was that the person wasn't a rogue. I saw all the men panic as they looked around their surroundings. One even ran to the car and said something to the mysterious person.

What snapped me out of my thoughts was the sight of Ian sniffing the air.

Oh shit!

I totally forgot they could smell me. So without a second thought, I ran into the woods like my life depended on it.

Well, I think it did.

The trees I passed were a blur as I ran for my life. I perked my ears up and listened to my surroundings. I heard some shouting in the distance and footsteps, but luckily, they weren't too close.

I think I could actually do this. All I have to do is lose them and make my way back to Aiden's pack.

I wonder what is he doing now. He probably found out that I am missing and is now looking for me. But how long would it take for me to run back home? Am I too far away? Who knows how long I have been sleeping.

I quickened my pace when I heard the footsteps get louder. I used my vampire skills to an advantage and ran as fast as the speed of light.

Not literally.

The sound of footsteps disappeared as I heard clothes being shed and growls coming from behind me.

Great! They shifted.

I felt like I was in the Twilight movies or something.

Now, that they had shifted, it would be easier for them to smell and gain on me, so I wasted no time in running deeper into the woods where it would be difficult for them to find me because of all the trees blocking their sight.

Suddenly I got an idea. I climbed up a tree which had so many branches and leaves and hid in the shadows so they couldn't see me. Once they passed the tree I was hiding in, they would smell my scent and continue to run, thinking that I just passed this tree and did not climb it.

I tried to control my breathing and beating heart as they passed me and shouted orders to one another. A couple minutes later, the forest was quiet, leaving me thinking that they have disappeared. No one was in sight, so I climbed down the tree and turned my head from side to side.

Which way do I go?

Before I could answer myself, a strong hand wrapped around my neck as the other held my arm in a death grip. I tried to break free, but the person holding me was too strong. It couldn't be the rogues because I would be able to smell them, and it couldn't be Ian because I was much stronger than him. The only wolf who would be stronger than me was someone with a higher ranking.

Before I could turn around and look at my captor, something wet came over my nose, and it took my breath away.

I felt my knees become weak as my vision blurred with black spots.

I felt myself being carried by strong arms, but before I could look up, my heavy eyelids closed, and everything around me turned dark.

* * *

I opened my eyes to darkness. It took a while for my eyes to adjust to the dark, not a single light in sight. The only thing I could make out was that I was in a small room, and in front of me was a steel door. The place smelled like rotten eggs and rats.

I didn't feel my body for the second time today, but this time I was much weaker. I was now tied to a chair, and ropes were again stinging my wrists.

Where am I?

Surprisingly I wasn't as scared as I thought I'd be. I knew I had to be strong and face what's coming.

If this didn't happen now, then it sure would have happened sooner. I just wonder what's my fate. Will I die today? Or will it be tomorrow?

Will I die knowing that I'll never get to tell Aiden how much I care for him?

Or love him?

Or will I make out of this alive but still watch someone so special to me die again?

I've lived for so long to know that I'm pretty scared. But these fears make me a stronger person. They make me who I am today.

Stella.

The Stella that at first hated Aiden, the Stella that wanted to have a normal life and live without fearing, the Stella that wanted to run away from Aiden but wanted to kiss him at the same time.

If I went through a much harder time, then I know I can go through this. And once I'm out, I will never look down on myself ever again. Besides, I can beat anyone.

Yes, I know that beating an Alpha might be hard, but I'm me! I can do anything as long as I put my head to it. If I say I will do it, then I will do it! Even though everyone might say it's impossible, to me, nothing's impossible.

I closed my eyes, trying to come up with a plan that will get me out of here alive.

I still don't even know why I'm here. Did I do something to enrage a certain Alpha? I don't think so. The only thing close to that is when I get on Aiden's bad side, and we all know that is never my fault.

I reopened my eyes when I heard footsteps coming closer to the room I was in. I took a deep breath and calmed my racing nerves.

I can do this. Whoever is behind that door doesn't know who they're messing with.

The footsteps stopped right outside the door, and the knob slowly turned. Light came into the room when the door creaked open. I closed my eyes and tilted my head sideways. I heard someone walk into the room and close the door. I opened my eyes and slowly looked up to see who it was.

I was afraid of who I was going to see but sighed out of relief when it was only Ian.

But the anger of betrayal came right back. I glared at him as I tried to kill him with my eyes. I wanted to spit at his face so badly and slap that smirk off his face. He looked at me with dangerous eyes.

This wasn't the guard I tried to get rid of.

This was a different person.

"Why?" I asked simply.

He stepped out of the shadows and walked closer to where I was tied up. He kneeled down so that we were at the same eye level.

"You'll find out soon," he said.

I couldn't hold it in much longer. I gathered as much saliva I could get in my mouth and spit it right on his face, showing my hatred for this person. He betrayed his pack, everyone around him. But most importantly, he betrayed his Alpha.

"I hope you're satisfied with yourself," I said.

He slowly wiped the spit off his face, and with that same hand, he slapped me right on my cheek, leaving it red as it throbbed in pain. I held back a hiss, not wanting to seem weak in front of the enemy. I lifted my head up high and glared at him for the thousand time today.

"Oh, if we didn't need you so badly, then I would be glad to get rid of you with my own hands," he growled out as he stepped back.

I raised an eyebrow.

"Why am I here?" I asked.

"You'll find out soon," he said again as he retreated and walked to the steel door. He made his way out of the room and closed the door, but before he could clearly disappear, I heard him murmur something that sounded like, "It's finally time."

* * *

It felt like days. But in reality, it was only hours. I think it was somewhere between ten PM to twelve AM because I felt myself starting to doze off. My head kept tilting to the side.

I was really tired, but I knew that wasn't the right time to sleep.

What if someone came and killed me in my sleep?

Okay, fine, maybe I'm exaggerating a bit because as Ian said, they wanted me for a reason, and besides, if someone really wanted to kill me, I'm pretty sure they would want me to be awake to witness it.

I was pulled from my thoughts when I heard footsteps walking toward the steel door again. But this time—I was not sure what got to me—I was breathing heavily and sweating as my heartbeat increased.

I felt power radiating from behind the door.

So much power. It was definitely the Alpha who was behind all this. I couldn't believe I was admitting this, but I was afraid. Afraid of what I was going to face. But I pushed all these emotions in the back of my head.

This is only my imagination.

This is only my imagination, I kept repeating to myself.

After several seconds of tension, the door finally slammed open. I was looking at the ground, but I gathered as much courage I had and looked up to who was awaiting me. Once I saw the face of the person who made my life these couple of days a living hell, I gasped.

There in front of me was a very powerful-looking man. But it wasn't his muscular body and perfect jawline that surprised me, neither was it the amount of power he had or those lonely yet scary dark eyes.

But it was because he was the same guy in my dreams.

Chapter 38

As much as I tried, I couldn't take my eyes off the person standing in front of me. He looked like he could kill anyone with just the touch of his finger. He didn't look quite friendly. He didn't look too old or too young, probably in his thirties. His dark brown eyes were looking through my soul, and shivers ran down my spine.

And not the good type.

He took a step forward after closing the door, making me gulp. I could feel sweat forming on my forehead.

This doesn't make sense. Why have I been seeing him in my dreams? I'm pretty sure I've never seen this guy in my whole entire life. Or did I?

Nope, he doesn't ring a bell.

Then why have I been dreaming about him? Or why did he keep saying, "Do it," in each dream like if I didn't, then he would snap my neck?

Not like that would affect me anyway, but you get the point.

There is something definitely wrong for me to be here. I just can't be here for no reason. And what about the ghosts that keep appearing? I'm pretty sure they're not just coincidence and that they are linked to this guy right in front of me.

"After all these years, I finally have the answer," he spoke in a low husky voice.

It took me a moment to gather as much courage I had and speak without stuttering.

"Answer to what?" I asked, or should I say whispered.

He seemed to ignore my question as he spoke, "Do you even know why you're here?"

He walked closer to where I was tied up.

"No," I answered as I shook my head.

He then kneeled down so that we were at the same eye level.

"You aren't normal," he whispered.

I gave him a confused look.

"Of course, I'm not. I'm a vampire," I said in a duh tone, but he shook his head at me then got up, standing straight as he looked down at me.

"What I mean is that you have special powers," he told me.

Okay, this is starting to freak me out.

"Powers?" I repeated what he had just said.

"Yeah, care to explain?"

I was so confused.

The only powers I have are my vampire skills, which are super strength and speed, but other than that, I have nothing.

"Oh, Stella, don't tell me you don't know what you're capable of?" he asked in a mocking voice as he started to walk around the chair I was tied to, which just irritated me more.

"Okay, first, how do you know my name? Oh, wait, never mind. Maybe it's because of the bastard Ian, but who do you think you are kidnapping me, then telling me shit that you think I'm going to believe?" I spoke, and it surprised me how strong I sounded.

All the courage I had simply went away when his eyes darkened as he kneeled down again but this time grabbed my shoulder in a death grip which seemed familiar.

Now that I think of it, this is probably the person who grabbed me from behind earlier.

"You do not want to anger me," he growled, pausing between his words, making his warning more threatening.

I gulped down all the words I was planning to say, fearing of what would happen to me.

"Who are you?" I asked.

He released his grip then stood up.

"I'm Alpha Argon," he said.

"Does that ring a bell?" he asked.

I thought and thought. That name sounded so familiar.

Where have I heard it?

Suddenly everything came back. That name, Alpha Argon, was one of the most feared Alphas many years ago, and not because he was so cruel, but because of the power he had at such a young age of nineteen.

"You're Alpha Argon? As in Argon Claze?" I asked in disbelief. I haven't heard of him in years after the tragic accident of his mate.

They were one of the most known couples in America. They had known each other for years and soon married, but in one tragic day, he lost everything. There was an attack from another pack that wanted to bring him down, and they knew that an Alpha's weakness is always his mate. So what did they do to defeat him?

The obvious.

They killed her.

I looked up at him nervously, still very confused. There were many missing pieces in this puzzle.

What did I have to do with anything?

"No one has heard from you in years," I said.

"Of course, they wouldn't. I was just too busy traveling the world to find an answer to my problems," he said, only increasing my confusion.

"What answer?" I asked for the second time today, causing him to stop right in front of me.

"Isn't it obvious?" he asked.

"The answer to how to bring someone back to life."

Okay, haha. Please tell me this guy is kidding.

But the look on his face told me that he isn't. He was definitely serious.

This dude is a total nut job. I mean, why would he try to bring someone to life? I mean, yes, I wished that a lot in my life, especially when Alice, died but it's impossible. Everyone knows that once someone dies, there's no going back. It's just the circle of life. Even us vampires have a day when we will die, it just sometimes it takes centuries.

"What?" I asked in disbelief.

That's when he began.

"When they destroyed everything I had—a pack that is long gone now—they took everything with them: my life, my soul, and my mate. They killed her! The love of my life, and you know what I did? I ripped every single one who dared to lay a hand on her,"

He paused. His voice was starting to get harsher as he spoke about his mate.

I was starting to pity him, but I had to remind myself that it was no excuse for kidnapping me.

"After the battle was over, I was left all alone. Nobody was there for me. She was gone! But I promised myself I wouldn't give up. For I had a witch friend. He knew secrets no one did. And I found out there could be a way to bring someone back to life."

Okay...This is getting creepy.

"So what is it you're trying to say? That it's possible? Okay, fine, I get that. But what does this have to do with me?" I asked. I was getting frustrated with all this nonsense.

He completely ignored my question, again.

"There's this prophecy," he began.

One day the weakness of the moon and the enemies of flesh will reunite,

>*bringing two kinds as one.*
>*A very strong fellow with a heart of stone,*
>*a courageous leader he will be.*
>*A creature that will melt his heart,*
>*despite her not having one*
>*has the ability to see what is gone*
>*and can bring back what was taken.*
>*With just a claim that will release the gift.*

Only one could be blessed, and only one could be brought back.

For a river of blood will be the key.

The room became quiet. I was still trying to register what he had just said in my mind. The prophecy sounded odd but made sense at the same time. That's when it hit me.

Is that what he meant when he said I have powers?

Can I bring back the dead?

"What do you want from me?" I asked in a very low voice, scared of his answer, but deep down inside, I knew what it was going to be.

Alpha Argon kneeled down and was just a couple inches away from my face.

"I want you to bring her back! Bring back Lilly Claze to life," he whispered right in my face.

He stood up and looked like he was looking for something in his pocket. I heard him mutter something that sounded like, "Where did that chain go?"

I shook my head furiously.

No, he definitely got the wrong vampire. I have no such powers.

"I can't do that! What makes you think I could? For all you know, I could be the wrong vampire," I said, and he chuckled coldly.

"You really don't get it, do you? You are the only vampire who's mated to an Alpha for years! It's what the prophecy says. And once your precious mate sunk his teeth into your skin, he activated your powers. Now everyone in the under realm wants you to choose them, for you could only use it once," he said.

"And you're going to use it on Lilly."

I really wanted to deny what he had just said. But what he was saying was kind of true. All the mysterious events have been happening right after Aiden marked me, like seeing ghosts for example.

But, wait, if I did have the ability to bring one dead to life, then does that mean I can bring Alice back?

Hope took over my mind and body as I thought about having my best friend back, of what we could do if she were alive again.

But I came crashing down to reality when it struck me that this man in front of me is going to force me to use it on his dead mate. I shook my head at him. There was no way I was going to do it.

"You can't make me!" I told him as my voice rose.

"Everything happens for a reason, and your mate's death too! Do you actually think she would be proud of you for doing this? Teaming up with rogues and kidnapping someone so that they could bring back someone so special? Well, reality check: life doesn't work that way! And there's no way I'm going to do that for you," I yelled at him.

I have to get out of here. How can someone be so caring for his mate be selfish at the same time? If I do have such powers, then I am going to use them wisely. There is no way I am going to give in.

"Oh, but you don't have a choice, my dear," he spoke then looked at his wristwatch.

"The time is eleven thirty, soon twelve AM. And your powers will only work under a full moon when the clock strikes midnight, as your blood falls down the peak of the mountain," he said.

I felt tears form behind my eyes, but I kept them in place. I'm pretty sure he was able to hear my beating heart. I started to struggle in my seat, trying to break free from the ropes that stung my skin, but it was useless.

"Don't waste your energy doing that. No vampire can escape from these special ropes," he told me.

"They were made especially for you," he said.

"You can't make me do this! My mate will save me!" I yelled, but he seemed unaffected by what I just said.

"I'd like to see him try," he said then snapped his fingers.

A bunch of rogues came into the room, about twenty of them. Two untied me from the chair, and five started to drag me out of the room, while the others scattered around the area.

This was going to be harder than I thought.

Chapter 39

It was dark outside, not a single star in the sky. The only source of light was the full moon shining above us; it reminded me of the powers I hold. If only I could just shoot an arrow into the sky and make the moon disappear so that I wouldn't have to do this.

I still couldn't believe Alpha Argon was going to make me use my powers on his dead mate when I could use it on Alice. I thought about escaping, but looking around, I found it will be much harder than I thought, for the place was crawling with rogues.

The only thing I could do was wait and pray for Aiden to find me as soon as possible.

I was being dragged by three rogues up a mountain. It would have been easy for me to defeat them because I was much stronger than them but the special ropes made me weaker.

So I just let them drag me to their destination as I tried to come up with a plan to get me out of here.

What if I stall them? I can do that and just hope that Aiden or someone will come soon and save me. I don't have any other ideas in mind.

But what if I just used the oldest trick in the book?

Pretending to faint. Surely they can't use my powers if I weren't awake right?

Right?

Well, there is only one way to find out.

I let a fake yet realistic yelp of pain escape my lips as I fell limp into the rogues' arms. I closed my eyes and steadied my heartbeat so that they wouldn't get suspicious. I felt the rogues holding me start to shake me and growled words like, "Wake up."

But I blocked them out as I focused on my steady breathing.

I heard one person call my captor, none other than Alpha Argon. I then heard footsteps come toward me. I was now lying in some rogue's arms as I tried to ignore his awful smell.

"What happened here?" he growled out.

I then felt the rogue's heartbeat increase in fear as he spoke, "A–Alpha, we don't know, she just f–fainted all of a sudden."

Normally, I would have smirked at his weakness, but I had to keep up with my act.

Which was probably a bad idea because I felt them change directions as they walked down the hill. The breeze was colder than earlier as the wind's pace increased.

Did they give up that easily? Were they finally going to take me home?

I wanted to give myself a pat on the back, but I should have known better because the next thing I know I'm thrown from the rogue's arms and into an icy pond.

I let a shriek escape me as I shivered, trying to keep my body warm.

I was soaking wet! I looked at them as if they were crazy and walked out of the water. I wish I could have wrapped my arms around myself to help increase my body temperature, but they were tied up.

"What was that for?" I yelled.

I heard someone mutter, "Problem solved."

The three rogues who were holding me earlier completely ignored me as they walked toward me and surrounded me. One gripped my arm, but I yanked it from his grasp and kicked him right between his legs.

I was pissed.

Even though I had a magical rope tied on my wrists, preventing me from using my strength, I still had enough energy to defend myself.

The rogue fell to the ground as he grunted in pain while the one behind me took a handful of my hair and yanked it toward him.

"You little bit–" he was interrupted by an angry voice which boomed through the night.

"Enough! It's almost twelve AM, and you are wasting my time!" he growled.

The rogue let go of my hair and pushed me forward. I heard the wolf I just kicked whisper something to the wolf next to him about him killing me if it wasn't for the angry Alpha in front of us.

Sure, he didn't stand a chance against me.

Everyone fell in silence as we continued to walk up the mountain. I was exhausted; all I wanted to do was be in my soft, cozy bed as Aiden played with my hair.

But no! I just had to be kidnapped by a crazy Alpha and a bunch of lunatic rogues.

What if I never saw Aiden again? It wasn't like after Argon got his mate back he's going to thank me then let me go home. Hell no! After watching so many horror and crime movies, they were definitely going to get rid of me when they have what they were looking for.

Sadness crept into my heart when I realized I might never see Aiden again. Or never tell him how much I love him.

No, I mustn't think like this! I have to believe in him. He will come, and I will see him again. It's just how on earth will he know where we are at? I mean, just looking at the place, it looks deserted.

Then it struck me.

We were in Alpha Argon's old pack that got destroyed many years ago. No wonder this place looked haunted and creepy. Thousands of wolves died here. I wouldn't be surprised if this place were really haunted.

Finally, the moment I had been dreading arrived. We were on the top of the mountain. I could see the unpleasant view as I looked past the rogue's shoulder. There were no trees in sight as crows flew above us. The sight made me cringe. I could already hear the screams of sorrow from the people who died here many years ago.

If I weren't so sure about my surroundings, then I would have thought I was in some horror movie.

I looked around and saw a chair that sat right under the full moon. I gulped nervously as I knew what was going to happen next. Two rogues dragged my soaking wet body to the chair and forced me to sit down.

In the corner of my eye, I saw Ian walking toward Alpha Argon. I still don't get why Ian was betraying us. I mean, there had to be a reason why he was helping Alpha Argon get his mate back. He couldn't just be here because he felt like it.

There was definitely something I didn't know.

The rogues stepped back once they were done tying me to the chair. I felt my skin become numb, for it has been stung by these annoying ropes from hell for ages.

Okay, maybe I was exaggerating a bit.

All the rogues then lined up right behind Alpha Argon— or who I like to call the psychopath who lost his mind.

He took a couple of steps toward me and was now hovering over me with his very tall frame. I then saw him take something shiny out of his pocket. My eyes widened when I saw what it was.

It was a blade, but not any ordinary blade. It was a chromium blade. It was known for being used on vampires when werewolves attacked. I thankfully never once saw it in my life until now. They say that it's really painful to us vampires, and they would use it because it would slow down the healing process.

I took a deep breath and tried to calm myself down, but it was nearly impossible with that torture device right in front of me.

"After all these years, tonight! In just a couple of minutes, I'll finally have what I have been looking for," Alpha Argon said.

His voice was loud and clear as all the rogues started to cheer, while Ian looked very happy for some unknown reason.

Geez, he talks about his mate as if she's an object.

I guess they had to wait for twelve AM exactly, because after a moment or two, Alpha Argon took one step closer, then in one swift movement, he dragged the blade from my shoulder all the way to my wrist.

I let out a piercing scream of pain as tears formed behind my eyes. I closed my eyes shut, not wanting the tears to fall out or it may show my weakness, but I couldn't hold it in for much longer.

The pain was too much.

It was as if I was beaten up then barfed all my insides and got eaten by a shark then came back to life and did it all over again.

"God it hurts! Make it stop!" I screamed as I tried to break free from my seat.

I wanted to rip the bastard's heart from his body so badly and drink the last remaining blood he had in his body.

"Oh hush, the pain will fade away soon, but now, it's time to wait until your blood reaches the bottom of the mountain," he said as everyone turned their attention to my running blood.

I then realized that my blood was running down the mountain, under a full moon, in a place that looks deserted.

Just like in my dream.

Oh goodness gracious! My dream is coming true!

My blood started to slide down the mountain, but thankfully it was nowhere near the bottom.

I still have time. I just need to think.

But my thoughts were interrupted when the sound of howls filled the air.

And one particular howl sounded so familiar. My lips moved upward into a big smile when I figured out who it was.

Aiden.

I don't think I've ever been this happy to see him in all my life.

All the rogues, Ian, and Alpha Argon turned their heads toward the direction of wolves running to them with wide eyes. I was the only one who looked happy and pleased. I noticed that there were about fifty to seventy wolves from our pack while there were only twenty rogues.

Warriors from our pack attacked the rogues by surprise, and they ripped them to shreds. I could already see that we were going to win, and I was proud. I suddenly felt Aiden's presence, but I couldn't see him anywhere. I was whipping my head from side to side, trying to find him when I saw a raging Alpha running toward me.

And unfortunately, it wasn't Aiden.

When nobody was looking, Alpha Argon rushed to me and untied the ropes that were binding me to the chair.

How could no one not notice a psycho Alpha taking away their Luna when that's why they were here in the first place?

I sighed when my wrists were freed, and I rubbed them, trying to make them feel better. I got up to my feet and took a step back, but Argon grabbed my arm and started to drag me away from the fight.

"Let go of me!" I hissed as I punched his chest, which seemed useless. I looked around for help, but everyone was too busy fighting for their lives. I couldn't help but feel guilty for putting my people at risk, but I had to believe in them.

After all, they were trained by none other than Aiden.

Alpha Argon stopped in his tracks suddenly, stopping me as well. I looked up to see a furious Aiden standing right in front of us as he sent death glares to the jerk next to me. His jaw and his fists were clenched. His eyes held anger as they turned into a dark shade of blue.

"Aiden," I cried as I tried to run into his arms but was held back by the dangerous grip on my arm. Aiden's eyes flickered to me for a second, and I saw them soften but soon returned to Alpha Argon.

"Let her go, and I won't make your death too painful," Aiden growled, but Alpha Argon just chuckled next to me emotionless.

"Get out of the way, Smith, and I promise I will return her once I have what I need," he said.

I rolled my eyes.

Everyone knows that's a lie. For if he did let me go, then I could just report to the elders that he kidnapped me. Especially because I'm a Luna, they will punish him. And I'm pretty sure he wouldn't want that.

I noticed his attention was fully on Aiden as his grip loosened a bit. I took this advantage and punched him in the stomach with my free hand, with all my force. Once he let go of my arm, I ran toward Aiden. He took me into his arms and hugged me so tight. I could hear his breathing calm a bit.

I then looked around and saw that our pack was winning while most of the rogues were either injured or dead. But I didn't see Ian anywhere.

"Are you okay?" Aiden asked as he looked down on me. I saw him cringe when he saw my gushing blood.

Oh shit, I almost forgot.

"I'm fine, but we have to do something. Once my blood reaches the ground, I will have to bring someone back to life," I said as I looked at Alpha Argon as he got off the ground.

"What?" Aiden asked. He sounded confused, and I couldn't blame him.

"I'll explain later, but now we have to get rid of him," I said as I pointed to Alpha Argon in front of us.

Aiden then pushed me behind his back and took a step forward, then turned toward me and gave me a pleading look.

"Whatever you do, do not interfere, okay? I will take care of this," he said.

At normal circumstances, I would have disobeyed, but now wasn't the time, so I just nodded obediently.

Aiden then ran toward the Argon and tackled him to the ground.

I know that Aiden is very strong, and he will win this, but I can't help but feel nervous. Seeing him fight with another Alpha scares me. I don't want him getting hurt.

What surprised me was that they didn't shift. They kept on fighting in their human forms. No one but me watched their Alpha fighting as they continued to bring down the rogues.

Aiden and Alpha Argon were throwing punches at each other with their bare hands as they growled viciously. It looked like Aiden was much stronger. Especially because he was a well-trained Alpha while Alpha Argon just spent his years mourning about his dead mate.

Not like I was blaming him or anything. I knew how losing someone felt like, but you didn't see me kidnapping people as I tried to bring them back to life.

It's just fate, and sometimes you just have to accept it.

I did a little happy dance in my mind when I saw Aiden on top of Alpha Argon as he punched him in the face. But I stopped breathing when I saw Alpha Argon take out the same blade he used on me.

I forced my legs to run toward them, but I was too late. He stabbed the blade right into Aiden's heart. I felt something inside me break as I stared at Aiden's almost lifeless eyes turn to me in guilt. He looked guilty because he wasn't able to save me, but that was the last thing on my mind. The pain on my right arm was completely forgotten as I felt a different kind of pain.

The pain of losing your second half.

A sob escaped my throat when his beautiful blue eyes closed. I then heard a scream of agony.

And it was mine.

Tears fell down my cheek as I saw Aiden fall limp on the ground while that bastard stood over him. Everything around me became a blur as I focused on his tired yellow face.

"No! Don't close your eyes! Look at me! You promised!" I screamed as I fell to the ground. I felt useless.

"Oh, Aiden, please wake up," I whispered to myself.

He can't leave me! He promised to stay by my side until he got old, but this was too early. I can't handle the thought of losing him. It's like losing my soul.

I felt everything come crashing down when I didn't hear his heartbeat.

And that's when everything turned black.

Chapter 40

I felt black, but I saw red. Everything around me was a blur as I focused on my target standing right in front of me. I wanted to see blood. I wanted revenge, and I wouldn't relax until I made sure Alpha Argon was burning in hell along with his pathetic minions.

I felt time stop as I ran toward him, letting my inner vampire come to life as my eyes reddened and my fangs came out of my gums.

Everyone said that it was impossible for me to beat an Alpha, for Alphas have a higher ranking than I do. They said that I couldn't do it, for I was weak. I was useless and didn't have the ability. But tonight, I will show everyone who doubted me they were wrong.

For nothing could stop me.

I tackled Alpha Argon to the ground and sunk my fangs into his skin, forgetting about everything around me. I gave my complete attention to the bastard in front of me. I couldn't go home until I was satisfied. I felt my sanity slip away as I ripped him to shreds, enjoying the sound of his screams of pain. He tried to fight back, but he was no match for me. I was going to bring him down, even if it were the last thing I do.

My humanity was crumbling to the ground.

Every good that was in me disappeared along with Aiden. Tears formed in my eyes as I screamed. I let everything off my chest as I sunk my nails into his chest.

"He was everything I had," I yelled while staring at the weakened Alpha in front of me.

The darkness crept closer as I wrapped my hands around his neck and lowered myself to his ears.

"Everyone doubted me," I whispered.

"Everyone told me I couldn't do it, except him. He took away my pain and gave me happiness. But you took away my happiness," I said as I stared at him with murderous eyes.

"So now, I will give you my pain," I said before inserting my hand into his chest slowly, making sure to hit every single bone and muscle as I saw the life drift before his eyes. I then grabbed his heart and twisted it painfully before yanking it out of his chest.

I watched him fall to the ground with his cold heart in my hand, but it didn't wash away the sadness in me like I expected. I still felt lonely.

I felt like a monster.

Tears ran down my cheek as I dropped his heart to the ground and rushed over to Aiden. Suddenly an idea came to mind.

What if I injected my blood into his body? What if his body reacted to it before it was too late and saved him?

But it was too risky. There were either two outcomes. Either I save him and he becomes a vampire when he wakes up. Or my blood will make it worse and kill him. Even though his heartbeat stopped, there could still be a chance of survival. But knowing that I was the one to kill him by inserting my blood, then I would never be able to forgive myself.

I would hate myself forever.

But I had to take the risk. If I never tried, then I know I would hate myself even more.

So I took a handful of my blood that was still dripping from my arm and poured it into Aiden's mouth. I didn't stop giving him my blood until I knew that it was enough.

I then lay my head on his stomach as I let everything out. I cried on his chest, still not paying attention to the fight around me. I cried for Aiden. I cried for Alice. I cried for Sarah. I cried for everyone who has suffered because of me.

And I cried for how lonely I felt.

I was alone.

I waited and waited for a heartbeat, hoping that it will work. That's when I felt Aiden arch his back, and a loud piercing scream escaped his lips. By now there were a couple pack warriors surrounding us, but I didn't pay attention to them.

I lifted my head up immediately and looked at Aiden's face. I heard his heartbeat increase as I saw pain in his now opened eyes. Hope flickered in my heart for a millisecond, but it disappeared when I saw Aiden cough out some of the blood I gave him.

He let out another scream of pain as his eyes held something I couldn't describe.

It was death.

I grabbed his face in my hands as his eyes started to close again and brought it to my chest. My breath stopped when his heartbeat slowed down then stopped as his body fell limp for the second time. But this time, it was all my fault.

I did it.

I killed my mate.

I took a handful of his hair in my fist and brought his face up toward me as I placed a lingering kiss on his lips. Then another sob escaped my throat.

"I'm sorry," I whispered as I looked at his white face.

He seemed so peaceful. Away from all the problems, away from reality, and away from me.

"I'm sorry for failing you."

Another tear escaped my eye.

"I'm sorry for being such a horrible mate."

Now mostly all the warriors were surrounding us, but I didn't dare look at their faces. I knew what they would hold, and I was afraid to see it.

"I'm sorry for never telling you how much I care."

One howl broke loose as another and another filled the night's air, mourning over their Alpha's death.

"I love you," I whispered in his ear then kissed his forehead.

"I love you so damn much! I don't want you to leave me!" My voice now was getting louder by the end of the sentence.

"Please don't leave me," I cried as I felt a familiar hand on my shoulder. I looked up in my blurry vision and saw Liam looking down at me with very sad, red eyes. He didn't say anything, which I was thankful for, but I knew what he wanted. The look of his eyes told me everything.

I pulled Aiden tighter to my chest and shook my head.

"No! You aren't taking him!" I yelled as my voice cracked in the end.

"He's still alive! You'll see. He'll come back, just wait," I told him and everyone else around me. One wolf took a step forward, but I just hissed at him, making him take one step back.

"Stella, it's too late. There was nothing we could have done to prevent this," Liam said, trying to reassure me, but I ignored him.

I looked down at Aiden's lifeless body and moved the strand of hair that was covering his face.

I know there could have been a way to save him. But I risked it. I've failed, and forever I will blame myself.

For eternity.

Aiden was there for me from the very beginning. He was there for me through the thick and the thin. He gave me a shoulder to cry on, and how did I repay him? By being selfish. I only thought about myself and my well-being when I could have asked him how he was feeling.

I must be one of the world's most horrible mate.

I was about to say something to Liam when I felt a strange feeling overwhelm my body. It didn't feel painful, but it felt odd. It's like my body was getting lighter. I looked around to see everyone face me with surprise in their eyes. Some even held panic.

"What's going on?" I asked.

It was quiet for a moment until Liam spoke.

"You're disappearing," he said.

I raised an eyebrow at him in confusion then looked down at my body. I put Aiden back on the ground so that I could see my lap and gasped. My legs weren't there.

But why?

Oh no! Shit, I totally forgot about my blood running down the mountains. I had to bring someone back to life, and since Alpha Argon wasn't here, then I wasn't going to bring his mate.

I felt hope overwhelm my body when I realized I could bring Aiden back to life.

Wait, but what about Alice?

If I bring back Aiden, then I would never get to see Alice again.

My thoughts were broken when I heard someone shout my name. I looked up to see Ian running furiously at me. He looked angry.

Wait, where was he the whole entire time?

He tried to get closer to me, but all the wolves surrounding me grabbed him. I then got up and pointed a finger at him.

"Keep a hold on him. He's the traitor. I'll deal with him when we go back home," I ordered them.

Some men looked surprised about my statement, but some weren't affected.

"Let me go!" Ian yelled as if he lost his mind and looked at me with dark, dangerous eyes.

"You have to bring her back! Bring her back or else I will make your life a living hell!" he yelled like a lunatic at me. I knew he was talking about Lilly Claze but why? Why was she so special to him?

The men started to drag a struggling Ian down the mountain as he yelled threats at us. But before he could clearly disappear, I heard him yell something that shocked and surprised me.

"Please! She's everything I had! Bring back my sister or else! I will kill you all!" he yelled.

My mouth fell open at his statement, and my widened eyes were clear proof I was surprised. Who knew that Lilly Claze was Ian's sister? I guess when she died, he moved into Aiden's pack.

Speaking of Aiden. I looked down at my body and saw that my stomach was gone, and soon my chest would be.

"Stella, what's going on? Why are you disappearing?" Liam asked in panic.

I knew he was scared. He may look strong, but deep down inside he was just a little boy crying over his dead best friend, and seeing me disappear might have scared him even more.

"Relax. Everything will be okay. It's just happening. I'll be back soon," I reassured him, but he just gave me a confused look.

"What's happening?" he asked as his eyes looked at my disappearing chest.

"My powers are activating, and I don't have time explain, but I will be back soon."

And just like that my neck disappeared then my head. I closed my eyes as I felt my body float. I took a shaky breath then reopened them to see that I was floating in a place that was white.

Not another single color.

I looked down at the ground to see that it wasn't clear. Fog covered the place. I looked around but saw no one. I was completely alone in this strange place.

But then I heard whispers coming from somewhere, so I decided to follow them. I moved slowly, not knowing what I was going to face. A minute passed and still nothing. I looked down at my arm and saw that the cut was almost closed.

I observed it and saw that it was healing at a fast pace. Just when the end of the cut was closed, I saw something flash before my eyes. I looked up and gasped.

Right in front of me were probably millions of people staring at me. I gulped nervously as I saw a couple take one step forward but stopped moving as they struggled against thin air. It was as if there was a wall between us, and they couldn't pass.

Maybe because there was an invisible wall, I saw no one take a step forward, like they were trapped.

I walked closer and saw the eyes of the dead. Surprisingly, they weren't as scary as I thought. Their eyes did hold sorrow and loneliness as they stared at me with pleading eyes.

I walked down the line that held millions of people staring at me as if I was the cure for cancer. I felt sad and guilty, but what could I do? It's not like I could bring back everyone. That simply was impossible. It's their fate to be here, but only one person in here is coming back with me because that's their destiny.

I was having a battle with myself as I continued to look for any familiar faces. My mind told me to choose Alice because this is what I have wanted in years, but my heart was yearning to see Aiden again. I felt tears of frustration form behind my eyes as I continued to think of who I was going to choose.

But deep down inside I knew from the beginning who.

Aiden.

As much as I wanted to see Alice again, Aiden's my other half. And without him, I don't know how I'll live. I've grown to love him so much it hurts. I've become attached to him, the complete opposite of what I wanted when I first met him.

I felt my heart stop when I saw a familiar face standing right in front of me. I let two tears escape my eyes as I stared at my best friend smiling sadly at me. I walked closer until I was standing right in front of the border that was keeping me from passing.

"Alice," I whispered.

I wanted to grab her and hug her, but it was impossible.

"I'm so sorry," I said.

She shook her head at me and gave me a reassuring look.

"Hey, don't cry. I know it's your only choice," she said as she put her hand on the border.

I placed my hand over hers and laid my forehead on it.

"I failed everyone, and especially you," I said as I looked at the ground, feeling ashamed of myself. It was quiet for a moment until she spoke.

"Look at me," she said.

I looked up hesitantly and was surprised to see her crying as well.

"Stop blaming yourself! None of this is your fault," she told me.

By this time, I completely forgot about everyone else here as I focused on my best friend in front of me.

"You know that when destiny bites you right in the ass, you always find a way to make things better," she told me.

"B–but what am I supposed to do Alice? I'm so confused," I said, and a sob escaped my throat. I didn't want to leave her after all those years. I finally had a chance to get her back, but it backfired on me.

She closed her eyes for a bit then opened them as she stared at me with glassy eyes.

"You know I can't tell you, only your heart can," she said.

I knew she was right, but I was too afraid to admit it. But I made so many mistakes in my life and messed things up, now wasn't the time. I'm going to do what I know I have to do and follow my heart.

"But I'll miss you," I said now, banging my fist on the border.

"How can I just walk away and leave you here?" I asked as I cried.

"It's simple," she whispered.

"Just turn your back on me and walk away knowing that someone else is waiting for you here," she said as a tear ran down her cheek.

"B–but—" I stuttered but was silenced by her stern look.

"Just go! You know this is what you have to do," she said.

I rubbed my eyes and wiped my tears. I looked at her and gave her a small smile.

"You know what made you special from all the others?" I asked.

She smiled and shook her head at me.

"Even though you were a goofball, you still cared about everyone around you. Always chose the decision that will keep them safe and not happy. As long as they were okay and fine, you thought the world was a better place," I told her.

She chuckled as she wiped a tear running down her cheek.

"I was motivated," she said.

"You were my motivation in life, and still are," she told me.

I smiled sadly at her.

"Now go, Stella. He's waiting for you at the end of the line. He's confused and needs you to be there with him," she said.

I nodded and took a step back. I was about to turn away when she called out my name.

"Stella!" she yelled.

I looked at her and saw her waving at me goodbye.

"Never forget me," she said.

I waved back at her and spoke.

"That's never happening. I can still remember the day we first met like it was yesterday," I told her and smiled.

I took a step backward slowly, wanting to cherish this moment.

"See you later, best friend. This isn't goodbye," I told her.

A tear ran down my cheek while she smiled at me, nodding.

"See you later, best friend," she said.

And with that, I turned my back on her and ran as fast as I could to the end of the line, trying to ignore the pain in my heart. I had one mission, and that was to bring Aiden back to life. Not just for me, but for Marie, Liam, his parents, and our pack.

Everyone is depending on me, and this time, I won't fail them.

Ignoring all the shouts from everyone around me, telling me to pick them, I stopped at the end of the line to see Aiden looking confused. I felt my happiness come back to life at the sight of him. My humanity and sanity slowly came back to where they used to be.

I saw light in his beautiful blue eyes.

"Aiden!" I yelled, catching his attention.

He looked happy but surprised to see me.

"Stella?" he whispered.

I ran to where he was standing and gave him a bright smile.

"Why are you here? Don't tell me they hurt you?" he growled, getting angry as he looked me up and down.

I was surprised that even though he was here, and he was the one to get stabbed in the heart, he still cared about me. It made me happy in a way.

"I'm fine. Don't worry. It's a long story, but right now we have to get you back home," I said.

He raised an eyebrow at me.

"How?" he asked.

I shook my head.

"Not now. I'll explain later, but right now we don't have much time," I said.

I'm not sure why, but I was able to cross the border, not like when I was with Alice. I guess it has to do with my powers, knowing that this is the person I wanted to bring back with me. I was about to grab his hand when something stopped me.

It was his eye color.

Just a while ago his eyes were blue, but now it had a color in them. Almost red. I then grabbed his hands but pulled away when I felt how cold they were.

"What happened?" I asked.

He looked the same to me, the same Aiden I knew, but his scent was also different. Something changed in him.

But what?

He ran his hand through his hair and sighed.

"I don't know, but when I got here, I felt different. I felt more powerful, and I think it has to do with your blood in my system," he said.

My eyes widened at what he said as I looked at him in shock. So what he was telling me was that he didn't cough all the blood out, only some. And that it has affected him.

Does that make him a...

"Stella," Aiden said.

"I'm half vampire and half werewolf," he said.

"I'm a hybrid!"

The words I was going to say completely disappeared as I looked at him with wide eyes.

I can't believe I did this? Does that mean when I bring him back to life then he will be immortal just like me?

"How do you feel?" I asked.

He smiled at me and took my hand in his.

"Much better now that you're here," he said.

I couldn't hold it in much longer. I jumped on him, wrapping my arms around his neck, finding comfort just by being with him.

"I love you," I said in his ear.

He pulled away once I said that and looked at me with surprised eyes. A big happy smile then broke loose, showing me his straight white teeth.

"You do?" he asked.

I nodded, then the next thing I knew he lifted me off the ground and twirled me in the air, ignoring everyone's stares. I squealed in surprise as he laughed happily. That sound was music to my ears. He then hugged me so close to him and kissed my lips.

"I love you too, Stella," he said, looking at me with sincere eyes.

"I love you so damn much! And I'm looking forward spending eternity with you," he told me.

His words made me smile brightly. I felt my broken heart repair as I looked at the gorgeous man in front of me. I finally found my happiness in Aiden's arms.

I couldn't wait to spend eternity with him.

I wonder what the future has in store. Whatever might happen, I know that no matter what, I'll be happy as long as I'm with Aiden. He's the light in my dark life. And I'm the dark in his bright life. Together we even it out.

He then grabbed my hand in his and looked at me with happy eyes.

"Ready to go home?" he asked.

I nodded.

"Ready."

And with that, I pulled him through the border, and everything around us disappeared. We went back to a place we call home. With everyone we love waiting for us there.

Our future awaits. All I have to do is open the door that will lead the way. The same door I opened that brought me to Aiden.

I remember when I first crossed Aiden's territory. I thought my life was going to end.

But little did I know that was just the beginning.

Epilogue

Ten years later

"Aiden!" I yelled furiously.

Words couldn't describe my anger for that man in this very moment. All I wanted to do was rip his gorgeous face from his sexy body and feed it to the annoying dogs that lived next door.

Ever since we've moved to our wonderful new house nine years ago, which was made by him, it was very peaceful. But a couple years ago, some members of the pack bought the house that was next to us and brought their dogs with them.

Now don't get me wrong. I love dogs and all sort of animals, but you start to get annoyed when they keep you up at night or even wake up your five-year-old son who was at the age of two when they arrived.

Which meant no sleep.

I slammed the fridge close and screamed for my husband to come down or else he wouldn't be getting anything tonight.

"I swear, Aiden, if you don't come here right now, you're sleeping on the freaking couch tonight!" I threatened.

Again, I was met with silence.

I continued to curse some colorful words in my head as I walked out of the kitchen and into the living room to see Aiden hiding under the dining table with Ryder by his side. I heard some whispers from under there as Ryder giggled.

I took a step forward and kneeled down to glare at Aiden.

"What are you two doing?" I asked, but it was mainly directed at Aiden.

Aiden gave me an innocent look as he pouted his lips.

"What? Can't a father just play hide and seek with his son?" he asked.

I crossed my arms over my chest and raised an eyebrow at him.

"You do realize that you both are hiding from no one," I pointed out.

"But we are, Mommy." Ryder's cheerful voice said, catching my attention as Aiden gave him a pleading look, not wanting him to say anything. My anger went away when I saw his toothless grin. I stared at him in awe.

"From who, baby? Has Daddy been telling you scary stories again?" I asked.

He shook his head at me.

"No, Mommy, but Daddy said there's going to be a very scary woman that will attack us, so we had to hide," he explained.

I then averted my eyes from my adorable son and looked to where Aiden was once at to see him gone. He was running toward the front door.

Oh no he didn't.

"Aiden!" I yelled as I waddled after him, trying not to cause any pressure on my growing stomach.

"You better slow down or else I will blow up," I said, knowing that was going to stop him dead in his tracks.

He turned slowly to face me as I stomped toward him. He looked at me with worried eyes.

"Baby, you look gorgeous as always," he said, but I smacked him right behind his head.

"Ow!" he whined as he rubbed the back of his head.

"What was that for?" he asked.

I rolled my eyes at his exaggeration.

"You know exactly why," I said, glaring at him.

"And don't think by complimenting me I will forget about you eating my slice of cheesecake," I hissed as I punched his chest.

"You knew that was the only one left, and you still ate it!" I said as I threw another punch at his chest, which I wish actually affected him.

"Baby, don't be mad. I'll buy you another one next time," He assured me, but I gave him a stern look.

"I'm having cravings right now, damn it! Tell me what I'm supposed to do! Huh? You better go to the supermarket right now and get me something that will ease my cravings or so help me, Aiden Smith, you're sleeping on the couch tonight," I threatened again, but this time I saw a reaction from him.

His eyes widened, and he nodded quickly.

"Okay, okay, love. I'll go grab the keys and get going. Just calm down. It's not good for the baby," he said then kissed my forehead as he rubbed circles on my stomach.

I nodded and watched as he retreated. He may be annoying at times but seeing him play with Ryder always makes my day. Thankfully the elders didn't take away his ranking many years back when he got turned into a hybrid. It took a couple months of meetings and discussing the situation with them, especially for what to do with Ian.

In the end, we ended up executing him. We couldn't let him go rogue because he did threaten us, so that was out of discussion.

I turn around once I made sure Aiden was out the door and saw Ryder still under the dining table while playing with his toys. I walked over to him and smiled.

I remember the day I gave birth to him like it was yesterday. Aiden and I didn't know what he was going to turn out to be, a vampire or a werewolf, but once we looked at him, we knew exactly what he was. He's just like his father, a hybrid.

"Come on baby. Let's get you to your room so you could play there," I said then took his small hand in one hand while the other held his toys. I walked upstairs and dropped him off to play in his room, leaving the door open.

I then walked down the hall and stopped right outside Sarah's door. I knocked on it then opened it to see Sarah packing her bags.

I felt sadness return in my heart when I remembered Sarah had to move out of the house with her mate. It's been years since I've adopted her, probably ten, and it was one of the best decisions I've ever made in my life.

Having her live with Aiden and me, along with our child, was one of the best feelings in the world. She's like the sister I never had. But unfortunately, she will have to move out tonight because she found her mate a couple weeks back, and he wanted her by his side.

I was sad to let her go but knew if this made her happy then it will make me happy as well. I then closed the door and walked into her now empty room and sat next to her on her bed.

"Do you really have to go?" I asked, looking at her with sad eyes.

"You're acting as if I'm moving across the globe. I'll only be living two blocks away," she assured me but still didn't make me feel any better.

"Yeah, I know, but I'm so used to seeing you here twenty–four/seven. I was the one to raise you for ten years after all," I said as I wrapped my arm around her shoulder.

She then gave me a sideways hug and smiled at me.

"Yeah, I know, and I thank you for that. I'm not sure what would have happened to me if I never met you," she said sadly as I noticed her eyes begin to water.

"Oh, you would probably be bored all the time since you've never met anyone as awesome as me," I said trying to lighten up the mood.

She shook her head at me while grinning. She then looked at my stomach and poked it.

I slapped her hand away and gave her a pointed look as she smirked at me.

"So did you and Aiden find out the gender?" she asked.

I nodded happily and placed my hand on my stomach.

"It's going to be a girl," I squealed, and she gave me a big smile.

"That's great, Stella! Do you have any names in mind?" she asked.

I looked at my lap as I played with my fingers and smiled sadly while nodding.

"Yes, actually, Aiden and I have decided that Alice is a perfect name," I told her.

She was about to say something when the door slammed open and a running Ryder came.

"Sarah! Sarah!"

He ran to her. She opened her arms and lifted him on her lap.

"What's wrong, Rayray?" she asked while using the same adorable nickname she always used. I just loved seeing them two together. They were like siblings who look out for each other.

"Why are you leaving me?" he whined while pouting. I'm pretty sure I noticed his eyes become glassy.

"Is it because I played on your phone without permission?" he asked.

"I'm sowy," he said.

Sarah then put her hands on his face and wiped the tears that fell on his cheek.

"Hey, don't be sad, and no, it's not because of you, Rayray. It's because I've found someone special, and I'm going to go live with him," she said.

Ryder looked up at her with sad eyes.

"Do you have to go?" he asked.

Sarah nodded.

"Yes, but don't worry. I'll come visit every day," she assured him then placed him on the ground. He then turned to look at me and smiled.

"Mommy, can I have a cookie?" he asked.

I smiled while nodding my head, then stood up and took his little hand in mine. I turned around and looked at Sarah.

"You can finish packing. Once you're ready to go, tell me, okay?"

She nodded and kissed Ryder's forehead. We walked out of her room and went downstairs to the kitchen. I opened the cabinets and took out a box of cookies and handed two to Ryder.

I took one myself to help ease the cravings, but it didn't do much. I then heard the doorbell ring and waddled to the door. I looked through the peephole and smiled when I saw who it was. I opened the door and immediately got pulled into Marie's arms as she squeezed me to death.

"Marie, you're going to kill her if you don't let go," Liam told her, which I was thankful for because she let go almost immediately.

I took a deep breath and placed a hand on my belly which became a habit of mine.

"Hello to you too," I said to Marie as she grinned at me.

"It's been ages, immo! Oh my god! Are you pregnant with your third child?" she asked.

I gave her a pointed look.

"No, Marie. You two have only been gone for two weeks. I'm pretty sure I wouldn't have enough time to go into labor and get pregnant again," I said as I shook my head at her.

She only shrugged her shoulders at me then walked in with Liam following behind her.

"So how was the trip?" I asked.

Liam and Marie were both away for two weeks celebrating their fifth year anniversary while they left their child, Lilia, in the care of her grandparents.

"It was nice and would have been a little more peaceful if Marie over here wasn't worrying about Lilia all the damn time," Liam grumbled.

Marie shot him a glare.

"Hey! I can't help it. It's a mother's instinct," she defended herself.

Liam rolled his eyes.

"Yes, I know, but she's perfectly fine with the care of my parents," he said.

Before Marie could say anything else, the door opened, and Aiden walked in while carrying a bag that held a delicious smell. I jumped out of my seat happily and walked over to where he was standing. I then grabbed the bag from him and kissed his cheek.

"Thanks, honey," I said and turned around so that I could take the cake with me to the kitchen, but he wrapped his arms around my waist, stopping me in my tracks. He then leaned over to my ear.

"Is that all I get? A kiss on the cheek, nothing else?" he asked.

I turned around and shook my head as I removed his hold on me.

"I would, but you're the one who ate my cake in the first place, so no." I then made my way to the kitchen and took a bite out of heaven. Once I walked back to the living room, I found Liam and Marie gone as Aiden sat on the couch watching TV.

I then saw Sarah walking down the stairs with Ryder by her side as she carried her luggage. Aiden got up and walked with me to her. I smiled sadly at her when she was standing in front of me.

"He'll be here any minute now," she said.

She then put her bags on the ground and gave me a big hug.

"Thank you so much for being there for me. Words cannot describe how much you mean to me."

She then averted her eyes to Aiden.

"Oh, and you too," she said and grinned.

Aiden smiled at her.

I took her hand in mine, grabbing her attention.

"The moment I saw you, I knew you were special," I said.

"How could I not have approach you when you were calling out for me?" I asked then hugged her again as I rubbed her back.

"Stella, would you stop acting like she's moving all the way to India?" Aiden asked, but I simply ignored his comment since now was not the moment to smack him when I was saying goodbye to Sarah.

"I better see you here every day or else," I threatened her playfully.

She nodded while laughing. We then heard a honking sound coming from a car, and Sarah carried her bags.

"That must be him," she said then kneeled down to kiss Ryder on the forehead.

"See you tomorrow, Rayray!"

We said our goodbyes and watched as her mate got out of the car to help her with her bags. We then closed the door when we made sure they were gone. I looked at Ryder to see him rubbing his eyes sleepily. I picked him up and walked to his room to put him in bed.

Five minutes later, he was asleep. I walked over to our room and saw Aiden coming out of the bathroom. I walked over to him and kissed him on the lips. He wanted more, but I pulled away and gave him a teasing look.

"Nope, I'm tired, and all I want to do is sleep," I said.

Aiden pouted and sighed.

"Fine," he mumbled and walked over to our bed. I got changed into my sleeping clothes and got under the covers with the love of my life. He kissed my forehead and wrapped his arms around my waist, bringing me close to his chest but not close enough to apply pressure on my belly.

"I love you," I said as I stared at his mesmerizing eyes. He smiled at me and kissed my lips.

"I love you too," he said.

We both closed our eyes and fell in comfortable silence as we listen to each other's heartbeat. I was about to get sucked into a deep sleep in my husband's arms when I felt a kick in my stomach. I ignored it and laid my head on Aiden's chest until I felt something wet between my legs and pain overwhelmed my body.

Oh shit, my water broke.

"Aiden," I whispered in pain.

He opened one eye to look at me.

"Hm?"

I took a deep breath and closed my eyes.

"I'm in labor."

"Shit."

THE END

Can't get enough of Stella and Aiden? Make sure you sign up for the author's blog to find out more about them!

Get these two bonus chapters and more freebies when you sign up at rua-hasan.awesomeauthors.org/!

Here is a sample from another story you may enjoy:

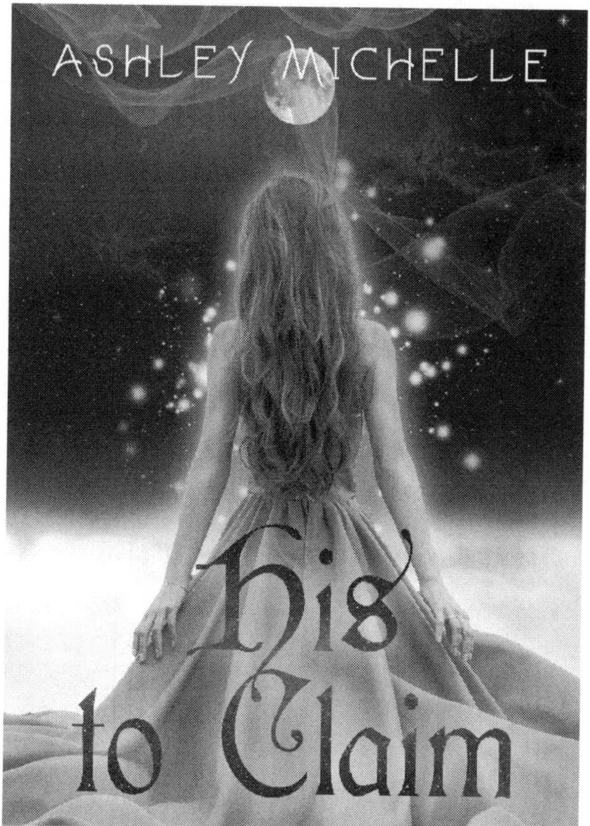
ASHLEY MICHELLE
His to Claim

01

Scarlett

"—Shift."

I was jolted out of my daydreaming by the sound of a loud voice ringing in my ear. I turned around with raised brows to find Darlene, the shift manager of the small family-owned diner, staring at me expectantly with a tray of dirty dishes in one hand. I had clearly missed the important parts of whatever she had been saying to me.

A sheepish grin worked its way up my face. "What was that?"

She rolled her eyes and blew a stray hair out of her face. "I *said*, do you mind covering the end of my shift for me? My babysitter called. Apparently, Graham is running a pretty high fever."

I nodded my head. "Sure, no problem." It wasn't like I had any plans for the evening anyway, other than obsessively checking the mail. There were only two weeks left before graduation, and I was yet to hear from any of the colleges I had applied to.

Darlene let out a small sigh. "Thanks, Scarlett. I owe you."

I waved my hand. "Don't worry about it. I know how hard it is on you being left to take care of Graham while Troy is away. I'm happy to help lighten the load." Her husband had to travel a lot for his job, and that left Darlene with extra parenting duties.

She gave me a grateful smile as she turned away with the tray of dishes. "You're truly an angel, Scarlett."

I snorted at her comment. "I already agreed to cover you. You don't need to kiss my butt anymore, Darlene."

She gave me a playful wink before turning away, disappearing through the kitchen door. I slowly turned back around with a sigh. This was going to be a long night of nothing but the virtual emptiness of the diner.

I was happy when a familiar face shuffled through the front door of the diner, setting off the little bell that hung above the door. He lifted his hand to his head, ruffling his dark hair which was starting to look shaggy around the edges. This boy would look like a mountain man if it weren't for my constant influence in his life. He met my gaze briefly as he reached out and grabbed one of the cheaply made menus from an empty table. He flipped through the pages quickly before setting it back down.

I pulled the pen and pad from the front pocket of my stained apron. "What can I get you, Wyatt?"

He shrugged as he moved closer toward me. "I think a cup of coffee will be fine. It's been a long day."

"It's going to be a bit longer. Darlene asked me to cover the end of her shift," I commented with an apologetic smile.

Wyatt had promised to pick me up after my shift ended while I was running out the door this morning.

He let out a sigh, running his hand through his hair. "Of course, she did. Well, there *is* a meeting tonight. Guess it's going to be extra long for both of us, sweetheart," he replied with a sarcastic grin as I poured him a cup of coffee and placed it on the counter in front of me.

Darlene approached us carrying her purse, her jacket slung over her arm. "You know the coffee here is shit, Wyatt. I don't know why you keep ordering it when you only ever have a sip and leave the rest."

Wyatt ignored her comment. The two of them were always at each other's throats for reasons unknown to me. He pressed his hands to the counter, breathing in deeply. His nose scrunched up a bit, and he looked over at me. "You smell." I frowned at my cousins greeting as he sat himself down on a stool at the breakfast counter, grabbing the coffee.

"Gee, you really know how to compliment a girl," I grumbled, my voice dripping with sarcasm. My cousin and I had a very close relationship, considering that my parents had taken him in after his father ran off and his mother got sick. He returned the favor when my parents died, taking me into his home and raising me like I was his kid sister.

"God, Wyatt…" Darlene remarked as she threw her arms into the sleeves of her jacket, pulling up the collar. "Even if a woman does stink, you shouldn't comment on it. And you wonder why you're still single."

Her words brought a smile to my face, and I gave him a pointed look. I snickered as I turned away from my cousin who was pouting at the blunt reprimand he had received. I could see Winston, our cook, slaving away over the grill through the small hole, singing along to some garbage being gurgled out of the old boom box he kept in the kitchen. The diner was my home away from home, and its motley crew was my self-created wolf pack even if they were only humans.

"Wyatt," she said his name in a flat tone. Darlene had never cared much for my cousin. Maybe it's because he had a knack for putting his foot in his mouth… or maybe because they had gone "grown-up" together and he'd been quite the fool back in his younger years.

"See you tomorrow, Scarlett. Thanks again," she called.

I turned around to give her a quick wave. "See ya, Darlene. Tell Graham I said hello and hope he feels better," I called back as she exited the front door, the bell ringing again.

Wyatt lifted his gaze to mine, staring at me expectantly with wide eyes as if he was waiting for something. I stared back at him, shifting my hands to my hips. "Why are you looking at me like that? Do I have something on my face?" I reached up with a hand and wiped it across my cheek, checking to see if there was any food splatter. It was a hazard of the job.

"Can't you feel it, Scarlett?" he asked me in a soft voice so that no one else could hear. Hell, if it wasn't for my extra-sensitive senses I probably wouldn't have heard him either.

I narrowed my eyes in confusion at his question. "What are talking about? Are you feeling okay, Wyatt?" I reached out and placed my hand on his forehead. He pulled back with a furrowed brow and looked at me as if I had two heads.

"After all the complaining and whining I had to listen to from you… are you seriously telling me that you don't feel even the slightest bit different?" he asked a little louder in an exasperated tone, waving his hand in the air dramatically. I had no idea what he was going on about or why he seemed so upset.

I looked around the small room at the other patrons who seemed content to ignore his outburst. I leaned forward, stuffing my notepad back into the pocket of my apron. "I don't know why you think I should feel different, but I feel the same as I always do. Unless you want to count the fact that my feet feel like I've been walking barefoot on hot coals. These ten-hour shifts have been killing me," I whined at him.

He gave me a slow blink, shaking his head. "Seriously, Scarlett?"

"What?" I questioned with a tired tone.

"Your scent—"

I held up a hand, cutting off his thought mid-sentence.

"I know. I know. I smell, but in my defense, you would smell too if you worked with greasy food all day," I snapped at him, growing tired of the conversation he was having with me. If I wanted to be insulted, I'm sure I could easily find one of my peers to satisfy that need without a problem. Human or shifter, they were all eager to tear someone else down to elevate themselves.

He shook his head at me. "No, your scent has changed, Scarlett. Your wolf has matured. I can smell her on you now."

I stared at him blankly as I digested his words. Had my wolf finally reached maturity without me noticing? I searched my mind for a sign of my wolf's presence. I had been waiting for this moment since I hit puberty. Most of my peers had already matured, leaving me as an outsider when it came to the pack.

All shifters had to go through two stages of puberty: the natural human one and the beast underneath. It could happen at any time, but basically, it meant that the connection between human and wolf was fully formed. It wasn't until this happens that we were allowed to attend actual pack events. Most of my friends had already matured. I had been left in the group of late bloomers. Sometimes, it happened that a wolf never matured.

These people were seen as Omegas. They were still a part of the pack, but they would never be considered true wolves.

I shifted back and forth on my feet, concentrating hard. "I don't feel any different."

Wyatt took a sip of his coffee. "You will, trust me." He pulled the mug away from himself, peering down into the cup with a small look of disgust before setting it down. "But you know what this means?"

"What?" I questioned with a raised brow.

He met my gaze with a knowing look. "You don't have to wait in the car like the other pups during the meeting tonight. You're a true wolf now," he teased as he gave me a wolfish grin. I rolled my eyes at his comment, but on the inside, I felt a bubble of excitement.

* * *

I had only ever seen the pack house from the outside, having never been allowed to enter it before. I found myself getting anxious as I followed Wyatt down the dirt driveway and around the side of the house. In the back, there was another building, about the size of a guest house.

I could hear the sound of happy voices carried on the gentle evening breeze. My palms felt sweaty in the pockets of my sweatshirt as my nerves got the better of me. Wyatt gave me a grin as he opened the door. "So it begins."

I rolled my eyes at him as I walked past him into the large open room. The smells of other pack members overwhelmed me for a moment. My eyes scanned the crowd warily, looking for familiar faces. I found my gaze gravitating towards the front of the room where the stream of bodies seemed to be moving.

That was the first time I saw *him*.

He stood near the front, greeting people with a friendly smile. My heart hammered in my chest as I watched him from where I stood at the back of the room. I had no idea who he was, but I knew he was perfect. His dark hair was shaved close to his head as if it had been shaved bare at some point and was finally being allowed to grow out. My eyes followed the length of his body, taking in every part of him. He had a lean body that spoke of endurance-honed muscles.

Wyatt elbowed my side. "Don't just stand there, Scarlett. People are starting to look at us." He urged me to move forward. I had to force my feet to move from where I had been anchored. My whole world seemed to be shifting on its axis, and I couldn't be sure I was standing on solid ground anymore.

My heart was in my throat as I approached my mate—at least that was what my wolf was telling me. This perfect male specimen was our mate, the one that the Goddess had ordained for us at birth. But what if he hated me? What if I wasn't what he was expecting? Insecurities that I had never felt before began to flood my brain.

I dug my heels into the floor. "I can't do this. Let's go home."

Wyatt grabbed onto my elbow and led me on. "You're being ridiculous. We all had to go through this, Scarlett. Consider it your official initiation into the pack." I gritted my teeth as every step brought me closer to the finality of my situation.

The Alpha and his mate were standing together, greeting the other pack members as they filed into the room, grabbing seats for the meeting. I remembered them from the times they had visited my home when I was much younger, way back when my mother was still alive and my father held a prominent position in the pack. They looked older and a little more worn down, but that had to be expected of people in their positions.

"Alpha Aaron," Wyatt spoke formally as he reached out a hand, a common human greeting. I danced on the balls of my feet, wishing that I hadn't accepted Wyatt's offer to join him. I was still in my work uniform, smelling like grease and probably looking unkempt from the busy workday... not the way I wanted to make my first impression on the pack.

"Wyatt," he replied, shaking the hand that had been offered to him with a firm grip, "it is good to see you again."

Wyatt beamed at the acknowledgment, turning his eyes toward the female beside the Alpha, bowing his head. "Luna Victoria."

She gave him a kind smile. "Wyatt."

Alpha Aaron's dark gaze shifted in my direction, a smile still on his lips. "And who is this beauty?" he questioned, lifting a brow as he examined me further. My cheeks rushed with heat, and I felt the sudden urge to hide behind my cousin like I did back in my younger years where I would cling to my mother's leg.

Wyatt wrapped his arm around my shoulder, pulling me in protectively to his side, and that only made me feel more embarrassed. "This is my cousin, Scarlett."

Luna Victoria gave me a knowing glance as she leaned into her mate's side. "Sweetheart, it's Conrad and Elizabeth's daughter."

"Of course, she is," he replied as if he had already known. My lips twitched with the urge to smile when she looked at me with a playful eye roll at his expense. Alpha Aaron crossed his arms over his wide chest, leaning forward toward me. "I can see it now that I've gotten a closer look. You've got Conrad's eyes."

"And Elizabeth's beautiful face," Luna Victoria remarked. "If I recall correctly, your mother was a late bloomer as well." I felt my head sink a little lower at her comment.

"David..." Luna Victoria called, turning toward my mate with a smile, "come over here real fast."

She glanced back at me. "Conrad helped train David when he was a young boy. I'm sure he will be very interested in meeting you." I felt my nerves spike as he turned in our direction, and I realized that he wasn't an average member of the pack. This was *their* son, the next heir: an Alpha born male.

I wanted to run, but my feet kept me firmly rooted in place. I was afraid to look up from the ground. What would I see staring back at me? I swallowed hard, trying to prepare myself for what was about to happen.

His shoes came into view, and I felt my wolf stirring under my skin. Wyatt elbowed me in the side. "Scarlett..." he hissed under his breath in a warning tone. I lifted my face to meet his gaze with a bated breath.

His dark eyes widened in surprise as we drank each other in. Something in my mind snapped. I could feel it all, everything everyone had tried to explain to me about having a wolf. Her emotions and thoughts surged through me as I watched the corners of his mouth lift upwards into a smile.. a heart-stopping smile that was meant for only me.

I felt my own lips begin to mimic his. There was nothing and no one else in the room for us at that moment. This is what it felt like to have a mate, and I knew he was feeling the same sensations by the look in his eyes.

The moment was broken when a tall dark-haired female placed a kiss on his cheek. "I'm sorry I'm late, David. My shift went into overtime. I had to help Doctor McCarthy deliver the

Johnson's twins. Those pups are going to be a handful. I can tell you that now." She finished with a soft chuckle of amusement.

I hadn't even seen her approach us I had been so lost in a different world. My smile faded quickly as my brows furrowed in confusion as I glanced between the two of them. He looked rather stiff as she grabbed a hold of his hand with hers, turning her face in my direction.

"Hello. I don't think I've seen you before." She tilted her head to the side.

"That's because she's only just matured, Eva," Luna Victoria commented toward her, both of them sharing a look of understanding like two people who've already been through it.

"This must be very exciting for you then," she remarked with a bright smile, completely unaware of what had happened between me and the male she was holding onto as if he were hers. My wolf was growling possessively in my mind, struggling to free herself so that she could eliminate the competition.

"David, this is Scarlett," Luna Victoria introduced me. "Conrad's daughter," she supplied as if it were my own special title.

I felt like the rug had been pulled out from under my feet and I was falling without anyone to catch me. My stomach was in my throat, but I forced myself to speak. "Hi..." I replied in a tense voice, finding it hard to hold his gaze.

David pulled his hand free from Eva's grasp and took a step towards me. He lifted his hand slightly like he wanted to reach out to me, but he thought better of it, deciding to stuff it into the pocket of his slacks instead.

"It's nice to meet you, Scarlett." Goosebumps rose on my flesh, and I watched his pupils dilate a bit as he took in more of me. "Your father was a great man. The pack lost a great warrior when he passed away. I lost a dear friend," he added, trying to keep things from getting strange in front of all the onlookers. None of them seemed to know what had transpired between the two of us.

I gave him a small smile that didn't reach my eyes. "Thank you." He looked like he wanted to say something more to me, his lips parted slightly. Alpha Aaron stepped forward, his dark eyes calculating as he glanced between myself and his son. I lowered my gaze to the ground, clenching my jaw tightly.

"Well, we should get this meeting going." He wrapped his arm around his mate and pulled her into his side. "It's wonderful to have another true wolf added to the pack."

Wyatt grabbed my elbow, and I tensed slightly at the touch. Now that I could connect to my wolf, the world seemed too overwhelming. Every sensation moved through me like an exploding bomb. I let him lead me away to some empty seats, but my mind was adrift as I looked around the room. I had matured and met my mate, only to find out that he already had someone at his side. How could I compete with her?

My gaze focused on the female in question, Eva. She was a fully matured female compared to myself, who was still growing into my body, which was mostly knees and elbows. She seemed kind, and she didn't waver under the gaze of all the people in the room. She looked like a queen. I certainly wasn't much compared to her. That was why she was the one standing on the stage, holding his hand.

I sunk down lower in my seat. I could hear Alpha Aaron's voice as he spoke to the group, but none of the words were able to pierce through my racing thoughts.

"We are happy to announce that the mating ceremony of Eva and David will be held at the end of next month," Alpha Aaron said with pride in his voice, clapping David on the back as he stood next to a smiling Eva, hand in hand. My heart dropped, and I sucked in a painful breath. This wasn't how things were supposed to go. I was his mate, not her.

I couldn't sit in that room for another moment and listen to any more words. I leaned over to Wyatt. "I need to go," I whispered. He looked over at me in confusion as I rose up out of my chair and hurried toward the exit. I didn't look back, but I felt David's eyes on me, my body heating up everywhere his gaze drifted to. It was getting hard to breathe as I pushed open the door and flung myself out into the night, letting the cool air wash over me.

I sucked in ragged breaths as I tried to overcome the ache in my chest. No one had warned me maturing would be so painful.

If you enjoyed this sample then look for
His to Claim.

Other books you might enjoy:

Mated to the Alpha King
Jennise K.
Available on Amazon!

Other books you might enjoy:

King of Beasts
Jamiee Lynne
Available on Amazon!

Introducing the Characters Magazine App

Download the app to get the free issues of interviews from famous fiction characters and find your next favorite book!

iTunes: bit.ly/CharactersApple
Google Play: bit.ly/CharactersAndroid

Acknowledgements

I'd like to acknowledge and give a huge thanks to Le-an Lai Lacaba who helped me reach my goal and dreams by giving this book a try. I wouldn't have been here if she didn't look passed my flaws and accepted my book. Thank you for being that person who once told me that I have potential.

I'd also like to thank my editor Klare Sencil who handled my countless mistakes and answered all my questions. Thank you for working your very best in making what you'd call, 'my baby' perfect and ready for the world. I truly appreciate your effort and hard work. I shall forever thank you for the help you've done and the support.

Thank you so much Malot for the amazing and wonderful cover you have designed. I truly love it. And thank you so much to everyone who gave my book a chance and looked passed my imperfections.

Author's Note

Hey there!

Thank you so much for reading *Fangs vs. Claws*! I can't express how grateful I am for reading something that was once just a thought inside my head.

I'd love to hear from you! Please feel free to email me at rua_hasan@awesomeauthors.org and sign up at rua-hasan.awesomeauthors.org/ for freebies!

One last thing: I'd love to hear your thoughts on the book. Please leave a review on Amazon or Goodreads because I just love reading your comments and getting to know YOU!

Whether that review is good or bad, I'd still love to hear it!

Can't wait to hear from you!

Rua Hasan

About the Author

Rua Hsan is a major book worm who loves to write and read. She was born in Palestine and grew up in California. She started writing at the age of fourteen and wrote her first book at the age of fifteen. She does not only love movies too but she can get addictive when watching an awesome series.

Like her Facebook Page: http://bit.ly/RuaHasanFB
Grab freebies from her here: rua-hasan.awesomeauthors.org/

Made in the USA
San Bernardino, CA
09 March 2017